I0613914

Junction

by

Katja Desjarlais

The Haunt Vault Series

This is a work of fiction. Names, characters, places, and incidents are either the product of the author's imagination or are used fictitiously, and any resemblance to actual persons living or dead, business establishments, events, or locales, is entirely coincidental.

Junction

COPYRIGHT © 2023 by Katja Desjarlais

All rights reserved. No part of this book may be used or reproduced in any manner whatsoever without written permission of the author or The Wild Rose Press, Inc. except in the case of brief quotations embodied in critical articles or reviews.
Contact Information: info@thewildrosepress.com

Cover Art by *Diana Carlile*

The Wild Rose Press, Inc.
PO Box 708
Adams Basin, NY 14410-0708
Visit us at www.thewildrosepress.com

Publishing History
First Edition, 2023
Trade Paperback ISBN 978-1-5092-5108-7
Digital ISBN 978-1-5092-5109-4

The Haunt Vault Series
Published in the United States of America

Pushing the gruesome images from his mind, Jonathan fixed his gaze on the low ceiling. "Do you see an end to this? Like, is this how it's going to be from now on?"

Louis scooted his bag beside his and lay down, flinching when his shoulder hit the ground. "No. Maybe for a few decades. A century at most. It depends on whether we decide as a species to return to hiding or if we're going to fight to stay out of the shadows. Now get some rest, newbie. I'll stay on guard."

Scoffing, he closed his eyes. "Remember that whole SUV discussion we had? The discussion I won?"

"When I let you win so you wouldn't cry about your bike," Louis corrected.

"Yeah, that's it." He looked over in the blackness. "A light-tight SUV would probably have come in handy tonight."

The cramped space was quiet for a solid thirty minutes, the sounds of the early morning shift buzzing around the nearby businesses filtering down until Louis finally replied. "Probably. But there's a certain escapist authenticity about cockroaches crawling up your pant leg you just don't get in a luxury vehicle."

Dedication

To Rheyna.
Your support for this book and these vamps was second only to the winter motorcycle road trip knowledge you bestowed on me when I texted you at all hours of the day and night.

CHAPTER ONE

Louis Forbes uncrossed his arms and ducked down to peer in the back window of the SUV. "Need the heat turned up?"

The Tender glanced up from her phone with a smile. "I'm still fine, darling."

With a shrug, he straightened and continued to monitor the deserted stretch of snow-covered dirt road spanning the American–Canadian border, listening through the gusts of wind for any sign of his contact. His gray eyes narrowed as another skiff of snow whipped across his face and settled along the collar of his thin jacket, dampening the back of his neck.

"Perhaps you should wait in here," the Tender called out, rapping her knuckles lightly on the glass. "I'm sure the road conditions are as miserable on his side as they are on ours."

As one of Rhys Kaius's vampire courtesans, she was not only trained to attend to the needs and desires of her master but those of every vamp in her vicinity.

It freaked him out.

But pissing off Rhys, who was both his friend and a vamp old enough to kick his ass with the single swing of a fist, freaked him out more.

Giving her a tight smile and a quick shake of his head, he hunched his shoulders and shoved his hands in his pockets.

No way in hell was he going to risk being caught by the heavily armed border guards patrolling day and night with their UV flashlights strapped to their hips and their mercury-filled bullets loaded into the automatics swung over their shoulders. Running a Tender along the icy backroads from Jackson Stojanovski's fortified vampire compound to the Canadian border was dangerous enough without him becoming lazy in the final stretch.

Risking his own neck was a deterrent to complacency, but the added pressure of guarding a woman linked to an old vampire with temperament issues was definitely a consideration in his meticulous assessment of the terrain. Between human bounty hunters and mis-turned vampire Deviants roaming the country, his back was already a prime target. Messing with the safety of the Tender under his watch would only make his existence a lot more precarious.

Tilting his head, he zeroed in on the faint rumble to the northwest, his eyes scanning the breaks in the trees for flashes of movement. He eased his phone from his pocket, opened his messaging app, and tapped on Rhys's number.

—This guy drive a motorcycle?—

Tracking the black bike's approach, he glanced down when his phone buzzed in his hand.

—Yeah. Weird as fuck. Hit me up on your way back—

The motorcycle slowed as the driver weaved leisurely between the potholes peppering the gravel road. He came to a rolling stop in the ditch and inched forward until the bike was hidden from view. Maintaining his slouched position against the car door, Louis watched while the rider swung his leg over the seat, reached back to grab a small satchel, and popped the strap on his helmet.

"Louis Forbes?" the vampire called out, swinging the bag onto his shoulder and striding over. His boots crunched the untouched snow between them, and he stopped with a grin a good distance away as he hiked up the leg of his jeans. "Jonathan Minks. Sixty." Pausing long enough for Louis to verify the vampiric age rings circling his ankle, he released the jeans and pointed the helmet at him. "Rhys said I couldn't miss the hair, even in the dark. Are we all set to hole up and get cozy for the day?"

Running his hands through the spikes of his fire-red hair, he pushed himself off the car, keeping one eye on the taller male while he hooked his thumb through his keys. "That Cockney accent of yours legit?"

Minks chuckled as he opened the passenger door and got in. "I can switch to the Queen's English on demand, but I see no reason to while I'm freezing my ass off in the middle of ice-hell, North Dakota." He turned in his seat and smiled at the Tender. "Pardon my language, ma'am. Jonathan Minks."

"Cecile Davies," the woman replied, holding out her hand and giving Louis a pointed look when Minks lifted it to his lips briefly. "Charmed."

"Indeed, I am." Minks grinned, settling back as the engine revved. "How far out are we?"

Using the light of the moon to guide his turnaround, he adjusted his rearview mirror and sped up along the icy gravel. "I'll be hanging a right up here and going eight miles into the bush. If you need to touch base with anyone, now's the time to do it before we're out of service range for a bit."

As Minks slid his phone from his bag, Louis slowed and turned down the narrow passage, waiting until they were deep into the cover of the brush before he flipped the headlights on.

Although he was reluctant to spend the day locked up in one of the Kaius haunt's bolt-holes, Nichol insisted that what appeared to be a short drive on the map was indeed a more time-consuming task than it seemed.

And if that miserable old vamp knew anything, it was scheduling.

Nichol Kaius was leading the entire North American vampire population toward the sanctuary city of Denver. It was a feat made almost impossible by the anti-vamp humans and their governments.

Add in a vengeful ancient female vampire with an army of mindless, Zombie-esque Deviants and a hate-on for the Kaius haunt? The job wasn't almost impossible. It was wholly impossible. And through his friendship with Mikhail Kaius and the rest of the haunt, Louis was now a part of the operation, one of the dozens of boots on the ground who answered to the terrifying Nichol Kaius.

As a dilapidated shack came into view, Minks lolled his head and winked at the Tender in the back seat. "Rhys arranged only the finest luxury accommodations for your trip, I see."

With a laugh, she crossed her legs and zipped her purse as Louis pulled the SUV in tight to the leaning walls. "Let's get you boys in there before the sun hits and I have to sweep your remains from the porch."

****

Jonathan flattened his hand on the fourth door and eased it open, nodding in appreciation at the size of the bed. "So you're saying there are dozens of these hideouts all around the country?" he called out to Louis as he tossed his bag on the bed and returned to the living room. "The Kaius haunt has some serious infrastructure in place for this migration."

The red-haired vampire nodded from his crouched position on the floor, his fingers fumbling with the wires of a black box. "Most of these are existing from pre-exposure times, but they're definitely coming in handy now." He sat back and draped his tattooed arms over his knees. "You have any idea how to read a wiring map?"

Glancing back to give the Tender a wave when she announced she was heading to bed, he accepted Louis's phone and looked over the photo. "I can give it a try. Can't be much different than hooking up a stereo." Carefully separating the wires by color, he turned the box over in his hands and began winding the red line around a tiny post. "What's this supposed to do?"

Louis leaned back on his hands. "It's one of Nichol's mashups he sent along to install. If it works, we'll have full wireless communication and a topside visual through the TV over there. I have a text with the passwords to get onto the haunt servers."

Reaching over to grab a small screwdriver, he tightened the first post and started on the green wire. "Are the rumors true?" he asked, exhaling when the wire tangled with the white one. "That the old bastard is connected and settled down with a woman?"

Louis pushed himself off the floor and walked over to the television, turning it on and lowering the volume when static punctured the quiet bunker. "That's the rumor, is it?"

Smirking as the elder vamp bounced the invasive

question back, he changed topics. "How's the sanctuary process moving? Last I heard, the militia training was complete and the boots on the ground were already patrolling the entire Denver perimeter."

"You heard right."

He waited for further information as he tightened down the green wire and switched to white. When nothing more was volunteered, he completed the rest of the work in silence until Louis finally spoke.

"Nice work."

The television lit up the room with the crisp whiteness of the snow under the sun's rays, the brightness assaulting his eyes. He set the box down, rose to his feet, and picked his jacket up from the sofa. "Mind if I have one?" he asked, sliding his cigarettes from the breast pocket. When Louis responded with a shrug, he lit it up and sat at the small kitchen table. "So, how are you linked to the Kaius haunt?"

Silence.

Taking a long drag, he leaned back. "My creator and Rhys go back a long way. And Theodonis, my creator's creator—my grandvamp, I suppose—was tight with Kaius Khthonios before he was staked last century." Watching his companion scroll through channels until he found a grainy news station, he exhaled loudly. "Those anti-vamp rallies are absolutely wild. You ever been to one?"

Louis got to his feet and looked down the hall at the closed bedroom door. The Tender's heart rate was slowed to a steady, sleeping pace. "Not yet." He sat down on the sofa and stretched his legs across the coffee table, remote in hand.

Flicking the cigarette cherry into the sink, Jonathan

turned on the water until the ash washed away. "The FANG group is almost as freaky as the Species Purifiers are. Rhys sent me a few links to some of the shit they're writing about Jagger and Bianca Schumann. He said it was something called fan fiction. Some of it was actually pretty damn good, but—" He rolled his shoulders out, crossed the room, and collapsed into the armchair. "There are some sick, sick people out there."

There was a faint twitch of Louis's thin lips. "Sure are."

While the older vampire settled on the station linked to the small camera he'd placed outside their hideout, he crossed his arms over his chest and relaxed back to catch a few hours of sleep before sundown.

****

Louis watched the Tender swing her leg over the back of Jonathan's bike and adjust her helmet. The two small bags she'd brought along were secured tight behind her, ensuring she would be crushed tight to Jonathan for the trip.

"You know where you're meeting up with her connected vamp, right?" he asked, leaning against the SUV, his eyes darting between the empty road and the motorcycle as Minks mounted it and started it up with a rumble.

Pushing his long chestnut hair back, Jonathan pulled on his own helmet, lowered the face shield, and reached back to help the Tender with hers. "North of Kenora. Nichol forwarded eleven possible routes and eight paragraphs of notes," he replied with a grin. "Gorgeous lakes up there."

The young vamp revved the engine a few times and turned his attention to showing the Tender where she could hold on while he drove. His accent morphed into a more regal pattern while he instructed the woman to cling tight. Once he appeared satisfied with her ability to remain on the bike, he gave a quick wave. "See you around, Forbes."

Waiting until the sound of the engine dissipated in the quiet night, he got into the SUV and drove down the dark road, watching the bars on his phone until he was sure the call wouldn't kick in and out.

"Hey, Louis," Rhys drawled through the speaker, the Kaius haunt's Tender trainer sounding relaxed against the loud thumping in the background. "Is Cecile with Minks?"

Easing onto a slightly wider gravel road, he turned on his headlights and squinted at the falling snow obscuring his vision. "Yeah. You sure he's good? He's young."

"Young enough to have his loyalty purchased for a good price and old enough to know who to align those loyalties with," Rhys replied casually before there was a loud crash followed by a string of obscenities. "Tell your fucking bestie here to back off during business. Fuck, Mick. Fine. Here."

Mickey Kaius whooped, and Louis grinned as his best friend took over the call. "When the hell are you swinging back through here? I...yeah, I...just a sec...Audra says hi. So does Molly. And...I'm just gonna put you on speaker."

There was a faint click before Louis heard the authoritative and confident voices of Audra and Molly clear as day. The respective mates of Mickey and Dominic Kaius took over communication immediately. "Can you hear us?"

"Yeah, yeah," he muttered, slowing to a crawl when he lost track of the road to the din of hellos echoing through the vehicle. "Hi, everyone. Any news?"

While the Kaius males shouted over each other to fill him in on the sanctuary housing crisis, the latest government-sanctioned vampire Deepfrying, and the number of Deviant killings, he turned down the volume and drove through the darkness, wondering how the lone motorcycle was handling the storm.

CHAPTER TWO

Louis sprawled out on the sofa in the main hall of the Stojanovski compound and watched Jackson Stojanovski welcome yet another small retinue of vampires. Their ragged clothing and wary assessments of the room instantly gave away their plight.

Another haunt seeking shelter.

Another young vampire forced to lead before he was ready.

Another hushed request for help. Pride was swallowed as desperation took hold.

Stojanovski glanced his way and shook his head before leading the group to the underground bunkers scattered throughout the property.

Louis's hypnosis skill wasn't needed for this group.

Or the last.

Or the one before that.

The once affluent compound—characterized by the nightly human hunts allowing vampires to embrace their baser natures between meetings displaying wealth and sharing intel—was now a safe house for the vampires fleeing their haunts while the humans closed in on them.

Some leaders remained behind to defend their turf, sending their offspring away to ensure their line wasn't completely eliminated. Others held off attacks from the anti-vamp vigilantes while the younger members escaped, knocked to their knees by the loss of their creators while they fled the cities on foot.

And one by one, they trickled through the midwestern Stojanovski compound in search of shelter, meals, and a few days of rest before they began the dangerous trek toward Denver and the Kaius haunt, drawn by promises of safety and freedom.

He tracked a pair of humans as they descended the stairs, their once fitted outfits and expensive jewelry exchanged for practical jeans and T-shirts, and their long hair pulled into ponytails for easy, efficient feeds. The women flicked their wrists at him as they passed, smiling when he shook his head and turned his attention back to the heavy doors.

Swiping his phone to life, he fired off a quick text to Nichol.

—Three from the Aloisios haunt—

The old vamp's reply was immediate.

—Three? Last intel was nine—

Staring at the empty room, he tapped out his response.

—Three left. Six lost in Chattanooga—

As it was every time he reported in, Nichol's reaction remained the same.

—I'll take care of it—

He watched the doors swing open, Stojanovski sauntering through the deserted hall before he looked around and slumped on the opposite sofa. "I do believe the mouth-breathers are winning more than just the battles."

The humans on-site walked quietly through the upstairs halls, a few trickling down the staircase with the empty trays of the evening's first meal.

"Jagger Kaius and Bianca are expecting a rush from

the south," Louis reported, scanning his messages while Stojanovski gave a few instructions to the men crossing the floor. "Most of those who jumped ship last year are being squeezed back into the US." Flipping through his emails, he pulled up a map. "These are the most recent locations of haunts who made contact within the week."

Jackson leaned over, shaking his head. "Where are Denver's numbers sitting?"

"Five? Closing in on the six hundred Nichol and the others have managed to house?" He tossed his phone onto the coffee table and stretched his arms across the back of the couch. "How are your hauntmates?"

Stojanovski stiffened a fraction. "They made it to Norway and have chosen to remain there."

Nodding in acknowledgment, he resumed his study of the intricate carvings in the wooden doors he knew wouldn't open again that evening. They wouldn't fling apart as another boisterous group of young vampires arrived, ready to partake in the hunt and indulge in the gossip the haunt elders carried across the continents. There would be no currying of favors, no vying for recognition from the ancients who traveled through, no displays of aggressive posturing.

The vampires arriving at the compound were now worn, dirty, and tired. They reeked of Deviant blood. Their kills were photographed and forwarded to the Kaius haunt for the payments and favors to ease their slow treks across the continent toward Denver and safety.

The few old vamps who strode through the doors brought orphans picked up along the way, young ones who didn't hold the scent of their bloodline. The highways were crawling with armed militia, so they took their chances on foot. Their progress was slowed by the unified hive of Deviants prowling the countryside on the hunt for vampire blood.

It had been six months since the Deviants rose. Khthonios, the female vamp who'd sired the Kaius haunt leader, made her existence known in the deadliest of ways. Across the earth, the mindless creatures crawled out of basements and sewers, out of abandoned mine shafts and ghost towns. The Kaius haunt was quick to act under Nichol's orders, and the haunt's second-in-command had been determined to keep the human death toll to a minimum.

But it wasn't the humans the Deviants were after.

"Will you be escorting these newcomers once they have time to regain their strength?"

He looked over at Stojanovski and shrugged. "Likely. Just waiting on Nichol's orders."

Nichol's orders.

Everyone obeyed Nichol's orders.

The miserable vampire's mind was likely flipping through the multitudes of requests piling in hour after hour, prioritizing each one with meticulous detachment against the reduced number of un-compromised bolt-holes, the most recent Deviant mob reports, and the dwindling safe routes across the land. Maps would be charted, calls made, payoffs transferred, and only then would Louis receive the text requesting his help.

Nichol was a miserable sonofabitch, but now he was miserable for a good fucking reason.

"Hey," he called out as Jackson stood. "Did the last payment come through?"

Stojanovski nodded. "Perhaps you could reiterate my refusal the next time you speak to him, as he seems unwilling to hear it from me."

With humans and Deviants closing in on all sides, Nichol was providing triple payment to Stojanovski for all vampires sheltered on route to Denver.

Quadruple for Tenders requiring safe transport.

Isolated in the northern corner of the state, Stojanovski had readily agreed since his bunkers were no longer filled to capacity with the dwindling vampire population.

Three months later, Jackson requested an end to the financial compensation.

"I can't profit from the demise of my species."

Although Louis couldn't be certain, the change of heart was timed with the arrival of a solo male to the compound. A vampire in his second year who was mutilated beyond recognition by Deviants as he crawled the fields with a bloodied map in hand. The quiet kid named Andy now inhabited the bunker next to Jackson's own. Skittish and easily spooked, he wasn't deemed well enough to make the trek to Denver.

Stojanovski refused to push the issue.

****

The laptop monitor cut out briefly, and Nichol's swearing blasted through the speakers until the screen stabilized and Louis could see the frustrated male again.

"Keep your fucking foot away from those cords or I'll rip your goddamn tongue out," the old vamp snarled at Dominic, the youngest of the Kaius hauntmates, before returning his attention back to the camera. "Okay, Louis, are you looking at the most recent map with the orange points along the Canadian border?"

He nodded and waved his phone at the screen. "So our route between highways fifty-nine and eighty-nine is compromised. Now what?"

Nichol ran his hand through his auburn hair. The faint sound of his grinding molars filtered into the bunker as the male's jaw flexed. "We've been preparing for the shutdown of Canadian routes. The haunts there are over max capacity with evacuees, and we can expect anti-vamp legislation to pass within the next two months given the recent change in government." There was an audible exhale from Jagger Kaius's mate, Bianca, and Nichol turned to her. "Evacuation contingencies are already in the works. We'll discuss them later."

The camera jiggled, and Jagger came on screen, his ice eyes less haggard than those of his de facto haunt leader. "Bianca and I are in the process of shoring up a new collection of safe houses through our contacts in the FANG movement. Once those are fully vetted and secured, we'll forward a list in preparation for the next stage."

There was a snort of disdain from Rhys as he swatted Jagger's hood to get the deaf vampire's attention. "I'm still trying to stomach that shit. Friends and Advocates of the New Gods. I can't believe we're fucking validating that bullshit."

Jagg turned back to the camera. "Bianca and I are ensuring we have routes through Canada and Mexico as well. Weird as some of the FANG members may be, they're more than willing to open their homes and make the necessary renovations to provide light-tight spaces."

As the group dissolved into arguments over the weirdness of some of the FANG members, Louis sat back and watched while Bianca and Jagg spoke quietly to each other. Their faces were synonymous with the pro-vamp groups across the globe, and they held the allegiance of what remained of the prominent haunt leaders in North America.

Jagg was now leading online Deviant attack training alongside Bianca for those younger vamps preparing to travel. Shipments of weapons were filtered through Jagg's hands and dispersed to his growing list of contacts. Select humans were sent specialized training videos adapted to suit the limited strength and speed of their biology, creating a small militia outside the Denver perimeter that was outfitted, trained, and ready.

"Louis?" Mick moved in front of the camera and grinned at him as his partner, Audra, draped manicured fingers over his shoulder. "If you're willing, we have an assignment taking priority right now. The evacuation contingency Nichol mentioned earlier."

If you're willing.

Every request made by the Kaius hauntmates began with those words, as though he had anything better to do.

"Lay it on me," he replied, lounging back on the sofa while his best friend nodded at someone off-screen, and he moved over.

Audra tilted the camera toward herself, her catlike eyes filling the screen. "We're surrounded on all sides. Access into Denver is almost impossible by land. So we have a plan."

The room went quiet while she laid out the situation, glancing toward Nichol periodically and receiving nothing more than a terse nod of approval.

He waited until she was done. "Forward me everything I need."

CHAPTER THREE

Louis spun his keys on his thumb as Stojanovski sat in the ornate wingback chair, his strong back hunched and black hair falling into his dark eyes. "Your release paperwork is already done," he finally said, looking up. "Now is not the time to be flexing and posturing for ego's sake." Pulling his phone out, Jackson tapped it to life and held it out. "Sign there."

With the swipe of his finger, he signed off on the contract dissolution, which tethered him to Stojanovski in exchange for the release of Nichol's connected mate, Simone. It was a trade Louis gladly made for the sake of a vampire he both respected and feared. And for Nichol's mate, who was equally terrifying and just as lethal. "Nichol said the paym—"

"Nichol's payment will be accepted and dispersed to our recent arrivals," Stojanovski responded, shaking his head. "You realize you'll be traveling through hostile territory with…how old is this Minks kid?"

Glancing up the staircase at the humans passing through, he gave Dahlia a quick wave. He and the Rhys-trained Tender developed a casual friendship a few years back, and her familiar presence always made him feel a little less like an outsider. "In his sixth decade."

Lolling his head back, Jackson closed his eyes. "I could perhaps join you until the bolt-holes are established and allies have been confirmed. Give you a fighting chance."

"The Kaius haunt needs you here," he countered, shoving his hands into his back pockets. "You're the last of the outposts still standing. The compound outside Dallas went up in flames last weekend. Dominic was able to account for all sixteen members of the LaSalle haunt, but there were a few rogues on-site at the time, and no one has been able to say whether or not they made it out."

Stojanovski's eyes snapped open. "Goddamn LaSalle. Are they en route to Denver?"

"Currently off the grid through the forests outside Santa Fe."

Pushing himself to his feet, Jackson extended his hand. "If you need anything, any favors called in, you have my number." Giving his hand a firm shake, Stojanovski released it and followed him to the exit. "No bravado, Louis. Turn back if you need to, watch your back, and remember loyalty never trumps survival. Those prone to flight have already gone, and all who remain are those programmed to fight."

Hefting his bag onto his shoulder, he opened the door and stepped onto the veranda. "Watch your own back, Jackson. There are a lot of vamps relying on you right now. It would put a pretty big kink in Nichol's plans if you went up in smoke or were ashed over an old grudge." He grinned when the older vampire snorted inelegantly. "Mickey will be in touch about the Aloisios crew soon."

He was halfway down the path when Stojanovski called out to him. "Any updates and intel will be forwarded to those in need. Rest assured. And if you happen to stumble across Khthonios...get the hell out of there."

The name alone sent a small shiver down his back. "Thanks for the reminder, asshole," he grumbled, his steps slowing a fraction as he waved over his shoulder and resumed his trek to the gates of the compound.

****

Mickey's voice cut in and out through the speakers as the road dipped.

"Shut up for a minute," Louis growled as the crackling pierced his ears. "Okay. Say that again."

"I said, you're a fucking idiot for going along with this," Mick enunciated.

"And you're a fucking idiot for thinking I wouldn't be on board. I'm riding this sinking ship into the bowels of hell right alongside you guys." He could hear the wind whistling through Mick's cell, and he knew his friend was hiding outside where he wouldn't be overheard. "You guys stay focused on Denver, and let me deal with the outposts."

Mick grunted in response. "We don't know what you're going to be walking in on. Audra and Nichol are tracking the Deviant movements the best they can, but the herds are moving with more stealth now. We could send you into an ambush without knowing."

His rear tires slid on the iced gravel, and he slowed. "Fuck it. How are you and Audra doing?"

He could hear the smile on Mick's face as he spoke. "Fantastic! I mean, we still argue every three nights, but it's good. Yeah. It's good. Real good."

Mickey and Audra's fighting had become such a staple of the Kaius haunt no one noticed it anymore. The whispered consensus was Audra poked at Mick just enough to push an unleashing of all the frustration that built up while the empathic vamp filtered through the emotional tensions of his hauntmates.

With Louis and his flat affect out of range, Mickey had nowhere to hide, no calm to anchor him while he was pummeled by every feeling his bloodline experienced. The small releases were enough to keep Mick from OD'ing on the stress pummeling him from all sides without respite since Louis left the haunt months earlier.

As the falling snow eased, he sped up again, anxious to make the bolt-hole in the Badlands before the threat of sunrise thwarted his plan. "So where does this Minks guy sit in the need-to-know range?" he asked, hitting the brakes when a small deer darted across the road and wincing when the vehicle skidded sideways for a few yards before it righted.

"Nichol has him on par with you for this mission," Mick replied, his voice muffled. "Gimme a sec...yeah, I'm out here. Just filling Louis in on Minks."

He could hear Rhys call over before a door slammed.

"You catch that?" Mick questioned, continuing without hesitation. "We have his creator and the rest of his haunt set up in the south side complex and working Nichol's perimeter rotation. So good reputation aside, he has enough of a link to us to keep him on the up."

Flashing his headlights on long enough to ensure he didn't miss his turnoff, he scanned the vacant fields for the telltale jerking movements of Deviants. "Stojanovski was shaken by the news of LaSalle." He zeroed in on a black shape in the distance before dismissing it as a cow.

"We all were, man," Mick said somberly. "Nic's still having a tough time with that one. Nothing on the radar said the compound was in the FBI Vamp

Division's sights, so it blindsided us. We know we probably lost a few strays that night, but we won't have any more intel until the remaining LaSalles make it here."

If they make it there.

It was left unsaid as it always was, but he knew as well as Mick did that between the bounty hunters, the FBI Vamp Division, and the Deviant mobs the government was quietly allowing to do the hunting for them, survival wasn't a guarantee.

Shoving the thought aside, he glanced at his phone and opened an email from Jagg detailing the first of his FANG contacts. "How's Nichol holding up anyways? Any more issues?"

He could hear the snow crunch under Mick's boots as the male put distance between the haunt's upper building and himself. "None. Rhys monitors him pretty tight, and we've had to really push him to walk away for his nights with Simone, but so far, he's holding it together. It probably helps Simone's on the same border patrol he is now. She keeps him in line better than any of us could."

Nichol's blood-high addiction was a blow none of the hauntmates were prepared for, and the realization their de facto leader was drowning while he held the others above water served as an intense wakeup call to all of them a few months back.

It was the spark to push Louis toward Stojanovski. He traded access to his hypnosis skills for the release of Jackson's hybrid Tender, Simone.

The hybrid Tender sold by Rhys to be used as a killing machine on the Stojanovski grounds before the compound became a refuge.

The hybrid Tender Nichol was unexpectedly linked to through his multitudes of online contacts.

The hybrid Tender the cranky male had also been unwittingly connected to for decades. His vampiric blood imprinted on her the moment she was born.

And given the intensity of vampire connection, Nichol Kaius was the only vamp in existence who could have survived year after year without knowing. His innate foul mood hiding most of the signs.

"I need to get back inside," Mick grumbled. "Dominic's temper is flaring again, and I'm certain Rhys is to blame, given the satisfaction I'm getting from the old asshole. Hit me up when you arrive on-site, and safe travels, brother."

The line disconnected, and Louis returned his full attention to the gravel road dipping with unfilled potholes and narrowing dangerously as snow drifted into the ditch.

He was pulling up behind the abandoned shed when his phone buzzed again. Ignoring Minks's call, he locked up the SUV and wandered the perimeter. He scanned for any signs of life before he ducked inside and crouched down, feeling the knots in the wooden floor for the latch to release the hatch. Descending into the hideout, he secured the locks and scented the small space, wrinkling his nose as he was greeted by nothing more than the pungent smell of dirt and rotting tree roots.

It was one of the less modernized bolt-holes, the entire place no more than a ten-by-ten room with a bed, a single gas lamp, and a stack of blades lining the far wall. Using the light of his phone, he lit the lamp and lay back on the bed, firing off a quick text to Mick.

—*This place is a dump*—

The minutes ticked by. Minks's unanswered call still sitting in his notifications as Mickey responded.

—Quit yer bitchin. It's nicer than 99% of the places you've lived—

Smirking, he tapped on Jonathan's number and waited for the deep Cockney accent to answer.

"Had me worried, Forbes," Minks announced. "You must drive like a grandma on her way to her Sunday knitting club." There was a loud exhale. "How are the accommodations?"

Tossing one arm over his eyes, he paused to listen as the easy trot of a coyote passed overhead. "Small and cold. Where did you hole up?"

"The base of the Big Horn," Minks replied after an audible inhale, his voice tight until he breathed out again. "At the rate you drive, we should hit Rapid City at the same time tomorrow."

Ignoring the slight, he scanned his memory for Jonathan's location. "You're on mountain paths? What the hell for?"

Most vampires avoided the mountains because the lack of accessible exits pricked at their ingrained survival instincts.

Of course, most also avoided the exposure of traveling on motorcycles, too.

"Where there are no vamps, there are no Deviants," came the response. "And if my holiday is going to be interrupted by a species war, I'll damn well enjoy the scenery on my way to my inevitable death." He chuckled, his voice echoing. "Though this cave leaves much to be desired, comfort-wise."

"Light tight?" he confirmed, the logical half of his mind knowing a vampire in his sixth decade would be well-versed in basic survival, while the other half was driven to ensure the young male was adequately protected from a painful end.

"We'll find out in twenty minutes, won't we?"

With his mind still pulling up the lay of the land, he frowned. "Rapid City is backtracking for you. If you remain on-site, I can shore up the connections at the rally and make it to your location tomorrow night."

"No deal," Minks replied, the usual relaxed tone of his voice taking on an unexpected edge. "First contact with the FANG leaders isn't something either of us should be walking into alone."

CHAPTER FOUR

Louis slipped through the shadows of the houses to avoid the UV lights lining the streets as he made his way toward the small crowd gathered in the stadium field where armed militia stood on the outskirts.

"We cannot remain silent while our own government murders members of our society," a woman hollered through a loudspeaker and a chorus of agreement rippled through the dozens of people surrounding her.

"They are our ancestors, our blood. They were here before us and deserve the right to exist with us and after us. Who are we to say they are no longer allowed to live? To thrive as they have for centuries and centuries? We must stand against our government, stand up to the barbaric laws being passed right now, and we must stand against the laws they've already forced on us."

"Compelling, isn't she?"

Crossing his arms, Louis leaned against the wall of a crumbling brick building and nodded without glancing over. "I'm convinced."

Minks lit a cigarette and grinned, showing off neatly clipped fangs. "You just arrive?"

Unwilling to admit he'd only hit city limits twenty minutes earlier, he shrugged. "Been here a while."

"Ah." The young vamp mimicked his pose against the wall. "The warm engine of your SUV threw me."

The group began to chant as a man took over control of the loudspeaker and whipped up the crowd with a list of vampires who met their end in one of the country's Deepfryers. The glass enclosures where UV rays publicly baked vamps for the crime of existing sat on the steps of nearly every courthouse from coast to coast, and every charred vamp was political proof the high price tags for each machine was money well spent.

He and Minks stood silent, their backs straightening while the names were read out. The cigarette was left to burn down until the man went silent and the voices of the FANG supporters swelled.

"A fucking travesty," Jonathan finally stated, nodding toward an unguarded opening in the field.

They walked across the snow-covered turf, nodding politely to a group dressed in all black who fell into step beside them. Slowing his pace to let them pass, Louis looked over at Minks. "Are they wearing capes?" he muttered under his breath, too quietly to be overheard. "If I see one drop of fake blood on their faces, I'm abandoning this mission and hiding in the sewers until this all blows over."

The young vamp laughed and tucked his hair behind his ear before he lit another cigarette and took a long drag. "Jagger forwarded the names Moira and Harris to me. I'm assuming that would be them," he said, gesturing toward the man and woman passing the megaphone between them, their calls for change being captured by dozens of phones as the audience grew at a slow, steady rate.

He followed Jonathan through the crowd, his presence wholly ignored while his companion was catching the eye of several of the women in their vicinity.

With the ease of a male used to the attention, Minks flashed smiles as he passed, his voice joining in the chants of the crowd while they made their way to the front where their targets stood on milk crates and egged their followers on.

"Take back the streets!"

The crowd shouted back, and Minks joined in with a grin.

"Vamps are people too!"

Again, his companion hollered alongside the others, pumping his fist in the air.

"Justice for all!"

"Yeah!" Jonathan bellowed, high-fiving a man beside him before he leaned over with a smirk. "If you're not with us, you're against us."

Narrowing his eyes, he crossed his arms and glanced at the people pressing up against his back. "Justice for all."

Apparently appeased, Minks returned his attention to the loudspeaker, leaving him alone to wonder why the hell he was there.

****

Jonathan declined the wrist held to his lips as he squeezed through the narrow hallway and gave the owner a smile. "No thank you," he said, arching away a fraction. "I'm afraid I filled up before I arrived."

The woman's eyes flickered with disappointment, and he turned away, scanned the living room for Louis, and found him backed into a corner. His hands were shoved deep into his pockets while Moira gestured around, her animated face almost making up for the complete discomfort on Louis's. Inching past the group of caped avengers in the dining room, he paused long enough to answer a few questions about the clip of his fangs before arriving at Louis's side.

"My deepest apologies," he drawled, interrupting Moira's spiel about the benefits of vampiric memory to historic societies. "I'm afraid I need to consult with my partner for a moment." He leaned forward, lowering his voice. "Jagger's orders."

Taking a deep breath and nodding solemnly, Moira stepped aside and turned her attention to the rest of her guests.

"I didn't sign up for this," Louis muttered, his gray eyes dark as they locked on the punch bowl of bright red juice. "Give me a herd of Deviants any night over this weird hero worship shit they've got going on here."

Elbowing him gently in the ribs, he smirked. "It's not all bad. You've got an A-pos, two B-negs, and an AB over there just itching to give you a crack at their veins."

"Go ahead."

He ran his tongue over his blunt fangs. "Screwed myself trying to fit in with our admirers."

"Benefit of being forgettable. None of these people will remember much about me by tomorrow." Louis pulled his phone from his pocket and fired off a text. "Ready to go? Mick's aerial surveillance of the hideout came back clear, but he wants ground confirmation within the hour."

It took almost the full hour to extricate themselves from the gathering. Moira and Harris finally put a stop to the onslaught of questions, following them with every step and ushered them out the door with promises to keep the members at bay until they were out of the area.

He followed Louis, struggling to maintain balance on his bike as the older vamp crept through the streets in his SUV, winding his way toward the small, windowless building no more than three blocks away as the crow flies.

It took thirty minutes.

Parking at the end of the street, he jogged up to Louis. "You just get your license?"

"Nope."

Taking the east side again to survey the lot, he waited quietly while Louis entered the code to the center unit and the lock opened. "How long have you been driving?"

"A while."

They closed the door behind them, flipped on the lights, and Louis entered a new code, signing it silently to him.

The room was simple—two narrow beds tight against the walls with a small TV hanging above a wood-burning fireplace. A cooler was wedged into the corner with two plastic-wrapped cups sitting on top beside a laminated list of phone numbers and addresses.

He tossed his bag on the closest bed and watched in disbelief as Louis scooped it up and tossed it onto the other bed. "Really?"

The older vampire shoved his newly annexed territory in front of the door and dropped his own backpack onto the mattress. "Your bed frame will collapse if it's moved."

Frowning, he gripped the headboard and gave it a shake. "It's fine." When there was no response, he sat down and bounced on it tentatively before stretching out and tracking the wiry red-haired vampire who sat hunched over his phone, grinning. "Holy damn, you're actually smiling."

Louis schooled his face immediately, and his thumb swiped across the screen before he set it down. "Nichol wants us in Big Horn tomorrow, en route to a FANG compound outside Dubois."

Cocking a brow, he pulled a cigarette out and lit it. "That *is* funny. At the speed you drive, we'll be lucky to make Spearfish." When Louis didn't crack a smile, he exhaled. "We'll hit the road a minute after sunset. You send in a report already?"

With a nod, Louie lay back and tossed his arm over his eyes. "I let Jagger know Moira and Harris are legit and the bolt-holes meet standards. Noted the parking issue and suggested a second exit be added."

Walking over to the fireplace, he flicked the cigarette ash onto the pile of logs. "Want me to fire this up?"

"No need to draw attention to ourselves by sending smoke signals into the air." Louis sat up and grabbed his phone. "I'll let Nichol know that needs to be traded out for an electric fireplace."

He made himself comfortable on the floor. "You're a little higher strung than Rhys led me to expect."

"I'm used to working alone."

"Bullocks," he scoffed. "Rhys said you've been with the Kaius haunt for years."

"And they left me alone."

With his point made, Louis tightened the laces on his boots, lay back, and closed his eyes.

****

Louis crossed his arms behind his head and stared at the ceiling.

"Nineteen times."

Jonathan opened one eye. "What?"

"I've driven nineteen times. Had no need to learn before I hooked up with Mick again. No license either." Frowning, he turned his attention to the far wall. "Nichol wouldn't even make up a passable fake one for me."

Minks was silent for a minute. "You're a hazard on the road."

"No lie there."

He could hear the bed frame creak as Minks shifted, the flame of his lighter illuminating the small room when it made contact with a fresh cigarette. "Maybe we should ditch the SUV."

"No fucking way." The cherry of the cigarette provided just enough light for his eyes to see clearly. "Why did you agree to this job?"

The red ember flamed as Minks took a drag. "I once told Rhys he could call on my haunt for anything." He chuckled low. "One of those mistakes of youth, I guess. Always add in the stipulations *before* offering services to one of the most badass vamps in existence." With a long exhale that curled smoke through the room, he swung his legs over the edge of the bed and stood, stretching. "Of course, I was also in the presence of Rhys Kaius. I would have bargained away anything he asked for just because, well, it's Rhys fucking Kaius."

He nodded knowingly, thinking back to his first months with the Kaius hauntmates. "Your hauntmates are in Denver already. Why not you?"

"Wanderlust," came the response between drags of the cigarette. "I was up in the Arctic tundra when everything went fully to hell. Which means my oldest brother probably decorated our room without me."

"You deal with Nichol much?"

"That scary bastard? Not if I can help it." Minks

31

crossed the room and flicked the ash before putting the cigarette out. "Is it true the youngest one survived a separated connection?"

Vampire connection was no laughing matter. While the unexplainable imprinting on a human wasn't common, it was even rarer for a vamp as young as Dominic. The separation from his connected mate, Molly, had made Dom feral and there was still a heavy holdover of possessiveness emanating from the guy on a constant—often amusing—basis.

"That's Dominic. Yeah." He smiled as he thought back to one of his favorite memories. Dom covered in river water and slopping through the pristine halls of a traitor vamp's impeccable house. "He's a good kid."

Minks gingerly sat back on his bed and slid the rest of the cigarette into his pack. "How tough a haul is this going to be? No holdbacks."

Fixing his eyes on the ceiling again, he contemplated cushioning it. "If we survive this, we're buying a shitload of lottery tickets."

CHAPTER FIVE

Jonathan's brows shot up when Moira smiled politely at Louis as though she hadn't spent an hour talking his ear off the night before. "Any friend of Jonathan's is welcome. Come on in, gentlemen."

She stepped aside so they could enter, and Harris waved from the living room. "Nice to meet you, Louis. How were the accommodations, Mr. Minks?"

Craning his neck to see into the living room, he nodded at Harris. "The accommodations were perfect, sir. Quite suitable." Turning his attention back to Moira, he held out the car keys. "We won't take much of your time this evening, but we were hoping we could store the SUV somewhere on-site for a few weeks."

Moira took the keys from his outstretched hand. "We'll guard it with our lives," she said solemnly. "I'll pull it into the back tonight."

Louis propped the door open with his foot. "On behalf of Jagger and Bianca, thank you for your hospitality. Jagg will be in touch soon."

Moira followed them onto the stoop. "Don't you forget you have friends here," she said as they clomped down the snow-covered steps. "We won't let them win."

Giving her a salute, he and Louis walked down the street silently until he was certain Moira was out of range. "They had no idea who you were."

"Told you."

He tugged Louis's bag from his shoulder and crammed it into the small cargo hold of the bike, pulling out leather gloves. "That has to be annoying, being forgotten so easily. Good thing it doesn't work on vamps."

Louis eyed the motorcycle warily, running his thumbs over the straps of the spare helmet as he put it on. "It's got its usefulness."

Securing his own helmet, he reached over, tugged at Louis's, and snapped the visor down to ensure the fit was adequate before handing him a pair of gloves. "Perfect. Put these on."

The older vamp wrestled them on, the fresh black leather standing out against his ragged jean jacket. "So I…sit?"

Stifling a laugh, he knelt beside the bike. "Feet go here. If you put your foot down when I stop, let me know so I don't take off and leave your leg a mile behind us. One hand can go here, but you're going to have to hold on to me, so if you have any hang-ups, now's the time to say it." When Louis merely nodded and narrowed his eyes at the back tire, he stood. "Let me lead the turns. Don't make any sudden movements, and hold on tight when I accelerate. Questions?"

"Probably. Let's go."

Snapping his visor down, he mounted the bike and booted the kickstand up, steadying it while Louis swung his leg over the seat awkwardly, kneeing him in the back as he did. "You and vehicles aren't a good fit."

"Nope."

When no arm appeared around his waist, he reached back and forced the issue. "Let me be real clear on this. If you don't hold on, your head's going off that rubber, we're painting the cement with your face, and I'm still going to make decent time because I have no problems dragging your bloody carcass behind me through the snow if it means we'll make decent time."

Louis's hand gripped the zipper of his leather jacket, and he started the engine, revving it a few times before he eased onto the street and wincing when his passenger's fingers dug painfully into his ribs.

****

Louis forced his grip to loosen when Jonathan's shoulders tensed, his hold admittedly a little tighter than necessary on the last curve. "Sorry," he yelled through the visor, knowing his voice would be drowned out between the noise of the road and the wind whipping at them through the passes.

Minks released the handlebars with one hand and gave Louis's arm a quick tap of acknowledgment, his laughter puncturing through the white noise when the vice grip resumed.

Motorcycles were fucking insane.

And so were the vamps who rode them.

They'd been winding through the side roads for over six hours, the extended winter darkness buying them ample time to skirt the interstate and avoid the roadblocks the FBI Vamp Division set up months ago. His ass was numb, and his fingers ached from maintaining a hold on the lunatic who simultaneously barreled down the icy roads and pointed out whatever interesting scenery he could in the darkness.

Nothing was more interesting to Louis than the driver maintaining a secure grasp on the motorcycle's handlebars.

The mountain pass they were whizzing through now

was wearing down what was left of his nerves which were already frayed by the tight turns taken sharply enough he was certain his knee grazed the pavement on the last one.

His exposed back pricked from the lack of cover, nothing more than his old jean jacket and a thin T-shirt standing between him and any weapon possibly trained on his spine.

But the thought of looking behind him, of seeing the road race beneath them, was definitely driving his focus. He kept his shoulders hunched and the visor of his helmet less than an inch from the back of Jonathan's.

The bike slowed, the angling of Minks's hips letting him know they were veering right.

"Three minutes ahead," the deranged driver called out, flipping his visor up and glancing over his shoulder. "You okay?"

"Fine," he ground out, forcing his jaw to relax before he snapped a fang.

Minks wound through the narrow pass and dropped one foot to the ground as he came to a stop. "I'll walk the bike behind those rocks, and we can hike it from here." He looked back again and grinned. "You can let go now."

With a dismount as graceless as his mount was hours earlier, Louis stumbled off the motorcycle, his balance wavering for a moment before he found his footing.

"This way," Minks called out, their bags already swung over his shoulder as he strode between the fallen boulders at the mountain base, his riding gloves hanging out of his back pocket. "You'll want to bring your helmet with you so it doesn't fill with snow."

Doubling back to grab it, he followed the young

vamp up the steep incline, the slippery slope a far more preferable journey than the ride in. He held back as Minks slung their satchels onto a narrow ledge outside a small opening, sizing up the cave's entrance. "You fit in there?"

"Not easily." Minks shrugged off his jacket and tossed it onto the pile before hefting himself up. "Good news is a tight fit for me means nothing bigger than I am will get in, either."

Watching as the broad-shouldered male flattened himself to the ground and inched into the cave, Louis shimmied up the final stretch and waited until the black boots disappeared inside.

"Toss it all in," Minks ordered, his hand reaching out of the opening. "Took me two tries to learn that lesson last time."

Firing their small stash of belongings in, he mimicked Minks's contortions and wedged himself into the cave, the temporary exposure of his legs to the unseen wilderness propelling him forward quickly. "For the record, no more caves after this." He inched across the stone and rolled onto his back once he was completely inside. "If we get cornered, we're fucked."

Using the light of his phone, Jonathan scanned the small enclosure, zeroing in on a faint marking as he reached into his back pocket and withdrew a small blade. "I'll add your name to mine in case they need to identify the ash," he grinned, kneeling in front of the boulder's face and scratching at it methodically. "There. No forgetting your name here, right?"

Leaning in, he cocked a brow. "You forgot the O."

****

Jonathan leisurely tossed his pocketknife into the air

again, catching it a split-second before it nicked his stomach. "I don't know how you deal with it," he stated, spinning the blade between his fingers. "I came from a large family and was brought into a large haunt, so the whole idea of being completely isolated for years, even months, is a weird concept for me. Even when I'm traveling solo, I'm in constant contact with the others." He pushed himself up on his elbows and glanced over in the darkness. "I guess being linked to the Kaius haunt is the same kind of thing for you, having to answer to someone else instead of staying rogue."

When Louis responded with nothing more than a grunt, he stretched back out. "Must be at least a little cool to be running with that powerhouse, knowing all you have to do is speak and shit gets done."

Another grunt.

Abandoning his blade for a small stone, he bounced it off the rock overhead, miscalculating the drop speed and cursing when it caught him in the throat. When there was a snicker from across the cave floor, he grinned. "So you're a slapstick guy. I'll remember that."

After building a precarious tower of helmets, bags, and jackets to block the small entrance, he'd done his damnedest to get Louis to say more than a few clipped replies. Even in total darkness, he could sense the unease in the older vampire. It didn't mesh with Rhys's description of the male he'd be working alongside for the foreseeable future.

"Chillest fucking vamp you'll ever meet."

Maybe by Kaius haunt standards, when placed beside Rhys's infamous temper or Nichol's notorious irritability, Louis was calm. But his ribs and sternum were still raw from the grip the male had on him on their ride up.

Sliding his blade into his back pocket, he tucked his arms behind his head. "How many days can you go without rest?"

There was a rustling as Louis switched positions. "Eight."

"Good to know," he muttered, closing his eyes. "So I only have six more to go before I'm not sleeping with an audience."

****

Louis listened to the rhythmic beating of the wings of a falcon taking flight outside the cave and tracked the bird until the rush of the wind carried it away.

Two hours to go.

Resting in close proximity to the Kaius hauntmates had taken some getting used to when he first moved into their haunt, but two centuries of friendship with Mickey kept his natural vigilance at bay during the initial weeks and months. But even then, he had the artificial security of walls and doors separating him from the others. A visual solitude appeased his instinct to remain isolated. Isolated and alive.

On the few occasions he found himself locked in bunkers or basement hovels with them, he fought injury and hunger to stay alert as long as possible, feigning rest while he kept his ears open for signs of attack.

Vampires who placed sleep over safety were easy targets.

Easy targets were easily ashed.

And being staked or beheaded in his sleep wasn't on his list of survival techniques.

Glaring into the blackness toward the pile of helmets and clothes providing a shoddy sunblock, he moved his foot closer to the wall of the cave. Inadvertently booting the precarious stack and exposing them to the sun's rays wasn't on his mental survival list, either.

He eased his phone from his back pocket and swiped it to life, shielding the bright glow of the screen to avoid waking his companion while he scanned his emails, his thumb hovering over Mickey's most recent message.

—*Sign here, brother*—

The attachment remained unopened. The documentation required nothing more than the swipe of his finger to make his integration into the Kaius haunt official and christen Louis Forbes as Louis Kaius.

Powering his phone down, he slid it back into his pocket and stared at the nothingness above him, wondering why he was hellbent on holding onto his bastard creator's name.

CHAPTER SIX

Jonathan slowed the motorcycle down and pushed his visor back, scanning the mountain terrain slowly. "Are you sure we have those coordinates right? Maybe we should double back to Dubois and check in with Nichol."

Louis's grip loosened as the bike came to a stop, and his foot thumped onto the fresh snow covering his shoe. "Turn this thing off."

Jonathan killed the engine and leaned back for a moment, jerking forward when he pressed against his passenger. "Sorry."

Unsnapping his helmet, Louis ignored his apology and stilled, his head cocked while he dismounted with slightly more grace than the previous evening. "Tuck this out of sight, and we'll go in on foot."

"Go where?" he muttered, the cloud cover limiting the moonlight. He walked the bike into the rocky ditch and pulled their bags from the hatch before he laid it on its side and kicked snow over it.

Louis stood on the narrow road, his thin lips tight as his nose wrinkled. "Northwest. I'm guessing a hundred yards, but they could be closer. The snowfall is fucking with the scent."

"You can't smell shit," he scoffed, swinging the bags onto his back and taking a deep inhale of the fresh air.

"No, *you* can't smell shit," Louis countered. "You young kids don't know how to filter." He took a dozen steps and paused, holding his hand out. "What do you hear?"

Freezing in place, he strained to listen through the faint wind trickling along the mountain pass. "Coyote to the east?"

Giving him a dead stare, Louis crossed his arms. "Try again. Lower. Get on your knees if you have to."

Crouching to the ground, he stretched his hearing as far as he could, glaring at the older vampire when he grabbed his head and forced it closer to the snow-covered earth. "I—" He hesitated, picking up a slight vibration. "What is that?"

"You tell me."

Focusing on the intermittent tremor, he lowered one hand into the snow to see if he could pick up the physical signs of life beneath him. "Voices?"

Nodding, Louis held his hand out and helped him to his feet. "Now that you know the tone you're listening for, show me where the entrance is."

Turning toward the northwest Louis had initially mentioned, he led the way, his ears capturing and losing the periodic pulses while they hiked between the rocks at the mountain's base.

"Okay, stop."

Keeping tuned into the voices, he stilled and scanned the wall of boulders.

"You get one shot to lead us to the entrance," Louis continued. "If you fuck it up, I drive for the rest of the week."

Snorting, he grinned and pointed to the northernmost boulder. "Right th—"

"Before you make what could be a very stupid and rash decision," Louis interjected, "I want you to scent the area. What are you looking for?"

"Vamp bloodlines," he stated, crossing his arms. "There's seven."

"Wrong."

Frowning, he bent down, one eye on Louis as he inhaled. "Six and two humans."

Nodding, his companion shoved his hands into his back pockets. "How old are the scents?"

He straightened with a shrug. "Two days?"

Another dead stare.

Crouching back down, he sifted through the smells, the individual odors strengthening as he untangled one from the next. "Three of the vamps arrived over a week ago. Two were there a lot longer. Maybe a month? One was in yesterday before the snow hit."

"And the humans?"

The two remaining scents were easily distinguishable, a B-positive and an AB-negative, with a hint of alcohol. "They passed through here three nights ago, but…they opened the entrance recently. Within the past few hours."

Louis stepped aside and gestured toward the mountain. "And that entrance is where exactly? Look very fucking hard."

He walked forward and stopped, studying his boots as they sank into the snow. Following the paths between the boulders, he hooked his thumbs in their bags and grinned. "That way, wise leader."

Louis followed silently as he wound through the jagged rocks, turning sideways to squeeze through the last one before he pulled a cigarette from his pack and fired his lighter up.

The entrance was shielded by a trick of the eye. The rock strata combined with the wind-eroded smoothness of the mountainside to create a solid visual effect masking a lipped opening. Taking a final drag of his cigarette, he pushed it into the snow to put it out, collected the butt, and slid it into the pack.

"Looks like there's no driving for you anytime soon," he exhaled, blowing a puff of smoke into the air as he crossed the final yards and stood in front of the small mineshaft door.

When he reached down to open it, Louis snatched his hand and shoved it back. "Lesson two. Opening unknown doors will get you ashed before you can finish gloating."

****

Louis listened to the silence which fell through the shelter under their feet and tracked the single rustle of fabric as it drew near. Standing between the door and the younger vampire, he prepared for an attack. "Louis Forbes, Kaius haunt."

There was an audible murmuring as his hosts relaxed. The locks on the wooden door clicked one by one until a man pushed the door open, eleven stakes strapped to his body. "Get in fast so we can seal 'er back up."

Leading them through the narrow passage, he blocked Minks from view when they hit the entrance to the makeshift seating area, which was little more than a collapsed tunnel recently cleared of the rocks and debris that had breached the last of the wooden frame affixed to the stone walls. Six pairs of eyes lifted to his, all familiar faces from the Stojanovski compound, all relaxing a fraction when he came into sight.

"Forbes," one of the older males greeted, nodding politely when Jonathan squeezed past him and sat on the cold ground. "Welcome."

Taking a seat beside Minks, he leaned back. "Are we expecting others? Jagger's notes had seven names."

The elder's gaze dropped as the others remained silent. "The youngest of the Chalone haunt over there felt the end of Chalone Tartarus last night. He was trailing behind to aid the evacuation of the Talon haunt." Glancing at the red-haired male sitting sullenly in the corner, the elder shook his head. "Goddamn bounty hunters won't be happy until we're wiped from the earth."

The humans flanked the entrance, watching the newcomers warily.

"Forbes," the younger one called over, leaning forward and extending his hand. "Jimmy Bellegard. This here's my brother, Brendan. It's an honor to meet one of Jagger Kaius's foot soldiers."

Fighting the lift of his brow, he shook the man's hand. "Honor is ours, Jimmy. Brendan." Nodding at the rows of coolers disappearing down a secondary shaft, he got to his feet and ducked as he entered it. "Anything to eat in there?"

"Nothing warm, but it'll pass," Jimmy called over. "Rations aren't too tight, provided the shipments from Jagger continue to come in."

He pulled out two bags, holding one out to Minks and the other to the young Chalone male. When the orphaned vamp merely turned his head from the offering, he knelt down. "How old are you, kid?"

Without a word, the Chalone youngster lifted his

pant leg, revealing a single ring.

Slicing the bag open with his fang, he held it out. "Eat." Met with nothing more than a hardened glare, he got comfortable and sloshed the cool liquid around, allowing the aroma to waft through the room. "Your eldest brother made Denver two weeks ago," he said quietly while he pulled his phone from his pocket and listened to the plastic rustling as Minks finished his meal. Opening his saved documents, he turned the screen toward the kid. "Right there on the bottom. He's in the east unit, apartment nine-D."

He stilled while the young vampire's green eyes scanned the list, waiting until the kid's fingers flexed toward the phone before he held the blood out. "We're going to need you at peak strength when we get the call to evacuate."

The male paused for a moment before he accepted the meal, his eyes locked on his brother's name.

****

Jonathan peered into the dimly lit shaft and examined the strength of the wooden frame with his hands before he snapped open the sleeping bag Brendan and Jimmy had provided. "Is the kid all set up in his area?"

Louis rolled out his own, flopped onto it, and tucked his satchel under his head. "Already out cold."

Pulling a cigarette out, he lit it and blew the smoke into the blackness of the mineshaft, stretching far past the boundaries of his heightened vision. "He's way too young to be on his own."

"He's not on his own."

Flicking the ashes along the rusting steel tracks that cut through the shaft, he sat and watched as Louis craned his head toward the area where the orphaned vampire was resting. "Is your creator already in Colorado?"

"My creator has been blowing on the wind for well over sixteen decades." Reclining back, he grinned. "So yeah, some of him may be in Colorado by now."

Butting his cigarette out on the stone wall, he draped his arms over his knees, his curiosity piqued. "How bad was the hit when he died? Was it as bad as they say it is?"

Louis crossed his arms behind his head. "Depends. If your creator is a half-decent guy, yeah, it will fucking hurt. Like being gutted without the gore. But if your creator is like mine? It feels absolutely fucking fantastic."

Thinking about his own indulgent, unflappable maker, a small shiver traveled down his spine. "How did he go out?"

"On his knees, begging like the pathetic loser he was."

His brows shot up. "You did it?"

With a smirk, Louis lolled his head to look at him. "Word of advice. Don't back me into a corner."

He dropped his gaze to the tunnel.

Having known only excessive leniency and attentive guidance during his early decades, the thought of ending the leader of his line turned his stomach and left a taste in his mouth sourer than the stale blood he'd ingested earlier.

He'd heard of vampires who had taken out their own creators for power, for wealth, for status. They were few and far between, always ostracized, and often hunted. Most who went that route possessed a dangerous ambition and a proclivity for violence.

What he knew of Louis didn't fit the stereotype. Nor did it mesh with the older vampire's connection to the Kaius haunt, a bloodline admired for their staying hands and swift justice for those who didn't adhere to the laws of their species.

Vampires who took out their own blood had no alliances, nothing to keep them in check should their actions or aspirations prove detrimental to their community.

On a social ranking, they sat firmly above the Deviants, those ID-driven turnings gone wrong and killed on sight.

"Don't overthink it."

He glanced over at Louis. "What?"

With one arm over his eyes, the older vamp chuckled. "I can hear the gears turning in your head, trying to figure out how a line-killer ended up linked to the most powerful haunt in the Americas." Lifting his elbow, he smiled, the shadows falling on his angled features making him appear more gaunt than he was.

"Mickey thinks my skinny ass is worth keeping around, so here we are, sleeping in a mine shaft, surrounded by refugee vamps, and guarded by two humans who have watched way too many apocalypse movies to be totally sane." He dropped his arm back over his eyes. "Lucky you."

CHAPTER SEVEN

Louis passed the pile of black boxes and multicolored wires over to Jonathan and shrugged. "If you can make sense of Nichol's instructions, go for it. I give."

Brendan arrived as dusk settled in the mountains, his back weighted down by the parcels he picked up in town while most of the vampires were resting, watched over by Jimmy and his impressive collection of stakes and ammunition.

Minks pulled the pile closer and carefully untangled the wires. He scanned the directions the de facto Kaius haunt leader had included among the plethora of disassembled speakers, microphones, and signal boosters scattered at their feet.

The young Chalone vamp sat silently between them, carefully organizing the dozens of screws and fuses by size while he nursed a cold bag of A-positive. Minks leaned over and demonstrated what he needed the kid to do before returning to his own collection, placing the instructions on the floor where they could both track the wiring diagrams Nichol drew by hand.

Satisfied the communication device the Kaius haunt needed set up was in good hands, Louis stood up and joined the others, keeping one eye on the young males.

"Once this is functioning, we'll do a test run to make sure you're in constant contact with Jagger," he announced to the older vamps as he leaned against a wooden pillar. "I want all voices fed through it so the guys can become familiar with who's who. When Jimmy and Brendan wake, we'll need to get them on as well."

Booker, a fair-haired vamp he recognized from the Stojanovski compound, hunched forward on his makeshift seat, the stone rocking a fraction as he did so. "So we get one shot at this and then what? If one of us drags our feet, our whole group goes down in flames."

Tracking the male's gaze, he stepped between Booker and the Chalone vamp. "How old are you?"

The male pulled his jeans up to reveal his rings.

"I'm pretty fucking certain a vampire in his fourth century can effectively subdue and assist a newborn," he stated calmly, crouching down to ensure they were eye-level with each other. "And if that newborn isn't on the plane when it takes off, I'll be issuing the shoot-down notice personally. Clear?"

Booker held his gaze for a moment before nodding tersely. "Crystal."

Righting himself, he smiled at the others. "Jagger and Nichol will get an update from me once we have that signal boost up and running and I get us connected to the Kaius haunt server. All names will be recorded. Any stragglers who make it here will be added up to and including the moment of takeoff." Taking his position against the pillar, he looked around the room. "Any plane landing without the young ones in tow will be turned away. And that will be a guaranteed death sentence."

Minks glanced up at him with a smirk before returning his attention to the signal booster, and the room went silent, save for the quiet creaking of screws as they were tightened.

The coordination of an air evacuation into Denver was a final attempt on behalf of the Kaius haunt to bring the last of the American vampires into the one city where they would be protected from the threat of the bounty hunters, Deepfryers, and vigilante groups prowling the streets.

The establishment of eight safe houses within a five-hour flight of the sanctuary brought him to the mine shaft. The responsibility of securing communications and confirming the security of the bolt-holes was now resting on his shoulders.

No one knew when the evacuation would occur. It was anyone's guess when Nichol would make the calculated call. Mickey was in charge of lining up the small aircraft that would be held in stasis until the announcement was made, and the pilots were paid heftily for their time, their patience, and their silence.

The Deviant mobs roaming the countryside were slowly making their way toward Denver as well. The coasts were clearing of the scourge as they stalked closer to their targets. Their hive mentality was led by Kaius Khthonios's own creator, who was nowhere to be found yet still managed to be at the forefront of everyone's mind.

The final evacuation held a two-fold purpose. Save the last of the American vampires and boost the numbers of the army who would fight the Deviant horde when it arrived on Denver's doorstep.

There was no room in the constantly evolving plans for any vampire who would leave another behind.

"Booker?"

The fair-headed vamp looked up. "Yeah?"

Gesturing down a dark track, he walked as far into

the narrow path as he could without being reduced to walking on his knees. His phone lit the way while he typed out a message to send once the signal booster was functional. "Are any of your bloodline already in Denver?" he asked, keeping his voice low to avoid being overheard in the chamber.

Booker nodded. "Two of the younger ones. Why?"

"They'll serve as a little extra incentive for you to keep the Chalone kid alive and fed," he replied as he pressed send on the email to Jagger and Nichol.

****

Jonathan hiked their two bags onto his shoulder while Louis gave his final instructions to the vampires and humans holed up in the mine shaft before he added a list of scrawled instructions and contact numbers to the grubby notebook Brendan kept by the entrance. With a last wave to the sullen Chalone kid, they walked out of the safe house, and the door closed behind them with a thud before the locks clicked into place.

"Better get that jacket done up," he called over his shoulder as he knelt down to lift the motorcycle from the snow. "Pocatello is a long way off on the side roads."

Louis eyed the bike and pulled on his gloves. "Remind me again why we didn't take the SUV?"

"Fuel consumption, terrain, and of course, the total coolness factor of this hog." Dropping his visor and mounting the bike, he revved the engine rhythmically until Louis joined him, one arm reaching around to grasp the zipper of his leather jacket. "Ready?"

"No." When the motorcycle didn't move, Louis grunted. "Fine. Yes."

They doubled back through the mountain pass, their progress slow until they hit the entrance to the main highway. Pulling off the road, he flipped his visor up and looked back. "You have two choices here," he stated, tugging at his gloves. "We go slow and steady through here, or we push this beast and get across this stretch in under two hours." Focusing on the snow-covered highway, he licked his lips. "Boils down to how much you trust me to get us there alive."

Louis visibly tensed. "The longer we're on the road, the greater our chances of discovery. By humans and Deviants," he finally said, his back hunching slightly. "Let's do this."

"Hold tight," he called over his shoulder as he gunned the engine and tore onto the icy road, swerving around the snowdrifts to avoid losing what was left of his limited traction. There were few other vehicles on the highway, the questionable weather system keeping all but the most ardent travelers off the dangerous mountain roads.

As he sped up out of a slide, Louis gripped him like a spider monkey, fingers digging into his ribs painfully until the bike leveled out.

Not that Jonathan minded.

He was a good rider, but even he had to admit the speeds he was reaching on the single-lane highway were quickly approaching hazardous levels. The heat of his tires did little to counter the thin layer of ice covering the pavement, the rubber finding nothing more than snow to grip. Black ice stretched for miles, hidden under the darkness of the night, and glazed with a skiff of snowflakes skipping over the road and buffing it to a sheen.

Maybe hazardous was too conservative.

It was downright deadly.

Katja Desjarlais

But so was slowing their progress.

Louis's anxiousness about their speed was tempered by the intermittent glimpses of movement in the shadows, the telltale jerking movements of Deviants pulling both pairs of eyes to the ditch every ten miles like clockwork.

Stopping wasn't an option.

Neither was crashing.

Adjusting his hold on his handlebars, he leaned forward and changed gears, tracking his revs while he sped up again. Both of Louis's arms tightened around him with enough force he questioned whether his ribs would hold up under the pressure.

If they survived until they hit Denver, he'd be hitting Nichol up for an encrypted Bluetooth device that would let him talk Louis's grip down to comfortable levels.

Swerving to the right as a Deviant stumbled out of the ditch, he put all thoughts of surviving until Denver aside and focused on surviving Teton National Park.

****

Louis stood in the turret of the opulent rural Pocatello manor and nodded absently while the hosts rambled on about the security precautions they'd taken to ensure the nineteen vampires housed in their walls were safe.

The owner, an elderly woman named Amelia, motioned toward the silos peppering the vast estate, her jeweled fingers glinting in the dim lighting. "Our guests have a choice of escape tunnels leading to various locations on our property. Inside each outpost are two vehicles with well-compensated drivers at the ready to transport them in light-tight transfer bays," she stated. "We're prepared for forty more should the need arise but

54

could accommodate upward of two hundred for a limited period."

Jonathan whistled in appreciation and flashed the woman a smile as he scanned the yard. "Miss Amelia, I must say you're making the thought of leaving here rather unpalatable."

Her blue eyes softened when the vampire poured on his Cockney accent, the slight bowing of his head obviously delighting the woman. "You're more than welcome to select a more permanent accommodation," she laughed, closing the curtains tight. "However, I suspect Jagger Kaius may not approve, and his word, as you know, is law."

Minks held his arm out to the elderly woman, and Louis trailed behind, making a final check of the perimeter before he followed them down the spiral staircase and into the foyer.

Amelia glanced at her watch, walked to her security system, and entered a lengthy code. Metal shutters unrolled over every window. "My apologies for the noise," she huffed as she led them through the living room to the stairwell leading to the basement suites. "I wasn't aware of the sound sensitivities vampires had until my first guests reacted. Had I known, I would have been more diligent in selecting a quieter brand."

"I suspect your first vampires were more sensitive to the unexpectedness of the sound, not the volume," he assured her as they descended into the underground rooms. "You'll have to forgive us for being a little jumpier than usual."

Passing a dozen closed doors, she opened one and motioned them in. "If you need anything at all, there's an intercom system in every room to alert my staff.

Bianca Schumann and Jagger have vetted each one, so you may rest easy today. Leave your laundry in the hall and someone will have it washed and pressed by sundown."

With a smile, she exited the room, her soft-soled shoes brushing along the tiled floor until she tip-toed up the stairs.

While he keyed a passcode into the door lock, Jonathan strolled through the small room, pressing on each of the four mattresses before selecting one. "Why would she do all this?"

Opening his email to Nichol's detailed notes on the property and its owner, he passed his phone over and walked into the bathroom. He turned the shower on and stepped under the hot spray while Jonathan read up on Miss Amelia Cornwall, her decade of vampire activism, and the fortune she built in the ranching industry.

With nights of filth and debris scrubbed from his skin and hair, he waffled between the pile of filthy clothes on the floor and the pristine row of bathrobes hanging on the wall, tags still attached to the sleeves. Deciding on comfort over practicality for a few hours, he tossed one robe on, tearing the tags off and tossing them in the garbage as he gathered his clothes and exited the room.

"Well, aren't you huggable?"

Refusing to acknowledge Minks's comment, he unlocked the door and placed his laundry in the hall, catching the eye of another robed vampire further down and nodding in mutual discomfort with their situation.

Securing the lock again, he claimed his bed and stretched out as Jonathan disappeared into the bathroom, frowning when a notification popped up on his phone.

—To place your meal order for dusk, press OK—

Scowling at the message for a moment, he tapped OK.

—For A-positive, press 1. For B-positive, press 2—

"Minks?" he called out over the rush of the shower. "What do you want for breakfast?"

"Surprise me."

Hunching over his phone, he followed the ordering instructions, ignoring the special request box before he sent it off.

Donning a matching robe, Minks sauntered out of the bathroom and keyed in the lock code. He called out a greeting to someone in the hall before he closed the door and flopped onto his bed. Rolling over, he grabbed the TV remote. "What are we watching while you pretend to sleep?"

****

Jonathan changed the channel for the third time in ten minutes, smirking when his bunk mate fixed him with a flat stare. "You stay up, I stay up."

Louis reached across to his bed, snatched the remote, and turned the TV off. "Then we wait each other out in the dark."

"Fine by me."

He knew the older vampire had the benefit of age, but he also knew Louis had been on high alert for enough nights to be sliding into exhaustion, the slight slowing of his movements giving him away. "Louis?"

"What."

Staring into the darkness, he listened to the padding of feet outside their door, the unmistakable sound of clothing being dropped into a plastic bag every few steps. "This might be the most secure we're going to be for a while."

"Probably."

Rolling his eyes, he turned his head toward his bunk mate. "If you don't rest now, I'm telling Nichol. You're bordering on becoming a liability."

He was met with a silence stretching out for almost fifteen minutes before Louis finally broke it. "Fucking tattle-tale is what you are."

Letting the words hang in the air, he bided his time until the older vampire's stillness hit an unmistakable level of rest. Satisfied Louis was actually down for the night, he sat up and tuned into the comings and goings overhead until sundown arrived.

CHAPTER EIGHT

Jonathan watched as Louis sat uncomfortably at the head of Amelia Cornwall's table. A retinue of vampires bombarded him with questions while their meals were carried out by a handful of wait staff, their militia-style uniforms at odds with the lavish decor.

Louis had woken with a start, shooting back against the bed's headboard when Jonathan eased the door open to collect their freshly pressed clothes. By the time the door was closed and secured, Louis was on his feet, a stiletto blade in hand and eyes darkened to a deep green.

The older vamp hadn't spoken a word to him since.

Even now, with his lips drawn tight and eyes narrowed while he addressed the litany of queries thrown at him, Louis held the look of a cornered fighter, lying low until the opportunity to escape arose.

Pounding back the last of his meal, he stood. "Hate to put an end to the info session, gentlemen, but I'm afraid we need to hit the road if we want time to dodge the Deviant mob outside Salt Lake."

Louis looked over at him, his shoulders dropping a fraction while the other vampires sat back in their seats. "Right." With a shrug of apology, he pushed his chair back and rose to his feet. "So, like I said earlier, only emails coming directly through the Kaius haunt server are deemed official. If any of you suspect you've received a trolling message, alert the others, take a screenshot, delete the email, and forward the information directly to Jagger and Bianca. We're out of here."

Jonathan bowed to Amelia, shaking his head when she started to stand. "We'll see ourselves out, ma'am. Thank you for the hospitality. And for assisting us in this endeavor."

Louis echoed his sentiments from the entrance to the dining hall, his bag and helmet already slung over his shoulder.

Once he paused long enough to memorize the faces of the vampires in the room, he joined Louis on the trek out the door, zipping his leather jacket on the way. "Not big on communication, are you?"

"Not my thing."

Rolling his eyes, he pulled his helmet on and opened the bike's hatch, handing Louis his gloves before he shoved both bags in and slammed it closed. "The Kaius haunt is all about communication, aren't they?" he asked, tightening his chin strap. "Must've been hell for you."

Louis mounted the bike and flipped his visor down. "Observing from the back of the room is a fuck of a lot easier than dealing with questions I can't answer and knowing answers I can't give."

Turning the engine on, he let it warm up against the bitter cold. "I know it goes against your no-talking thing, but we should hit up Nichol to send some communicators we can use while we're on the road. Maybe have him ship them to the Vegas stop?"

With a grunt, Louis pulled his phone out of his back pocket, fired off a quick text, and popped the collar of his jacket up. "Let's go."

****

Louis had always known the existence of a rogue

vampire was precarious, that living without the protection of a haunt would lead to an early end.

He hadn't figured that death would arrive dressed in leather and riding on two wheels.

All shame aside, he clung to Minks while they sped across the secondary highways and gravel roads, the silhouettes of Deviants lurching through the snow-covered fields keeping Jonathan's foot heavy.

His driver was almost giddy with the chase, the challenge of weaving between snow drifts and gnarled fingers apparently making him bolder as he flattened down over the handlebars and took another corner a little too tight for comfort.

The bike finally slowed when they reached a dead end, and Minks circled around slowly while they assessed the empty fields surrounding them.

"Isn't this where we're supposed to hang a right?" he asked, flipping his visor up and yanking one glove off. Opening the aerial shots Nichol had sent them, Jonathan sat back and scowled into the darkness. "What the fuck?"

Tugging his own cell out, he fired off a text to Nichol. "He's tapping into our coordinates now," he muttered, craning his neck to see behind them until his phone buzzed. "Yeah, we're where we need to be." He looked at the snow-covered path to their right. "Can we get through that on this?"

Minks tapped his thigh and pointed eastward at a dozen dark figures stumbling their way. "Let's find out."

Angling his phone so they could track the progress of the Deviants, he leaned in tight and grabbed onto Minks. The bike spun to the west, spraying snow and ice behind them.

Eleven miles to go.

The tires fought to cut a path, the white powder hiding divots in the earth until they were bouncing over them. Minks's grip was tested when a larger hole sent the front tire lurching to the left, both of their feet dropping to the ground to keep themselves upright.

"This is fucking stupid," he yelled through the wind, knowing the driver wouldn't hear him but needing to voice his thought before they wiped out at the heels of the Deviants emerging from all sides.

He could feel the tension in Jonathan's muscles, his formerly fluid movements holding a more calculated rigidity while he drove them within three miles of their base and slowed to a stop to assess the scene.

"Louis?"

"Yeah?"

"How good at hand-to-hand are you? On a one-to-ten scale?"

He eased his stiletto blade from his back pocket. "Eight."

Nodding, Minks opened the small compartment between the handlebars, pulled out a switchblade, and passed it back to him. "And where's your trust factor sitting with me? On a one-to-ten?"

"Why?"

Jonathan revved the engine, and the advancing Deviants paused. "Turn around."

He arched his neck back.

"No," Minks ground out, his feet balancing the bike. "Turn around completely."

Fuck.

Pulling one foot up onto the seat, he hefted himself up and turned, straddling the motorcycle backward.

"Hook your feet on the pedals, move your ass back,

and be ready to slice and dice," Jonathan instructed before his arm shot back and his hand gripped Louis's hip.

The bike lurched forward, and he jolted, his balance faltering momentarily until the speed leveled out. The closest Deviant jumped at him, its malformed fangs making contact with the rear tire when Louis's blade swiped across its face. The wheel spun up, spattering his visor with a mix of ice and foul mutant blood while Minks swerved to the left and dodged the next one readying for attack.

Gripping the lip of the seat, Louis attempted another strike of his blade through the throat of a Deviant coming at them from the right. The spray coated his visor, leaving him blind. Shoving it up, he cursed into the wind and lined up his next hit, sending the stiletto through the air and whooping when it embedded into a mutant eye.

Jonathan's hold on him tightened painfully, and he braced himself as the bike keened to the side, propelled back up by Minks's booted foot. The motorcycle fought to remain upright, steadied by a single hand while they forged ahead, putting a little distance between them and the Deviants.

"Three hundred yards!" Minks hollered back, his death grip faltering when they hit another divot hidden beneath the snow. "Two hundred."

The Deviants began to fall back when they approached the ring of dilapidated shacks, the dozens of red stains peppering the white powder around the buildings serving as a warning to the mutants.

A gunshot pierced the air, and Louis flattened down, swiping his hand over his face to clear the snow and ice coating his skin and blurring his vision.

"Slide that beauty right in here," a voice yelled out, and the bike's rear tire kicked out to the left. Minks's grip the only thing keeping him from sliding off the seat at the unexpected turn.

As they slowed, he straightened up and nodded to the man lining up his scope with a Deviant persistent enough to break the line in the snow.

"That," Minks announced as he eased the bike into the wooden barn, "was downright invigorating." He patted Louis's thigh and steadied the motorcycle. "Off you go, old man."

Regaining his whereabouts, he swung his leg over the rear tire and put as much distance between him and the damn death machine as he could. "Invigorating. Yeah," he muttered, brushing the caked mix of Deviant blood and snow from his jacket.

Minks flipped the kickstand down and dismounted, unbuckling his helmet, shaking his hair out before he bent down and flicked the ice buildup from his jeans. "Those things have some fucking claws," he snarled, grimacing as he tugged a mutated finger from his calf and held it up for inspection. "Gross."

Frowning, Louis walked over to his companion and crouched down to examine the shredded muscle. "Yup," he agreed, standing as their host walked over, gun slung over his shoulder. "Gross."

****

Jonathan stretched out on the dirt floor of the basement, wincing when his wound made contact with the seam of his jeans.

"Here," Louis muttered, passing his own blood ration over. "Muscles take a lot for regeneration."

Accepting the offering, he sat up and tore into the

bag, ignoring the chemical taste of preservative in favor of filling his gut. "Thanks. Everything set up here?"

"Nope."

Leaning forward, he scanned the multitudes of vampires sitting in groups in the bunker, their tiny spaces carefully eked out with lines etched into the frozen soil. "What the hell?" he whispered.

Louis stood up and held out his hand, pulling him slowly to his feet before he turned and walked to the ladder leading topside. "We have twenty minutes until dawn," he stated as he ascended and gave the humans guarding the makeshift fortress a nod. "Just checking on the bike."

"Fuel's in the north building beside the tractor," one of the men replied, his eyes on the barren terrain. "Don't get caught in there. Lots of cracks in those walls."

Pushing past the pain in his leg, Jonathan steadied his walk while he followed Louis to the barn. "Not quite Miss Amelia's setup, is it?"

Louis lifted several gas cans and shook them before finding a full one. He scanned the yard and crossed the open grounds, slowing his pace to stay at Jonathan's side. "I figured haunt politics would rear its head at some point." He passed over the gas can when he couldn't locate the bike's tank. "But I thought the Vegas safe house would be the one."

"So that's what's going on with the little mapped-out kingdoms down there?" he asked, fueling the motorbike. "It looks like a chessboard."

Flicking a melting icicle from the bike's bumper, Louis snorted. "That's essentially what it is. Sixteen vampires from four different bloodlines, all with grudges and feuds stretching back for centuries. Notice there wasn't a single straggler down there?"

He nodded and passed over the empty gas can, leaning on the bike to relieve the pressure on his leg. "Why is that?"

"The more social Cali vamps will travel through to the Vegas safe house. These are the northern ones, the ones who prefer more solitude. Going by the ages and what I know of those lines and the territory disputes in Oregon a few centuries back, I wouldn't be surprised if there was a haunt war in that basement within the week."

He wandered the barn, grabbed a few small rusted tools from the wall, and shoved them into the inside pocket of his bloodied jean jacket. "We'll stock a travel arsenal in Vegas, but these are passable for now."

They exited the barn, pulling the doors tight and scanning the fields.

"Minks?"

"Yeah?"

"The haunts down there are obeying the Kaius word, but I'm not too keen on testing how deep that obedience runs. Stick close to me down there. And if anything erupts, fall back toward the exit." He ran his hands through his hair and spiked it up. "I'm not learning how to drive that thing anytime soon."

Smirking, he followed Louis inside, their steps hastening as dawn crept closer. His companion assessed the patches of claimed territory before motioning to the dark area behind the ladder.

He could feel the eyes of the other vampires tracking them, their whispers little more than hushed static in the barren room. Louis placed their bags against the wall and sat, his knees bent and arms draped over them as he watched over the sullen groups.

"Minks." His gaze zeroed in on one of the more hostile haunt leaders. "Sit."

Joining the older vamp on the floor, he felt the wooden handle of a trowel slide against his uninjured leg. He wrapped his fingers around it and watched Louis motion to the leader of the largest group, a blond, bearded vampire with an impressive sash of knives strapped to his chest.

"Damon Ricardo." Louis welcomed the male approaching them cautiously. Rising to his feet, Louis lifted the hem of his damp jeans, revealing five complete rings and a single, incomplete one. Jonathan squinted at the charcoal lines marking Louis's age at shy of sixty and frowned with the realization he'd never thought to check or question Rhys's claim Louis was well into his second century.

Damon's rigid posture relaxed significantly the moment he saw the rings, exposing his own to reveal his near five hundred years. "The Kaius haunt sends child foot soldiers," he proclaimed loud enough to gain the attention of the others.

Maintaining a stoic expression, Louis looked up at the male, his gray eyes shifting to a light blue in the dim light. "There will be no turf wars in this bunker," he stated calmly, his voice holding a peculiar levelness. "All grudges you hold against the other haunts inhabiting this place are forgotten. Set aside. We're facing bigger problems as a species than petty arguments among haunts."

Damon nodded. "There's no room for petty grudges."

"As one of the elders," Louis continued, his cadence almost lyrical, "you are responsible for the safety of every vampire entering this place. They're yours, and those of the other elders, to protect until you find safety in Denver."

Crossing his arms, Damon nodded again slowly. "I'm bound to shield them."

Leaning back against the cement wall, Louis waved the vampire off. "Winston Antonio, your turn."

CHAPTER NINE

Jonathan eased the bike off the street and onto the gravel road leading to a Kaius haunt bolt-hole located outside Ely, Nevada. His eyes moved between the coordinates Nichol sent them and the rugged terrain doing its best to destroy his motorcycle's suspension.

He felt Louis's fingers tap his ribs, and he glanced down, turning in the direction his passenger pointed. He glimpsed moonlight reflecting off a steel latch and slowed, killing the engine, and stopping long enough for Louis to jump off before he walked the bike into a clump of dried bushes. Grabbing their bags, he lowered the motorcycle to the ground and walked away, scanning the area to ensure the bike wasn't visible from the road.

Louis descended into the bunker first, using his phone for light as he prowled from room to room, his wiry form hunched in preparation for unexpected company. Waiting until the older vampire gave the all-clear signal, he locked the latch and climbed down the ladder.

Within moments, the reluctant rumbling of a generator filled the spacious bolt-hole, and a single light in each room flickered to life. Without a word, he peered into the three bedrooms, assessing each before selecting the one at the end. He tossed his bag onto the bed and joined Louis in the living area, flopping onto the opposite sofa.

"This one's been used within the past eighteen months," Louis stated as he unlaced his shoes and threw them toward the ladder. "The dust level is almost tolerable."

He grunted in agreement and loosened the laces of his own boots, lifting his jeans to check his healing calf muscles.

Louis leaned over to assess the wound. "Not healing as fast as I'd like."

Shoving his pant leg down, he sat back, pulled a fresh cigarette pack out of his pocket, and carefully peeled the plastic wrapping away. "Rhys said you were over two hundred."

The red-haired vamp cocked a brow. "Holy fuck, he speaks. I was wondering how many more hours you were going to toss the silent treatment my way."

Refusing to respond, he eased a cigarette out and flipped his lighter open, inhaling deep as he lit up.

Louis shook his head and stretched his arms along the back of the sofa. "I was a little younger than you when I ended my creator and the age rings stopped appearing. My sixth never closed, so on quick inspection, I'm easily mistaken for a young one." Thumping his feet onto the coffee table, he grinned. "It has its advantages."

"Advantages," he echoed, exhaling with a cloud of smoke. "Advantages like hypnosis?"

"Kinda like that."

When Louis didn't expand, he took another drag. "When the fuck were you going to tell me you could do that?"

"When the fuck it became relevant."

Blowing three perfect rings across the table, he

flicked the ashes into his palm.

He was pissed.

The skill of hypnosis was rare, and the talent to control it even rarer.

But vampire hypnosis? Not only was it unheard of in any circles he'd encountered, but it was also an ability equivalent to a death edict if it became common knowledge. A vampire capable of manipulating the minds and actions of other vamps was a dangerous weapon.

"Me," he breathed out, watching the smoke waft through the room. "Have you pulled that shit on me? Fucked around with my head?"

Louis leveled him with a flat stare. "Why the hell would I do that?"

Pacing the floor, he took another drag, wrinkling his nose when the cherry singed his fingers. "You tell me."

When he'd gotten the call from Rhys weeks earlier, he hadn't questioned the Kaius male's assessment of Louis.

Stoic.

Quiet.

A few weird quirks, but, in Rhys's words, nothing too annoying.

Above all, Louis was a survivor.

He had ways, Rhys stated. Ways of getting out. Ways of landing on his feet.

Ways of ensuring he could make the thousands of miles needed to complete the mission with a young vamp in tow and get them both out alive.

He should have asked for more details.

Louis crossed his arms behind his head. "Better put that thing out before it lights you up."

Dropping the cigarette to the floor, he stomped it out with his bare foot. "Yes or no," he growled, stepping closer. "Have. You. Fucked. With. My. Head?"

Louis slid his fingers through his hair and sent it in all directions as he scoffed and rolled his eyes. "No, Minks, I haven't fucked with your head. Any vampire nuts enough to ride a motorcycle like you do doesn't need anyone else scrambling his mind."

He stared at him, eyes narrowing. "Will you?"

"Nope."

Taking another step closer, he crossed his arms. "What's backing your word?"

Louis eyed him for a moment before he dropped his feet to the floor with a thud. "What's backing the word of a line-killer, you mean," he stated, leaning forward. "Let's get something very fucking clear right now, Minks. The only thing backing my word now, or ever, is me. No bloodline, no haunt name, and no sire dictates where my loyalties lie. If I decide you're worthy of my word, you'll have it."

He tugged another cigarette from the pack and lit it. "Does the decision come via courier, or do I have to wait for snail mail?"

Crossing the floor at a leisurely pace, Louis sauntered past him toward the tiny bedrooms. "The decision comes when you prove you're more than the spoiled spawn of a rich daddy."

Louis's door clicked closed, and he stood alone. He took a final drag before he crushed the half-smoked stick under his toe and stormed to his room.

****

Louis dropped another blue plastic tote onto the living room floor and popped the lid, scanning the collection of weapons available for them while they waited for dusk. "I don't know why I always assume Kaius and Nichol would stock these places with wooden crates and straw mattresses." He picked up each blade and turned it over before laying it on the coffee table. "You prefer stilettos, switches, or jacks?"

Minks finished refueling the generator and capped the gas can. "Whatever."

Tilting his head to admire the edge of a silver jackknife, he glanced over at his pissed-off bunk mate. "Never underestimate the power of a good blade in good hands."

When Jonathan responded with nothing more than the snick of a lighter, he returned his attention to the weapon stash.

He couldn't blame the kid for being angry.

His ability to hypnotize vampires was known only to the Kaius haunt and to Jackson Stojanovski, and both the haunt and Stojanovski guarded his secret rabidly.

He was a weapon.

Minks had every right to be wary of him now, having witnessed the casualness of his hypnosis talent outside Salt Lake City. The time spent developing his skill with Mickey had paid off, his ability to slip into the minds of vampires and place his will without detection perfected. Only a close observer would notice the subtle shifts in the victims, the slight rounding of their oval vampiric irises and the nearly imperceptible relaxing of their muscles.

Close observers were something he actively avoided.

Leaving the larger swords in the bin, he knelt in front of the coffee table and began laying the weapons out in a row, placing his favorites to one side and what he felt would be Jonathan's to the other.

He didn't want to think too hard about why he'd allowed—encouraged—Jonathan to observe.

It was a reckless decision, one made without consideration of the consequences when he'd sized up the turf war ready to erupt in the bunker. He saw no other way to ensure the young vampires hiding out would survive the egos and feuds of the elders.

None of the vamps he spoke to would know or suspect, their change of mind easily attributed to the dire situation their species found themselves in. The only one who knew what happened was currently smoking a foul-smelling cigarette while pacing the room with his dark brown eyes locked on the floor.

His skill, should it become known to others, would put a scope between his eyes and a target on his back. One that would be placed on the backs of all in his sphere.

And Minks was in his sphere now, whether either of them liked it or not.

Tossing two stiletto blades at Jonathan and pocketing three of his own, he perched on the sofa and loaded their bags with the rest. "Kill the generator. We're Vegas-bound."

CHAPTER TEN

Jonathan unbuckled his helmet and tugged it off, shaking the fine desert sand from his hair while he scanned the barren terrain surrounding the Las Vegas outpost. "Who is this guy again?"

"Wolfgang Vicente," Louis replied, spitting on the ground with a look of disgust. "I can feel grains of dust crunching between my teeth." He adjusted his position on the bike and narrowed his gaze on the dark, grandiose hotel up ahead. "He owned a few places on the strip before everything went to hell. Decent vamp, for an entrepreneur and a kiss-ass."

The rumble of the freeway traffic a few miles back continued to overpower the skittish movements of the nocturnal animals hunting among the rocks and sand. "What's his link to the Kaius haunt?"

Louis dismounted and sauntered up alongside him. "Remember the video released after Rhys's Deepfrying? The Derry McConnaughey one with the UV lights?" Shoving his hands into his pockets, he rocked on his heels. "Vicente was the one who orchestrated it."

Whistling low, Jonathan shook his head and pushed his hair from his eyes before putting his helmet on and strapping it tight under his chin. "That wasn't easy to watch."

The video of Derry McConnaughey being blasted with UV flashlights as retribution for selling out his own species had gone viral through the vampire world. It closed the chapter on the media circus surrounding Rhys Kaius and his mate, Lis, as they were captured, tried, and sentenced to the Deepfryer. The twenty-four-hour news reporting on the proceedings was addicting, and he freely admitted he'd watched with rapt attention when the face of the wild Rhys Kaius was splashed across every tabloid and newspaper in the country.

The fact it was one of the male's own Tenders who had triggered the frenzy in the first place made it all the more interesting. Haunts around the globe placed bets on how and when Rhys would end the woman who turned on their species, murdering her master before running to reporters with the sordid details of the vampire Tender trade.

He himself lost good money on the pool when word got out Rhys not only allowed her to live, but he also shacked up with her.

Straddling the motorcycle, he steadied it while Louis got on. "Were you part of the rescue?"

The rescue had pulled a charred Rhys and drained Lis from the glass shower-like enclosure equipped with UV lights to fry vampires publicly. It was an ambush now touted by vampires worldwide as the epitome of guerrilla warfare in urban centers.

Louis's hand took its place on the hem of his leather jacket. "Sure was."

Another gust of wind picked up the loose sand, pelting them as they made the final leg of the night's journey.

The UV lighting punishment Derry McConnaughey was given was remarkably satisfying for him. The smarmy vamp's role in Rhys's Deepfrying earned him an existence of isolation from vampire society for eternity or until death, whichever came first.

Jonathan didn't involve himself much in vampire politics, but he knew a traitor to the species when he saw one. And his personal Rhys hero worship aside, he wholly believed the cowardly Derry McConnaughey received precisely what he deserved.

Slowing the bike as they approached the gated driveway, he waited until Louis texted Vicente. The massive steel doors swung open slowly, the guards hidden in the alcoves nodding their way. Sidling up as close to the hotel as he could without damaging the stunning floral displays surrounding the building, he killed the engine and held still for Louis.

"So what should I expect?" he asked, unbuckling his helmet and sliding the straps over the handlebars. "Is this guy…should I be watching my back?"

Louis spiked his hair up and scoffed. "Wolfgang prides himself on being a lover, not a fighter. The only thing you'll be watching are the dancers he pushes at you every ten minutes."

"Every fifteen minutes," a voice boomed from the entrance to the hotel. A black-haired vampire strode down the marble steps toward them with a grin and his fangs fully on display. "War-time rations and all, Mr. Forbes." With a bow, he extended his hand. "Wolfgang Vicente."

"Jonathan Minks," he replied, shaking the proffered hand while keeping one eye on Louis.

"Minks," Wolfgang said slowly. "Is Minks Silas your creator?"

"He is."

Vicente's smile widened, and he motioned to the

open doors. "Then let's not waste any time acquainting you with the indulgences your sire and older hauntmates have attempted to shield you from."

****

Louis unhooked his fangs from the throat of the brunette who had taken up residence at his side. "Take it easy," he warned when another shot glass spiked with ancient blood was passed to Minks. "That stuff hits hard." He waved off the server's offer of one for himself and turned back to Vicente. "I can see how you're suffering out here."

Wolfgang lounged back in his seat and feigned weariness. "The payoff regimen required to keep this operation going has been exhausting on my signing hand." The music's volume amped up a fraction, and another dancer took the stage. "I had to cut the duet and trio acts last month to ensure I could maintain the entertainment schedule expected from the guests arriving at my door."

"A hardship you bear with grace," Louis chuckled. "No issues with the FBI Vamp Division or the Species Purifiers?"

Vicente set his empty glass down and waved his hand around the room. "Everyone laughed when I purchased this abandoned casino for what was admittedly a million over market. But two decades later, who's laughing now?" He let loose a barking guffaw that drew the attention of everyone in the room. "That would be me, collecting and gaining favor with every haunt in a thousand-mile radius who needs a secure launch point for their final trek into Denver."

Jonathan rose to his feet before slumping back in his chair. "Yeah. Okay, that's potent."

Louis scooted his seat closer to the young male. "You about ready to call it a day?"

"Let the kid relax," Wolfgang crooned as he motioned for another round of spiked shots. "Traveling the country backroads with your quiet ass can't provide nearly as much stimulation as this boy needs." The older vamp divided up the small cups and pounded one back. "He has Minks blood in him. It would take another ten of these to take him down."

Jonathan's fangs were extended far over his lower lip, his eyes dulled by the intake of the ancient blood, which gives vampires a high unlike anything else. "Yeah, I better go."

Louis stood and grasped Minks's arm, hauling him to his feet. "Suite eight-seventy-six?" he clarified with Vicente, accepting the key card when it was passed to him. "Until tomorrow night, then."

"Yeah, yeah," Wolfgang huffed. "It's all business talk tomorrow evening."

Steadying Jonathan while they walked to the elevators, Louis pressed the button and rolled his eyes when his companion leaned on the mirrored wall for balance. "The initial hit will wear off in an hour," he reassured him. "Then you're just going to feel really, really, off."

Minks grunted as the doors opened and accepted Louis's help to get into the elevator without argument. "I didn't know we could get drunk."

Nichol's face flashed across his mind, the highly strung vampire's addiction to blood highs nearly costing every member of the Kaius line their lives a few months back. "Once won't kill you," he stated. "But it's not anything you want to get mixed up in more than that."

The doors slid open, and he led Jonathan down the hall, swiping the key card and almost shoving the young vamp inside. "Get comfortable," he called out as he entered his own code into the electric lock, and Minks stumbled through the doors of the closest bedroom. "I'll be in to check on you in a bit."

Orienting himself to the enormous suite, he popped open every door and drawer, rolling his eyes at the amount of normalcy Wolfgang maintained in the middle of the desert during a species war.

The plush bathrobes, scented shampoos, and travel toothbrushes were a nice touch.

As was the tray of iced blood cubes in the kitchenette.

And the movie guide propped in front of the fifty-eight-inch wall-mounted television.

Listening through the rush of water as he showered, he tracked Jonathan's tossing and turnings, unable to shake the visions of Nic from his head.

If a vampire with the age and control of Nichol Kaius could fall victim to the draw of the blood highs, a young vamp in his sixth decade was a prime target for the dissociated reality ancient vampire blood provided. And during a period of unrest and uncertainty, anything reality numbing was tempting to even the most moderate of vamps.

Combing through his short hair while he exited the bathroom, he approached Jonathan's door and rapped his knuckles on the wood. "Leveling out yet?"

"Yeah," Minks grumbled, swinging his legs over the edge of the bed as Louis peered into the room. "Everything's just warm and fuzzy."

Grabbing the remote, Louis flopped onto the sofa

and smirked when Jonathan followed suit with significantly less grace. "Lucky for you, a single night of that shit won't have any lasting effects. Not even a hangover." Frowning while he scanned the plethora of movie selections, he tossed the remote over to Minks. "But as the old guy in the room who's been there, done that, I'm obligated to tell you not to try that crap again."

"Noted," Jonathan mumbled, sinking deeper into the cushions and flicking through the channels. "I never realized my sire was such a lech. He was so fucking strict about avoiding places like this. Said it was a gateway to hell."

Unable to maintain a straight face, Louis broke into a grin. "He wasn't wrong. He just left out the part about how fun hell could be. In doses."

"If it's so fun, why weren't you diving into it all?" Minks demanded, settling on a police drama. "No shots, no dancers…you didn't even take your meal up on any of her offers." A look of realization came over him, the expression amplified by his drunken state. "You have a Tender or something back home?" His dark eyes widened, and he pushed his hair from his face. "Hot damn, you do, don't you?"

Snorting, he leaned back, crossed his arms, and tried to catch up on the plot of the film. "No."

Minks went silent for a few minutes and continued to stare at him, the slight haze to his eyes giving away the blood high still worming through him. "Ah," he finally said with a knowing nod. "You're hung up on someone. I'd put money on it being one of the Kaius vamp's mates."

"I'm not an idiot."

Minks hunched over a fraction and side-eyed him.

"Then I'm putting my money on one of the Kaius hauntmates."

Giving his roommate a flat stare, he grabbed the remote and cranked up the volume. "Don't hit the tables in the casino tomorrow. You place poor bets."

Jonathan snatched the remote back and turned the volume down again before settling onto the sofa, his attention flipping between Louis and the screen. He pulled a cigarette from his pocket and lit up, arching his neck to blow clouds of smoke into the air.

"Why the hell do you do that?" Louis asked as two perfect rings floated up and evaporated.

Minks walked to the bathroom with a slight unsteadiness and there was a rush of water in the sink, the pungent scent of tar beginning to wane. "Picked up the habit on my first tour overseas as a human and it kind of stuck," he called over, reemerging with the wet cigarette butt in hand. He dropped it into the garbage and sat beside him. "I don't get the little buzz from it like I did before I was vamped over, but it's kind of relaxing in its own way."

Louis shrugged and settled back in his seat. "You're still young. Lots of kids hold on to human habits for the first century. The Kaius haunt's youngest, Dominic? He still breathes. And I don't think he could be still to save his fucking life." Motioning to the screen, he glanced at Minks. "Are we good to leave this on until dawn?"

Jonathan stared at him for a few moments before nodding and pulling another cigarette out, inhaling deep as he lit it up.

"Damn, Minks," he grunted while he angled away from the smoke. "Maybe do that over th—"

Vampires were always attuned to the speed of life

around them. Their minds could process fast movements with meticulous accuracy, allowing them time to react to things a human brain wouldn't categorize until seconds later.

And when you were dealing with a species that could move with impressive speed, milliseconds meant the difference between existence and sludging.

Of course, for the vamp processing speed to work, a basic level of alertness was required, and, at the moment, Louis was definitely falling short of the necessary level.

The shock of Jonathan's lips on his own temporarily disoriented him. As his mind caught up with what was happening, he leaned away from the kiss and gently moved Minks's hand off of his neck. "And that settles it," he stated, standing up swiftly. "I think you need to sleep that blood high off. Let's go."

Jonathan sat motionless for a moment before rising unsteadily and nodding, passing his lit cigarette over. "Yeah. You're…right."

Louis stepped aside and let the young vamp pass by to his room, waiting until the door closed before he ran the cigarette under water and collapsed back on the sofa. Running his hands through his hair, he returned his attention to the TV and shoved back the litany of thoughts churning in his mind.

CHAPTER ELEVEN

Jonathan tucked his hair behind his ear and stepped out of the elevator, scanning the lobby for any sign of Louis. He walked slowly through the opulent surroundings, his eyes drawn to the mirrored ceilings where he could monitor the comings and goings of the vampires strolling around him. Others were doing the same thing, their gazes moving with stealth across the reflective walls while they chatted amongst themselves casually, the quiet banter wholly focused on the changing dynamics of vampire society.

Many powerful haunts were decimated over the past year, with others fleeing into hiding. Wealth was shifting, as was influence.

And none of it was on his mind at the moment.

He'd awoken from his rest in a rare state of confusion. Facedown on his bed and his legs dangling off the edge, it wasn't until he stood under the heat of the shower spray that the memories of the prior evening came barreling back.

Craning his neck to see around the vampires and dancers relaxing in the dining hall, he backed out and continued his search for the bunkmate who was probably halfway to Albuquerque without him by now.

Not that he could blame him.

He'd emerged from his shower in a mild panic, listening for any signs of Louis while he dried off and dressed, brushing through his hair longer than necessary while his thoughts looped.

He was never touching ancient blood again.

And that settles it.

He had no idea what reaction he'd expected from Louis, but he was damn sure that even in his drunken state, he hadn't expected such a calm response. Though, replaying the memory in his head over and over, he was fucking lucky the older vamp hadn't de-fanged him.

Pushing open the door to the smaller ballroom, he hesitated and listened to Vicente's voice echoing in the emptiness.

"...following Nichol's lead. While the financial hit could be sizable, the media spin is genius." There was a pause before the booming voice called out. "Don't just hang in the doorway, Minks. Take a seat."

Keeping his gaze averted from Louis's position, he pulled up a chair and sat. "What's Nichol doing?"

"Buying up Denver properties from anti-vampers who are hoofing out of the city and reselling them to the influx of supporters moving in," Louis replied, nudging a goblet and a carafe of AB-negative toward him. "He's buying high and selling low, but the press has picked up on it and public opinion has shifted up a tick in the northwest."

Pouring a glass, he took a long drink, his fingers itching for the cigarettes in his jacket pocket. "And you're looking to do that here?" he asked Wolfgang, keeping his attention on their host.

Vicente smirked and held up his own glass. "I'm not too proud to steal a good business plan when I see one." He downed the last of his meal and stood. "I'll track you two down later to discuss a few finalizing details I may have overlooked in the evacuation plan."

The old vampire left the room with a flourish, and Jonathan rocked the stem of his goblet on the table rhythmically, at a loss for what to say.

"Don't get fucking weird."

His brows shot up, and he looked over at Louis. "What?"

"Weird," Louis repeated, hefting a box onto the table, and unloading it, passing over a sheet of paper covered in Nichol's precise writing. "This whole nervousness thing you have going on right now. Cork it and help me figure out how this thing works."

Reading over the instructions, he picked up the batteries and chargers and carried them over to an outlet. "He sent four times the number of batteries needed."

"Because Nichol's not an idiot," Louis replied with a grin, holding up the tiny ear pieces for inspection. "We aren't guaranteed to have electricity at every stop, so backups are good. Where the hell do I talk into?"

Rifling through the box until he found the microphones, he began assembling the communicators. "Here," he said, handing Louis a completed headset. "Once they're activated, you can swear at me all you want on the road."

"And I fucking will," Louis retorted, trying it on and walking over to the mirrored wall. "I look like a member of a boy band."

Finishing his own headset, he put it on, adjusted the fit, and joined Louis. "You aren't wrong."

Louis pressed his hands against his head, flattening the set and frowning when the microphone jutted forward half an inch. "Let's head out to the bike and check the fit under the helmets while the batteries charge."

Tugging his headset off, he followed Louis out of the banquet hall, lighting a cigarette when they stepped onto the veranda and scanned the terrain. "So, which member are you?"

Louis glanced back at him while he descended the stairs. "Member of what?"

"The boy band," he exhaled. "There's always a formula to their makeup. Like, if the Kaius haunt was a boy band, Dominic would be the boy next door because he's the baby. Rhys would obviously be the bad boy. Jagger would probably be the strong, silent one since he doesn't strike me as the kind of guy to talk just to talk."

"Unlike yourself."

Grinning, he puffed out a cloud of smoke. "Mikhail would be the funny one, at least according to what my hauntmates have told me. And Kaius is probably the hot leader holding the group together. Though, again, guessing since I've never met him."

Louis passed him his helmet. "What about Nichol?"

"Nichol wouldn't be in a boy band, so I'm not touching that minefield."

Adjusting his headset under his helmet, Louis jiggled it back and forth for a moment. "I'm in Nichol's non-band."

Dropping his cigarette to the sidewalk, he ground it out with his boot. "Not an option. Pick one."

"You pick one."

Trying his helmet on with the communication system on, he adjusted the straps a bit and took it off, shaking his hair out. "Fine. I get to be the bad boy."

Leveling him with a flat glare, Louis hung the helmets on the handlebars. "Really."

"Damn right. The bad boy doesn't have to be bad, he just has to look like he would be." He turned slowly on the spot, stretching his leather-covered arms out. "And I totally have the look."

"I'm the guy who waits out his contract and walks away," Louis finally stated, crossing his arms. "There's always one of them, right?"

Lighting another cigarette, he rolled his eyes. "Yeah, yeah. You can be that guy. What's on the docket for the rest of the night?"

"Formal sit-down with the vamps on premises and then touching base with the Kaius haunt," Louis replied, leaning against the marble railings of the stairs. "I'll make sure to update them on your boy band assessment."

If he had a pulse, it would have sped up a fraction with the threat.

"Sounds good," he breathed, blowing a perfect ring and watching it float toward the sky. "So before we go back in, I, uh…" He hesitated, not certain what he wanted to say but knowing he needed to say something. "I'm sorry for the whole…thing…last night."

Louis shrugged and started up the stairs. "Blood highs are unpredictable, kid. Don't stress it."

He waited for Louis to disappear through the doors and snuffed out his cigarette, collecting both butts and shoving them into his depleting pack.

The only unpredictable thing about kissing Louis was how badly he wanted to do it again.

****

Louis paced the floor of the suite, his hair spiking in all directions while he recounted the evening's meeting with the Vegas evacuees to Nichol and the others over video. "I don't think he's open to negotiation," he warned, thinking back to Vicente's demands that his staff be included in the count. "Wolfgang has managed to secure eleven planes and has four airstrips ready for your word, so the details are done on his end."

Nichol's hazel eyes flashed as he growled. "Tell that smarmy bastard the vamps are first in the air," he relented. "The humans have the flexibility of turnaround if things go to hell."

He looked over at Jonathan, who sat silently at the table, his nimble fingers sliding rows of tiny batteries into the Bluetooth communicators. "Anything I missed, Minks?"

The young vamp startled and looked up from his work. "Uh, yeah?" He angled his seat so the Kaius males could see him. "I overheard a few vamps talking about the power shifts on the continent. Not sure if it's something important now, but—"

"We're developing a plan to redistribute in both the short and long term," Nichol interrupted. "Good to have confirmation the issue is coming to light, though."

Louis smirked when Minks visibly relaxed a fraction in his chair. "Jagger," he called out, winking when Jonathan pulled another cigarette out, lit it, and took an abnormally long drag. "I forwarded the list of missing and unaccounted for vamps from the haunts present tonight. Rhys, I cc'd you since there were a few Tenders on another list of those stranded in larger centers."

The blond head of his best friend leaned into the screen. "Enough about the boring shit. Is the dancer with the missing rib still working there?"

He could see Audra standing behind Mikhail, and he bit back a laugh as she exchanged an exasperated look with someone off-screen, likely Jagger's mate, Bianca. "Yeah, she's here," he confirmed.

"Minks!" Mick yelled out. "Louis, move. Minks? That chi—ouch. That woman has the most amazing O-pos blood you'll ever have."

Jonathan gave a thumbs-up and dropped his eyes back to the communicators.

Mickey wrinkled his nose and moved closer to the camera. "I haven't received a response to the email I sent you," he said pointedly, looking smug when Rhys and Jagger mumbled behind him before breaking into a barking laughter. "Hear that? Embroidered towels with your name on them are being ordered as we fucking speak, man."

"I'm thinking on it," he muttered, leaning his elbows on the dresser. "Yeah, I'm thinking on it."

After a chorus of signoffs, he hooked his phone to the charger and joined Minks at the table. "We'll be overnighting in Flagstaff tomorrow, so we better enjoy the hotel amenities while we can."

"I'm good up here," Minks replied, bagging the spare batteries and placing them into his jacket pocket. "You can head down if you want."

With a snort, Louis flopped onto the sofa and stretched out, turning on the television and looking for a strong distraction from Mickey's email. "This is the only amenity I'm interested in. Stojanovski doesn't have half these films."

He tracked Jonathan's reluctant approach, swinging his legs onto the coffee table so Minks could join him. When the young vamp perched on the far edge of the sofa, he swung his leg out and booted him. "Sit back and relax, or I'm putting on a cartoon, kid."

With a flat glare, Minks obeyed. "Enough with the 'kid' thing. I'm hardly a newbie."

"Anything under a century," Louis retorted, settling on a war flick. "Now shut up."

Jonathan lasted all of ten minutes before he spoke. "What's the email thing?"

"Nothing important," he muttered, turning up the volume.

"Obviously," Minks scoffed. "You went from chill to totally fucking wound in a split-second. You don't have to tell me what the deal is, but I wouldn't ignore a Kaius haunt email for long."

He sat back and crossed his arms. "And that's why you're a kid. Because you don't know shit about anything."

"Whatever," Jonathan grunted, mimicking his position and turning his glare to the television.

For a moment, a debate surged in his head.

Minks came from a large haunt, one with structure and rules and expectations. One where the sire was both indulgent and protective, perhaps overstepping his bounds to keep the youngest hauntmate sheltered from the less noble sides of vampirism, though with good intent.

But Jonathan was also driven to wander, to push back against the cushioned lifestyle he'd been born into. Although he'd joked about the state of some of their accommodations, he hadn't once griped as many of the young, spoiled vamps were prone to do. He'd approached haunt leaders and newborn orphans with the same deference, turned his charm on for both stunning waitresses and elderly hostesses.

And Jonathan had nothing invested in Louis's

decision. Nothing that would make him anything more than a sounding board.

"Yeah, maybe turn the cartoons on," Minks said, grabbing the remote and tearing him from his internal deliberation. "This war thing is hitting way too close to home right now."

He looked over as Jonathan hunched over the remote and squinted at the television until he selected a show, and the screen lit up with bright animations.

Minks was right. The war thing was hitting too close to home right now, even if he wasn't wholly certain what *home* was.

CHAPTER TWELVE

Louis's grip on Jonathan's jacket tightened when they hit an unexpected patch of gravel and the rear wheel spun out to the side. He forced his eyes open to watch the road fly past as Minks's foot dropped instinctively to keep them upright while he regained control.

"Sorry 'bout that," Jonathan hollered louder than needed with the new headsets.

Releasing his death grip, he patted his driver on the ribs and straightened up. "Fuck this bike."

Minks laughed and revved the engine, sending them flying down the empty backroad toward the outpost located northeast of Flagstaff. He resumed his monologue on the changing landscape, pointing out the rolling clusters of rock before trees surrounded them on all sides.

"Shame we couldn't take in the Grand Canyon," Jonathan stated as he slowed, and the wheels kicked up stones on the graveled road. "Maybe when we aren't in the middle of a species war."

"In a goddamn SUV," he muttered, wincing when his foot slipped off the pedal and skimmed across the rock.

Minks tensed for a moment, bringing the bike to a stop and slipping his phone from his breast pocket. "Up there?" he asked, nodding toward the small mountain to the west.

Resigning himself to another twenty minutes on the back of the damned motorcycle, he rolled his head back and slid his thumb under his helmet to adjust the headset. "Yeah. There should be three humans and eleven vamps on-site." He scented the air and frowned. "Pull over when we get to that alcove."

Waiting until his arms were wrapped firmly in place, Jonathan eased through the brush and trees, going heavy on the gas as they began the incline.

"Hold on," Minks warned when they hit a dip in the path. "This is going to suck for you."

"It always sucks for me," he grumbled back, tightening his grip. "Just don't slam on the brakes or something stupid."

As uncomfortable as the communication devices were under their helmets, he had to admit it was a good idea. He'd even managed to relax a fraction on the paved roads, knowing Minks could easily warn him if anything up ahead required a strong hold.

They climbed higher, swerving fallen logs and branches until they hit the alcove.

"Kill the engine," he said as he climbed off the motorcycle and moved away from the exhaust. When silence overtook the area, he walked further up the mountain and scented the air. "Minks?"

"Yeah?"

"How many humans are you picking up?"

Jonathan lowered the kickstand and dismounted before jogging over to him, his brows furrowed. "Seventeen, I think. No…nineteen. Hard to break through that smoke smell."

Tugging his phone from his pocket, he fired off a quick text to Nichol. "Let's hold out until the boss advises."

They continued to circle the area, murmuring to each other with every new human scent until Louis's phone buzzed to life.

"Hey, Nichol. So w—"

"Get the fuck out of there," the old vampire snarled. "Jagger's locating another safe house within an hour's drive."

Signaling to Jonathan, he sprinted to the bike and leaned back to allow the driver on. "Why? What's going on here?"

"Breach," Nichol replied tersely as the bike growled to life, and the hum of four other engines followed suit in the distance. "Whoever answered my contact's phone didn't know the code word."

Minks spun the motorcycle around and his balance wavered. "Look, Nichol, I gotta go."

Flipping his high beams on, Jonathan maneuvered back down the path. The lights of a pack of side-by-side ATVs flickered behind them, gaining speed.

"I'll watch ahead, you watch behind," Minks called out, zigzagging through the trees toward the gravel road.

Craning his neck, he quickly counted the headlights racing down the mountain, tracking their distance as they closed in. "Three hundred yards off," he reported, cursing when a bullet zipped past them. "This is gonna hurt."

Minks flattened himself down over the handlebars, and he followed suit, preparing for a hit in the ass.

They sped down the mountain, skidding onto the gravel road and doubling back down the road they'd taken in with the ATVs hot on their heels and shooting off round after round. One grazed Louis's helmet, and he flinched. Jonathan's hand flew to his to steady him as he adjusted the position of his visor.

"I'm good," he yelled. "Drive with two fucking hands."

The cloud of dust behind them made visually tracking their attackers almost impossible. The only surety he had they were still closing in was the nearly imperceptible time between the bullets firing from the gun and when they ripped past his ear.

His phone buzzed incessantly, ignored until Minks took a sharp left at full speed, buying them a few extra yards.

"Answer that," Jonathan ordered, reaching back to tap Louis on the ribs. "I need directions."

Releasing Minks long enough to tug his phone out, he slid it under his helmet and ducked against Jonathan's back. "Get us out, Nic."

"Why the fuck else did you think I was calling so fucking much?" Nichol snarked. "You have four miles to go before I can veer you into the bush."

He relayed the info to Minks. "Then what?" he demanded, gripping the driver's hip with what had to be a painful force. "We have four side-by-sides on our ass, eight humans and three shotguns."

"Minks, I've patched into your headset. Don't get shot," Nic stated. "And don't let your wheels get shot out. Wheels are priority, then your ass. Three-point-eight miles to go."

The hooting and hollering behind him fell back a few more yards, and he grimaced when another two bullets whizzed past them. "Is it too late to be put on internet-monitor duty?" he grumbled when Nichol called out their distance again. "Boots on the ground sucks,

Nic."

"Yeah, so does listening to you bitch."

He could feel Jonathan's shoulders shake as he laughed.

"Can you give me the layout after we make the first turn?" Minks called into his mic.

Nichol delved into a detailed description of the path they'd eventually take, his voice patching through to both headsets. Louis shoved his phone into the waist of his jeans and reached back to pull a blade from his pocket.

"Minks?" he interrupted, earning a grunt from Nichol. "I'm turning around."

Jonathan nodded. "What switchbacks are we coming up on, Nichol?"

There was a pause before Nic barked into the earpiece. "In zero-point-four, veer right then left. Repeat zero-point-six miles after that."

"Better move fast," Minks called out as he reached back. "I got you on my left side."

Steeling himself for the switch in position, he drew his feet onto the seat, braced himself on Jonathan's shoulders, then spun and dropped awkwardly while Minks grasped his hip. "I'm good."

The bike sped up, and he held tight to the edge of the seat, lining up his shot.

"Angling to your left," Minks yelled, and he braced himself, sending the blade flying through the air moments before the bike careened to the side. "Now right!"

Hooking his feet backward on the pedals, he held on as they hit the second half of the switchback, grinning at the sound of an ATV spinning out. "I think I hit one."

"Don't get cocky," Nichol barked in his ear. "One-point-six miles to go. You have the layout memorized, Minks?"

"Got it," Jonathan replied, tapping Louis's thigh. "Left again."

Centering himself on the sound of the three remaining ATV engines, he waited until the motorcycle steadied before he opened the small storage compartment and dug into his bag, yanking out two more blades and slamming the hatch shut.

"I'm taking out the rest," he called out, giving Jonathan's hand a quick pat and lining up his next hit. "Keep steady and...*fuck*!"

A bullet pierced through his shoulder, the searing pain second to his annoyance in the hole now marring his favorite jacket. Zeroing his focus, he let the first blade fly, nearly tipping to the side in celebration when it embedded in the thigh of one driver. The ATV veered wildly off the road, taking out another on his way.

"One to go," he snarled, sending the last blade through the air and watching in triumph when it pierced a front tire. "Okay, Minks. I'm counting on you to get us the hell outta here."

****

Jonathan scanned the east side of the industrial park. "Why don't we just bust through that window up there?"

"Never thug out what you can accomplish with finesse," Louis replied, the click of the deadbolt punctuating his statement. "See? Smooth as silk."

Knocking the motorcycle's kickstand up with his toe, he squeezed it through the door and angled it toward the exit for a swift escape. "And this place is empty?" he asked, snatching a drop cloth from the floor and tossing it over the bike.

"According to Jagger's intel, it's up for a foreclosure auction." Rolling out his injured shoulder, he grimaced. "But be prepared in case."

Nodding, he followed Louis across the cement floor, hesitating when Louis propped open a narrow hatch with his foot. "Down there?"

"Down there."

Slinging their bags over his shoulder, he tugged his phone from his pocket and swiped it to life, using the light to examine the crawl space. Dropping in, he nudged a few abandoned boxes aside and crouched. "Cozy. I suppose it was nice to have clean clothes for a few hours."

Louis hopped in after him and knelt as he eased the hatch shut and tested it to ensure they could open it later. "Could be worse. Could be flooded."

Grunting in agreement, he set their bags down and lay on his. "Any more from Nichol?"

"Nothing you need to see."

Booting Louis's foot with his, he rolled onto his side. "That bad?"

"Yup."

They lay in silence for a few minutes, the madness of the evening settling over them.

"Louis?"

"Yeah?"

Flopping onto his back, he tried to get comfortable on the dirt. "How many do you think you killed?"

There was a rustling of fabric in the dark. "None, I think. I aimed for non-lethal strikes. Possible one or two were lost in the crashes, but the speeds weren't excessive. Nichol can update us tomorrow night."

Falling back into silence, they both shivered as dawn came.

"Rest up," Louis ordered, the light of his phone illuminating his angled features. "We can anticipate a hard trek out of the area at dusk once word of our escape travels. Which is actually a better scenario than getting hunted during the day, so let's cross our fingers for a rough ride tomorrow."

Staring at the cement above him, he tucked his arms behind his head. "You think they'll find us?"

"Possible. That's why I'm closer to the door."

Cracking a grin, he looked over at Louis. "You going to take on a mob of rabid humans?"

Louis's phone light nearly blinded him when it was angled toward him. "If—and it's a big if—we get found, I'll hold them off while you toss that bike sheet over your head and barrel straight for the residential. Aim for a basement and drain whoever you need to recover from the sun damage. Long shot, but better than nothing."

"Fuck that," he scoffed. "We take out the mob together and ride off at dusk, spinning out on the blood of our victories."

He could see Louis's expression flatten. "You're an idiot."

Smirking, he grabbed the phone and swiped over the maps Nichol had sent. "Yeah, well, unlike you, I don't do this kind of shit, so it's still exci—" He froze when he swiped too far. "Damn."

Louis inched back to him and glanced over at the phone. "Damn is right," he said as the photos flipped slowly. "That's what we're up against. There wasn't a human or vamp in that outpost who could've survived that much explosive."

"How…" He fought to form his question. "How did Nichol get these?"

"Jagger pulled them off an online forum dedicated to vamp slayings," Louis replied, taking his phone and tucking it under his bag. "The vampires knew the risks they were taking. But the humans who helped them? I don't think what they know and what they understand meshes."

Pushing the gruesome images from his mind, he fixed his gaze on the low ceiling. "Do you see an end to this? Like, is this how it's going to be from now on?"

Louis scooted his bag beside his and lay down, flinching when his shoulder hit the ground. "No. Maybe for a few decades. A century at most. It depends on whether we decide as a species to return to hiding or if we're going to fight to stay out of the shadows. Now get some rest, newbie. I'll stay on guard."

Scoffing, he closed his eyes. "Remember that whole SUV discussion we had? The discussion I won?"

"When I let you win so you wouldn't cry about your bike," Louis corrected.

"Yeah, that's it." He looked over in the blackness. "A light-tight SUV would probably have come in handy tonight."

The crawl space was quiet for a solid thirty minutes, the sounds of the early morning shift buzzing around the nearby businesses filtering down until Louis finally replied. "Probably. But there's a certain escapist authenticity about cockroaches crawling up your pant leg you just don't get in a luxury vehicle."

CHAPTER THIRTEEN

"Ready?" Minks called out, his foot balancing the bike in anticipation.

Louis turned the knob on the door, nodded, and flung it open. He jumped back as the bike rumbled forward enough for him to jump on. "Ride like the wind, Minks."

With Nichol barking directions through their headsets, they spun on to the road, tearing west for several hundred yards before doubling back down a business route.

"First blockade is two blocks south of you," the Kaius male reported, his aerial navigation system providing a bird's-eye view for them. "Just follow my orders, and I'll have you racing the clock into Albuquerque in thirty minutes."

And he did.

With Minks pushing the limits of the bike's balance, they slid through back alleys, skidded across empty parking lots, and wound their way along narrow walking paths cutting through the suburbs of Flagstaff. Traveling between the trees and fences lining playgrounds and dog parks, they rumbled through until they hit the unblocked gravel road leading them out of town.

"You have seven hours to make a seven-and-a-half-hour trek through the backroads," Nichol called through their headsets, and Jonathan sped up, kicking sand and dust up in a cloud behind them. "If you make it, check in."

Minks glanced back at him. "He's messing with us, right?"

He shook his head and adjusted his feet. "Nichol doesn't mess around. Speed up, kid."

And speed up he did.

Stopping only long enough to siphon gas from a truck parked outside a dark farmhouse, they hit the Albuquerque city limits with forty minutes to spare.

"So, am I skirting along the south or north?" Minks asked, slowing as the gravel side roads they were traveling met the paved highway.

"Neither." He slid his phone under Jonathan's arm and showed him the map. "We're going straight in."

He could feel Minks tense up as he looked at the map. "That's a goddamn townhouse. Inside the city."

"Funny," he said, pocketing the cell. "That was my reaction."

Though a solid guy to begin with, Jonathan's muscles hardened when they hit the freeway and found the predawn traffic heavy. Louis could feel the hesitancy in his movements while the motorcycle dropped its speed to stay among a slower pack of commuters. The fear of standing out, of being singled out, guided every clear shoulder check and signal.

He hadn't realized how lax Minks was with the rules of the road until he was obeying every one.

They pulled up in front of the address Nichol provided and eyed the rows of homes.

"You sure about this?" Minks asked, tugging his gloves tighter onto his wrist.

Confirming the address with Nic, he nodded while

he read over the incoming text. "This is it. Pull around the side and park along the shed. Two guys going by the code names Mr. A and Mr. B will meet us around back."

"Original."

They crept along the side of the house, scanning the perimeter and watching for signs of an ambush. The bike went silent, and they dismounted, shoving their riding gloves into the hatch and swinging their bags over their shoulders as the fortified steel door opened and two men stepped out, armed to the teeth.

"Which one of you is Forbes?" the shorter man demanded, his grip loose on his weapons.

Raising his hand, he stepped between the men and Jonathan. "Are you confirming against a visual?"

Waving a phone in his direction, the taller man looked him up and down before his stance relaxed. "Name your companion."

"Jonathan Minks," he stated, crossing his arms. "Now if you two gentlemen would do me a favor and remove those ski masks, I'd like to do a confirmation of my own."

The men exchanged glances before the shorter one pulled his off, his shaved head standing out against his black uniform. The taller man hesitated a moment, then tugged off his own slowly. "Who's the primary contact for the southern division?"

Louis grinned and took a step closer, ensuring he had a good lock on the men guarding the entrance. "Bianca Schumann," he replied, giving the code name. "Rolls off the tongue, doesn't it?" The men visibly relaxed when he handed them the full confirmation, and he seized the opportunity. "Mr. A, what do you stand to gain from assisting vampires during this evacuation?"

The man's brown eyes blinked with a slight unevenness. "My best friend," he responded without a second thought. "My best friend was turned last year. He made it as far as Wichita. He's holing up there with a group keeping him safe and I'm paying it forward."

Satisfied, he turned to the shorter man. "Mr. B, what do you stand to gain from assisting vampires during this evacuation?"

There was a faint swaying to his stance as he answered. "That's my brother. In Wichita. He…" The man stammered for a moment, his blue eyes reddening. "He's a good man. He doesn't deserve to be hunted and killed like a rabid animal."

Releasing their minds simultaneously, he motioned for Jonathan to follow and entered the cookie-cutter townhouse, listening as the men secured the multitude of locks at the entrance.

There was a noticeable shift in Minks after Louis confirmed the intentions of their hosts. The young vamp was on edge the whole drive, his carefree demeanor hampered by the sobering events of the previous evening.

He didn't like it one bit, so he decided a personal screening of their hosts was important while they made their trek to Albuquerque. If it gave Jonathan some peace of mind, it was necessary.

Pausing at the base of the stairs, he scanned the faces of the other evacuees, mentally comparing the numbers to the list Jagger messaged him an hour prior.

"Most of the upstairs rooms are claimed," Mr. B stated as he leaned against the handrail, his thumb absently tracing the barrel of his gun. "But these guys insisted on keeping that one over there open for your arrival."

"So there are two vamps upstairs?" he asked, eyeing the closed doors for any sign of the two unaccounted vampires.

Mr. A shook his head. "They left three nights ago to assist an outpost to the west that was having some troubles."

His stomach sank.

Flagstaff was the closest western outpost.

"These guys here got real agitated yesterday before sunset," Mr. B added. "Almost like they were in pain or something. Then they just went quiet. Like this."

Jonathan took a step closer to him, the muscles in his jaw tensing.

Mr. A cleared his throat. "Maybe you two can find out what's up. We asked, but yeah, they ain't responding."

Louis walked slowly through the center room, where eleven vampires sat silently, each one lifting the hem of their pants to reveal their age as he passed by.

"I'll…" He scanned the room again, ensuring he wasn't mistaken. "We'll be out in a few minutes."

Minks followed him through the bedroom door and closed it behind them, gesturing toward it as he spoke in a hushed whisper. "What's up with that? There isn't a single vamp over five years old in there."

Tossing his bag into the corner, he sat on the edge of the bed and spiked his hair up in frustration. "What did you notice about the scents?"

Jonathan sat beside him and mimicked his pose. "Eleven vamps, two bloodlines. Does Nichol or Jagger know this is a goddamn nursery? That the sires are…?"

Shaking his head, he stared at the door. "The Kaius

haunt doesn't keep track of lineages, so I'm guessing they received names and just accepted those based on haunt affiliation. They wouldn't know newborns were among the lists. Just that it was six members of the Alejandro haunt, seven in the Georgio haunt." Digging his finger into the knots forming in his shoulders, he hunched forward. "This isn't good."

Minks continued to gaze at the floor, his dark hair falling into his eyes. "What do we do?"

"What we always do when we don't know what the fuck to do," he stated, pulling his phone out and swiping it to life. "Call Nichol."

****

Jonathan paced the room while Louis wrapped up his call, listening for any movement in the center room where the young vamps continued to wait.

"So?" he pressed as the cell went dark. "What's Nichol going to do?"

Louis rifled through his bag, pulled out his charger, and plugged his phone in beside the bed. "He's going to swear nonstop while he fixes this shitstorm. Problem is, we're on babysitting duty until he figures it out."

Leaning on the door, he opened his cigarette pack and lit the last one up.

"Once you finish that, we'll go out there and figure out where their hunger levels are sitting," Louis grumbled, his eyes locked on his silent phone. "Maybe send the humans to the store to pick up a few packs of those nasty things for you. No sense in me talking to them, though. They've probably forgotten I exist already, and I'm not in the mood for re-introductions."

Flicking the ashes into the empty pack, he exhaled loudly. "Eleven newborns. Why so many?"

107

With a shrug, his roommate stood and stretched his arms over his head, his injured shoulder still moving stiffly. "Apparently, it's becoming a common discovery, these passels of newbies. Threats to the species seem to have caused a switch to turn on in some bloodlines, and they've gone into hyper-drive, filling the ranks with little thought as to how much fucking work young ones are."

Butting his cigarette out, he set the empty pack on the dresser and ran his hands through his hair. "I'll follow your lead out there."

Louis gave him a tight smile. "No, you won't. Tonight, you've graduated to elder vamp status. I'm not taking the fall alone for this potential disaster of a babysitting gig."

CHAPTER FOURTEEN

Louis took the stairs two at a time as his phone buzzed in his pocket, and he met Minks at the bottom.

"Are the kids all in bed?" Jonathan asked with a grin, ignoring the glare he received in response. "A and B just texted me. They'll be back with the mail and cigarettes in an hour."

Answering his cell, Louis put it on speaker and motioned Minks to their bedroom, where there was a modicum of privacy. "Nichol. Tell me you have good news."

"This is a fucking war," Nic spat. "I have news, and that's as good as it gets."

Plugging his dying cell into the charger, he sat on the edge of the bed and waved off the bag of lukewarm blood Jonathan held out to him. "Fine. What's up?"

"Is Minks listening in?" Nichol asked, the rustling of papers coming through the speaker.

Swallowing his meal, Jonathan moved closer to the phone. "Here. Just downing a B-negative."

There was a muffled murmuring before Nichol spoke again, his voice strained. "Okay. We have a few vamps in their fifth centuries willing to divide the newbies up until they hit Denver. Problem is, you need to get them there."

"Get them where?" he said slowly, already not

liking the turn the discussion was already taking.

"Amarillo."

He flopped his head back and ran his hands over his face. "You want us to transport eleven new vamps three hundred miles without detection?"

"Four hundred miles," Nichol clarified. "I have your route mapped out, along with four alternatives should the side roads you'll be traveling have more Deviants or militia than expected."

Jonathan balled up the plastic bag and dropped it in the trash before sitting beside him. "How are we doing this? A convoy?"

"A motorhome."

Louis stared at the wall as Minks elbowed him in the ribs. "I'm not driving a motorhome." He could hear Mickey laughing in the background and he closed his eyes. "Tell me this is a fucking joke."

"You aren't driving," Nichol stated, a loud thump followed by Mickey's silence, indicating Nic had pulled rank. "You drive like a fucking blind grandmother. Minks, you're behind the wheel. The unit I have a line on has a toy hauler. Your bike should fit in there."

Rubbing his jaw, he shook his head. "This wasn't in the job description."

"Too fucking bad," Nichol snorted. "You're one of us, dipshit. The only job description we have is 'save the goddamn species.' "

"I didn't sign off on squat," he argued, trying to wrap his head around the idea of eleven young, hungry vamps barreling down the highway in a RV with the only thing standing between them and final death being him, the hotshot beside him, and a switchblade.

Mickey's voice called out through the speaker. "Not

yet anyway. But it's totally up to you on this. I mean, we have no other viable option to get those newbies out alive, but whatever. Minks, you'll step up, right?"

Bastard.

Closing his eyes, Louis flopped back on the bed and tossed his arm over his face. "Yeah, yeah. I'm in. We'll need a stash of blood and weapo—"

"Not my first rodeo," Nichol interrupted. "They'll be ready for pickup by Mr. A and B by noon tomorrow, along with a change of clothes since your partner there emailed Jagger saying you're stressing out over a hole in your jacket."

Lifting his arm, he glared at Minks. "What the fuck?"

Jonathan shrugged. "You must stick your thumb in that bullet hole five times an hour. I figured it wasn't a distraction we needed right now." He grinned, his fangs on full display, along with his perfectly straight teeth. "And I prefer my passengers to look as badass as I do when we're on the road."

When Mickey's laughter came through the speaker again, he flipped Minks the bird and snatched the phone off of the nightstand. "You're all assholes. I'll call in at dusk."

Jonathan continued to smile at him as he slid his cell back on the table. "If it makes you feel better, I asked Jagger to include a new set for me, too. Road rash hurts as bad as Deviant claws." Laying back and copying Louis's position, he swiped through his phone and fired off a few texts. "One hour late in checking in and my hauntmates are climbing down my throat."

Opening one eye, Louis glanced at the multitudes of messages buzzing in. "This isn't a time to get lazy on updates. Your sire is well within his rights to be pissed when you're unreachable."

Flipping between the conversations, Jonathan continued to respond to his brothers. "He'd have felt it if I was ended, so he's overreacting." He grumbled as the incoming texts slowed. "Their perimeter patrol took a hit last night. Lost one vamp in his fourth decade and put a human in the ICU."

"And that's why they're on high alert about your whereabouts," he stated, swatting at Jonathan's arm. "Be grateful you have someone worrying about your annoying ass."

Smacking back at him, Minks sat up and plugged his phone in. "Pots and kettles, loner." Laying back, he tucked his hands behind his head. "So what haven't you signed off on yet?"

"If you don't shut up, your death warrant," he grunted, toeing his shoes off.

Minks chuckled. "As long as you need someone driving that motorhome, I'm pretty secure. 'Fess up."

He stared at the ceiling for a moment and sat up, swiping his phone to life and scanning through his emails. "Here."

Jonathan hesitated before accepting the cell, hunching over it while he read over the message. "Can I open the attachment?"

"Go for it."

The silence stretched for what felt like hours while Minks read through the formal decree naming Louis as an acknowledged member of the Kaius bloodline, his lips moving until he got to the end of Nichol's long-winded edict.

"That's some intense shit," Jonathan finally stated,

passing the phone back. "There are hundreds of vampires who would be jumping at the chance to be brought in as an official Kaius hauntmate."

Standing up, he began pacing the small room. "Yeah, well, hundreds of vamps are used to the haunt existence. I've been an independent for almost two centuries, and it's worked out pretty damn good."

"Fair enough," Minks replied, rising to his feet. "But where would you be today if you weren't out here saving newbies from extermination?"

Prowling the length of the room, he shrugged. "Lying low in a city. Somewhere without snow or inbound motorhomes or cold bags of blood. Maybe eastern Texas."

Jonathan stepped directly into his path. "Lying low? You mean watching your own ass for a few decades until it was safe to come out of hiding again, right?"

Crossing his arms, he widened his stance in challenge. "Yup. Nothing wrong with survival."

"Then what's stopping you?" Minks asked, copying his pose. "I can get these young ones into Amarillo. With Nichol and Jagger backing me, I can take care of the Amarillo outpost and the Wichita one. You can head out tomorrow night, disappear into the darkness for thirty or forty years, and step out into a new world of vampire rights. Or subjugation. Or annihilation. Whichever comes first, I guess."

He refused to respond, his tongue running along the tips of his fangs as they lengthened in anger.

"Know what I think?" Minks pressed on. "I think you're full of it. I think you've seen what haunt life can be and you want it. I think you like being needed. And I think it freaks you out because being forgettable is your thing. What you are."

Rolling his shoulders out, he took a step closer. "I think you talk way too fucking much for a kid."

Jonathan rose to his full height and looked down at him. "Do I now?"

The four-inch height difference piqued his ire, and he growled. "Stand down, Minks."

"Naw, Forbes. I don't take orders from rogues."

His tongue sliced open on his fang, and he took a step back, knowing he was moments away from using his age's strength and speed to flatten the cocky bastard. "Discussion's over, kid. We have a lair of young ones we need to watch over at dusk, and I'm not doing it by myself because you're too goddamn tired."

Jonathan's expression morphed into amusement as he shook his head and turned away, walking to the door. "I'm heading upstairs to see if they returned with those cigarettes. See you in a few minutes, *honey*."

****

With a fresh pack of cigarettes in hand, Jonathan exhaled, turned on the bathroom sink, and ran the ember under the water as he fanned the smoke and mulled over his argument with Louis.

He hadn't meant to confront him about the contract. It was, in reality, none of his business. He'd been shocked when Louis had passed the phone to him, open to Mikhail Kaius's email proclaiming Louis a Kaius hauntmate in name and blood.

Shocked but not surprised.

From what he knew about the Kaius males, they trusted no one outside of their line to carry out missions, large or small. Outside haunts were granted rare opportunities to assist in the groundwork, but never in key positions and certainly not with full knowledge of the operation or its endgame. For Louis to be tasked with a major mission he was obviously well-versed in, he had to be in tight with the Kaius haunt.

His own involvement was nothing more than being a chauffeur, and even that was considered pretty damn impressive.

Nothing wrong with survival.

Lighting one last cigarette, he perched on the edge of the sink and inhaled.

Louis gave off the air of being a rather apathetic bastard, one who thrived on watching his own back above those of any others.

Yet here he was, holed up in the suburbs of Albuquerque with a horde of newborn vampires and a partner in his first century, watching all their backs and lowering his chances of survival incrementally with each passing night, with every mile the two of them spent out in the open moving from outpost to outpost.

He arched his head back to blow the smoke directly toward the bathroom ceiling fan.

Honey.

He was unable to resist when Louis had given him orders like a mother fed up with bearing the brunt of the childcare. If he thought back long enough, he could probably pinpoint a moment his own mother had made the same statement, rest her soul.

Putting the cigarette out under the water again, he tossed the wet butt into the garbage can and turned off the light. He picked up the large box Mr. A and Mr. B had brought from their mail run and punctured the tape with his thumb. He slid his nail along it to pop the top open while he crossed the floor, giving the bedroom door a quick knock before he walked in.

"Honey, I'm home," he called out as he set the box on the dresser and pulled a leather jacket out, squinting while he sized it up. "This must be yours."

Louis sat up and caught the jacket in mid-air as it was tossed toward the recliner in the corner of the room. "Enough with the 'honey' thing, asshole."

Throwing the matching leather pants over his shoulder, he turned around and leaned against the dresser. "So we'll move on to the Kaius haunt thi—"

"The Kaius haunt thing is a closed topic," Louis interrupted, not bothering to look away from the television.

Nodding, he walked to the bed, lay down, and crossed one arm behind his head. "Took the words right out of my mouth." He stared at the TV for a few minutes, his fingers absently tracing the cigarette pack tucked into his sleeve. "The whole forgettable thi—"

"I'll reintroduce myself to the humans at dusk."

Rolling his eyes, he looked over at Louis. "Great. Anyway, I was just going to say you're kind of a dismissive guy in general, aren't you?"

"Trying to be at the moment, yeah."

"So when I kissed you—"

This time there was no interruption, only a slight tensing of Louis's jaw.

He pressed on, his stomach knotting. "I mean, you just…it's just forgotten, right?"

Louis's fingers tightened on the TV remote. "My memory is infallible, Minks."

Nodding slowly, he tossed his arm over his eyes to block out the television light.

Two more episodes of the crime drama Louis was

watching went by before the red-haired vamp spoke again.

"Minks?"

"Yeah?"

"Why'd you do it?"

He lifted his arm off his eyes and tapped his cigarette pack a couple times. "Reasons."

Louis snorted. "And you say I'm the dismissive one."

"Fine," he stated, gripping the cigarettes through the fabric of his shirt. "I wanted to because I might have a thing for you. Even if you are an apathetic old bastard." Tugging his lighter from his pocket, he flipped it between his fingers and stared at the ceiling. "Probably just some warped hero worship bullshit or something. I don't know. It's a non-issue."

They fell silent as the theme music from the TV series announced the next episode.

When minutes passed and Louis didn't respond, he tossed his arm back over his eyes and tried to get some rest before their babysitting duties commenced.

CHAPTER FIFTEEN

Louis looked across the table at Mr. A and B and leaned back in his chair, his re-introduction to the men having gone relatively well considering they'd encountered him in the stairwell, their weapons raised until Jonathan stepped in and smoothed things over.

"On Nichol and Jagger's orders, we'll be hitting the road tomorrow at sundown." Disappointment crossed their faces, and he continued. "I know you were preparing for the evacuation, but with the elder vamps no longer around, it's too risky to leave these kids here."

Mr. A's brows furrowed. "We're completely fortified. No one's getting in to hurt them. I swear it."

Jonathan dropped his elbows to the table. "Look, man, you two have done an amazing job. And this place will stay on the list as a safe house in the future since we know more will pass through at some point. But those vamps downstairs…" He trailed off and looked over for help.

"Those vamps downstairs are your biggest threat right now," he stated. "Young ones have control issues. Feeding issues. Guidance issues. And without old vamps around to wrangle them and monitor them, there's a very good chance one or both of you will become a good meal."

Both men straightened in their seats. Mr. B's lips drew into a tight line as Mr. A nodded. "Okay, then.

What do we do now?"

"You two are expected in Wichita," he replied, glancing over at Minks when the men visibly relaxed. "I spoke with Nichol an hour ago, and he said the outpost there could use a few extra hands to do patrols and assist in the final evacuation."

Mr. B took a deep breath. "When do we leave?"

"Tomorrow night, same as us," Jonathan piped in as he pushed away from the table and stood. "You'll follow us to Amarillo, then carry on to Wichita. It's a long drive, so get some rest now while we're up."

Joining his partner, Louis shook the hands of both men before he walked to the basement stairs. "Jagger said to tell you Avery's well, and he's looking forward to seeing you two."

The men grinned as the door shut, and he followed Minks downstairs.

"Time to eat," Jonathan announced, opening a cooler and holding up the top two bags. "We have a B-negative and an AB-positive up first. Takers? Don't try holding out for the O-negs at the bottom because those are mine."

As the young vamps walked over to the cooler and began naming their preferences, Louis leaned against the wall and watched while a few of them lingered at Jonathan's side, quietly discussing the plans for the next evening.

Whether it was due to his age or his demeanor, they were more at ease with Jonathan. With Louis, they were deferential and obedient, speaking only when spoken to and providing only the most concise of responses. The short meeting they'd held at sundown was quick, Louis laying out the plan and the young vamps nodding silently.

"Any questions?" he'd asked.

Nothing.

But now, mingling around the cooler, he could hear them asking Jonathan a litany of questions about the upcoming weeks. As more approached him, the warier ones in the peripheries moved in, listening with interest, while Minks provided as much intel as he could.

The rest of the night passed slowly. The lack of imminent danger was almost boring against the constant adrenaline rush of the past two weeks. Every hour or so, Minks would go topside for a cigarette, and the room would go silent, the young vamps giving Louis little more than polite nods of acknowledgment. Alternating with Jonathan's nicotine breaks, Louis would venture outside periodically, scanning the quiet suburban neighborhood for signs of trouble and reading through the Kaius haunt email loops.

When sunrise threatened the horizon, he went back inside for a final time and joined Minks upstairs as he supervised the young vamps.

"Everyone rest up," he ordered, peeking inside each room to do a head count. "It's going to be a long night tomorrow, and I need everyone in peak fighting condition."

Jonathan elbowed him in the ribs and leveled him with a dead stare. "All of these guys were in their twenties when they were turned, dumbass. Add that to vamp impulses no longer controlled by their sires, and I promise you, all they need to be ready to fight is the word 'go,' They don't need you riling them up before bed."

"Right." He closed the last door and called out a final instruction. "Anyone caught fighting without my direction will ride on the roof tomorrow."

Minks grinned and shook his head, tucking his hair behind his ear. "How old were you when you were brought over?"

Thumping down the stairs, he double-checked the locks to the outside. "Thirty-two. Drained dry in a back alley, woke in a moldy cellar in Birmingham. You?"

Jonathan walked through the basement living room, straightening up the sofa cushions and tying the garbage bag closed. "Twenty-nine. I'd just returned from my fourth tour overseas when my sire approached me."

He hefted the plastic bag from the can and tossed it toward the stairs. "It was too tempting an offer to pass up, so here we are." Eyeing him as they entered the bedroom, Minks closed the door and crossed his arms. "Not a trace of that Brummie accent when you talk."

Setting aside the new leathers and jeans Jagger had sent, he smirked. "Dropped the accent after I ended my maker. Figured it was too identifiable if anyone was on the hunt for me."

Jonathan emptied his own bag and refolded his clothes, tossing his jeans and tee over the back of the recliner. "So did they? Come after you?"

"Nope. Being forgettable definitely has its benefits." Placing his fang clippers on the dresser, he grabbed the TV remote and flopped into the chair. "That, and my creator was an asshole, so I don't think his absence was missed."

Minks stretched out on the bed. "Are you sure you don't want to switch places for tonight? I can sleep anywhere."

"So can I. Now shut up and rest."

Jonathan wrinkled his nose but obeyed. "Fine, you

miserable sot. Good night."

Lowering the volume on the television, Louis got as comfortable as he could in the old recliner. Glancing over at Minks periodically to ensure he was sleeping, he listened to the comings and goings of the neighborhood until he drifted off himself.

****

Jonathan held the clipper to his fang and hesitated. "Yeah, I can't do it again. The memory's too fresh from last time, and I just…no."

Pushing himself out of the recliner, Louis joined him at the mirror and held out his hand. "Gimme those and stay still."

Bracing himself for the sound of metal scraping against bone, he gripped the edge of the dresser, opened his mouth, and fought the urge to flinch away when the first cut was made.

"One to go." Louis grinned, showing off his intact fangs. "Open wide."

Stilling until the second tip was sliced off, he ran his tongue over his blunt teeth. "There's no way the young ones will go for this. It'll leave them completely defenseless."

Leaning toward the mirror to take care of his own fangs, Louis met his eyes in the reflection. "Not a choice. Teeth and contacts are the easiest way to survive a visual inspection, and if we're going to pass this motorhome off as a frat party bus, we damn well better look like frat boys."

Raising a brow at the rugged hardened lines on Louis's face, he shoved his extra shirts into his bag and hiked it over his shoulder. "What does that make you, old man?"

"The chaperone," Louis replied, shrugging his new leather jacket on. "You know, the guy who doesn't get paid nearly enough to put up with everyone's bullshit." Spiking his red hair up, he examined the fit of his jacket. "I make this look good."

Did he ever.

Shoving the intrusive thought aside, Jonathan walked through the living room and scanned the area one last time to ensure they hadn't left anything behind.

"I'll clip fangs, you check rooms," Louis stated as they climbed the stairs. "Under beds, behind doors...pretend you're hunting for a porn stash."

Snorting while he walked past the young vamps milling around in the kitchen, he examined the makeshift bunkers, collecting the odd sock left behind and listening to Louis explaining the reasoning behind the clippers.

When Louis's spiel wasn't followed by the bone and metal sound that pierced his brain, he returned to the kitchen to find the vamps standing as far from Louis as they could in the small space, their arms crossed and eyes narrowed.

"Open wide, gentlemen," he announced, showing off his own blunt teeth. He lifted a heavy box onto the table and sliced it open with his thumb. "They'll regenerate in forty-eight to seventy-two hours, okay? Once you're humanized, we have contacts in here for each of you and...yup...enough blades for everyone to take two."

The males hesitated until the eldest, a tall vamp in his fifth year, stepped forward and opened his mouth.

Louis approached him slowly. "This is going to feel real wrong," he warned him. "But try to hold steady or they'll clip unevenly."

Jonathan couldn't help but notice Louis left out that tugging away at the wrong time could result in a complete defanging.

The vamp nodded, his hands clenching into fists at the first cut. Louis gave him a moment to compose himself before clipping the second and dropping the tips into a small baggie.

Passing two stiletto blades to the kid, Jonathan motioned toward the exit. "Wait there for the others," he ordered, lowering his voice as the vamp passed him, a slight tremble in his hands. "You okay?"

The kid nodded again. His knuckles were white from his death grip on the knives.

Until young vampires had the strength and speed benefits of age, their fangs were their only defense in the event of an attack from another of their species. Protecting them was as instinctual as their drive for blood. The added threat of Deviants and bounty hunters only heightened the anxiety.

And given the awkward hold the kid had on the blade's handle, his sire hadn't made weapon training a priority for the newbies.

One by one, the vampires opened their mouths for Louis's clippers, a few becoming visibly pale when the first snips were made despite the older vamp's attempts to calm them before he started. Mr. A and B sat silently from the table, their eyes down to avoid drawing attention to the sympathy they couldn't mask.

When the last fang was blunted, Louis shoved his clippers into his bag and held out his hand for the box of contact lenses Nichol had shipped in. "Okay, boys. These aren't as invasive, but they're annoying as all hell. Grab a pair and find a mirror. If you don't know how to do it, follow me to the bathroom, and I'll demonstrate."

The quiet procession followed him, with Jonathan bringing up the rear after all the contacts were dispersed.

"So you just lean in and do this…," Louis muttered, his attention on his own reflection as he balanced a brown-tinted lens on his finger. "And then…this…and…yeah, blink. And there! Next one…"

Several of the young vamps broke off from the group, a few managing to pop their lenses in without a mirror.

"Did this for ten years," one of them mumbled, blinking a few times. "I don't miss it at all."

Waiting for his time at the mirror, Jonathan held up a blue lens and clenched his teeth, flinching away for the first few tries until he finally got one in. The second took a few more attempts, causing Louis to poke his head into the bathroom.

"Hot damn, Minks. Hurry up."

Blinking furiously, he shoved his hair out of his face and turned. "Yeah?"

Louis's brown-tinted eyes narrowed. "Not a fan of the color. Let's move."

CHAPTER SIXTEEN

Louis stepped aside with a flourish, bowing to Mr. A when he moved into place and began a series of hand motions Jonathan was obviously finding easier to follow than Louis's gestures, given the fluid movement of the motorhome as it backed tight to the house.

Mr. B stood beside him, eyeing Louis for a moment before he spoke. "He worked in a warehouse for a few years," he explained weakly, nodding at Mr. A as he gave Minks the thumbs-up and unlatched the ramp.

"Yeah, yeah," he grumbled, walking along the side of the RV where Minks was leaning out the window and grinning from ear to ear. "Are we good to load?"

Jonathan tossed the keys to the motorcycle to him. "I'll assign seats. You drive that beast into the back once everyone's in."

Pocketing the keys, he jogged back and ushered the young vamps into the motorhome, scanning the area for danger until the last was inside. Toeing the motorcycle's kickstand up, he walked it up the ramp, the steep angle making it more difficult than he'd anticipated.

Grunting as he pushed it up the last foot, he popped the kickstand down and knelt at the opening, extending his hand to the humans. "It's been a pleasure, sirs," he said, backing up when they bent to lift the ramp. "See you in Wichita."

The hatch swung up, and the lock clicked into place.

Using the cords Mr. A had tossed in, he secured the bike to the walls and walked through the tiny bathroom into the bedroom.

"This place is nicer than anywhere I've ever lived," he announced, reaching up to touch the chandelier hanging over the bed. "How the hell is this a camping unit?"

One of the young vampires cracked a smile, his lips closing tight when he remembered his clipped fangs.

Doing a final head count, he collapsed into the passenger seat and passed Jonathan his bike keys. "Ready when you are."

Easing onto the road with the enormous RV, Minks smirked. "You didn't drive it up the ramp, did you?"

"You know damn well I didn't."

The motorhome inched through the narrow streets of the suburb, the passengers silently obeying when Louis called out an order to lower the shades over the windows.

"Think I'm getting the hang of this girl," Minks announced as he turned onto the freeway and hit the gas. "I'm gonna open her up and see what she can do for me."

Louis snorted, his eyes drifting between the speedometer and the road as he pulled the motorhome manual from the glovebox. "Maybe hold off on pushing limits until we're on the highway. Or, you know, not actively trying to avoid being taken down by the FBI Vamp Division."

"You're no fun." Jonathan grinned and signaled for the turnoff onto the secondary highway Nichol recommended. He slowed his approach and checked for traffic. As he increased his speed and left the lights of Albuquerque behind them, he settled into his seat. "That was easy."

With a glare, Louis groaned. "What the fuck did you go and say that for? You just tripled our chances of a Deviant attack."

Jonathan's barking laughter caught the attention of the young vamps, and one of them scooted a little closer to them from the dinette.

"The, uh, Deviant thing…," the kid stammered, looking over at the others. "What do we do if that happens?"

Louis undid his seat belt and spun his chair around, wiggling it back and forth a few times while he scanned through the RV spec list. "Well, we sure as hell aren't stopping to offer them a ride. If we can, we'll run 'em over. If there's too many of them or we get blockaded, we'll get out and kill 'em face to face."

Several of the males nodded solemnly, while others shared concerned looks.

"But," Minks called over his shoulder, "we have this badass guy right here leading the charge. He was in on the Kaius haunt Deepfryer extraction mission out in Los Angeles, and I know from experience he can take out Deviants one-handed while riding backward on a motorcycle."

Leveling his travel companion with a stare, Louis cocked a brow, picked up the TV remote, and turned on a movie. "And Minks can take them out single-handed while driving that bike through snow, so we got you guys covered."

Jonathan laughed, and he spun back around, turning the manual to page one. "Nothing like creating false heroes to boost the troops," he hushed, checking behind to ensure the males stayed engrossed in the film.

"Nothing false about it," Jonathan countered. "We're the best shot these guys have of survival. And I happen to think we're doing a damn good job taking care of them."

Wrinkling his nose, he skipped over the introduction and dove straight into the warnings peppering the pages. "We'll make that determination in Amarillo."

Hours passed, Louis getting up periodically to distribute the blood bags Nichol had shipped in. Every so often, he'd put on a new movie, monitor the empty roads, and allow the vamps to lift the shades and look out into the darkness.

"Louis?"

Balling up the last of the empty blood bags and tossing them into the trash, he joined Jonathan at the front. "Yeah?"

"That doesn't look like Mr. A's headlights, does it?"

Checking out the side mirror, he shook his head. "How long have they been behind us?"

"Five minutes and gaining fast."

He tracked the lights as they drew closer and tapped his pockets for his blades when a second vehicle sped into view. They both pulled up tight, holding steady behind them.

The motorhome slowed.

"I'll see if they pass," Minks said tersely. "Maybe alert the others to lower those blinds."

"Already on it," he replied, walking through the motorhome and motioning toward the windows. "All right, kids. We have a potential situation. Keep those curtains closed, stay low in your seats, and wait for orders. Anyone caught acting without direction will be left on the side of the road. Got it?"

There was a noticeable shift in the atmosphere as the vamps muttered their agreement. One lowered the volume on the movie, and all heads tilted slightly to the driver side.

Taking his place again, he glared at the side mirror and pulled out his phone. "I'll update Nichol."

Minks sped up again, and the lights tightened to their bumper. "What's the plan?"

Reading over Nichol's confirmation, he set his phone on the dash. "Wait until they make the first move and go from there."

The tension in the motorhome skyrocketed when the first of the vehicles pulled up beside them, and the passenger looked up into their cab, his semi-automatic on his lap and a UV flashlight in hand.

"Minks," Louis ground out, maintaining a calm facade. "You're about to be hit by light. Don't. Fucking. React."

The moment the words left his mouth, the beam striped through the cab, catching his jaw while Jonathan bore the brunt of the hit, hiding the charring of his skin with his hair.

"Fuck, that stings," Minks whispered, opening his cigarette pack and lighting one up as another flash streaked across his face. He unrolled the window and blew the smoke out, masking the wisps rising from his burns. "Motherf...goddamn."

Louis tilted his head enough to ensure the young vamps were lying low to avoid any stray light. As the beam flicked off and the vehicle sped up, he leaned forward to get a good look at Jonathan's burn. "Damn, Minks."

The second truck pulled up beside them for a

moment, then revved its engine and tore ahead.

The eldest of the young vampires inched to the fridge, opened it, and passed Louis a bag of A-positive.

"Thanks, kid." He watched Minks exhale a billow of smoke and toss the dying cigarette out the window. "That's not going to heal quick enough with this bagged shit."

Holding his hand out, Jonathan swallowed and winced. "I'll put in an order for a tall brunette with washboard abs once we hit Amarillo." He moved to tear into the bag with his fangs and paused. "Could you slice that for me?"

Flipping his blade open, he cut a clean line in the bag and stilled.

Fuck it.

Handing the bag to the kids behind them, he shoved his sleeve up as high as it would go and scored his own wrist with the knife before he held it in front of Jonathan. "One vein, three minutes."

****

Jonathan flinched as the RV lurched forward thanks to his foot dropping onto the gas pedal when the scent of Louis's blood hit him. "I, uh, can't?"

"Just shut up before I bleed all over the floor mats," Louis grumbled, his eyes tracking the trucks disappearing in the distance. "That means now, Minks."

Releasing the steering wheel with one hand, he grasped Louis's arm and brought it to his lips, the searing pain of his burns keeping him centered as he latched on.

"Funny story," Louis whispered, glancing back at their passengers. "Last time I did this, it was with Dominic Kaius's connected female, Molly. It was all good until I bit her back, which, in hindsight, wasn't the smoothest move on my part."

Lowering his arm, Jonathan adjusted his grip on the steering wheel. "Did Dominic kill you?"

"No, dumbass. You have two more minutes." Louis tugged at his sleeve and returned his attention to the road ahead. "Straighten the wheel. Yeah, so I kind of overrode the link he had with her. It was a nightmare. You know those people who are just moving and scratching and fluttering around every fucking second? That's Molly."

A ripple of jealousy slithered through him. Shoving it aside, he focused on keeping the motorhome on the road while he drank.

Louis cleared his throat and shifted in his seat. "One more minute. Anyway, there were a few months there where I had this constant buzzing in my head, and on top of that I had Dominic Kaius stalking me in the halls of the haunt. All lurky and shit." He paused and flipped his blade closed. "Time's up."

Releasing Louis's arm, he ran his thumb across his bottom lip and gripped the steering wheel, the older vampire's blood already setting off the tingling sensation of the first stage of healing. "Thanks."

"Whatever," Louis grunted, pushing his sleeve back down. "I don't need you injured and whining."

They drove on in silence, Louis staring out the window and Jonathan forcing his attention to the road.

He knew their passengers were watching them, stealing sly glances their way. Bloodletting outside of haunts wasn't something their species encountered frequently. The potential for accidental links was more than enough of a deterrent for most. It went against their instincts, against their self-preservation. With links came information, intimate information that could be wielded with more force than any other weapon.

The risk was high, as Louis well knew.

He swallowed and tilted his chin to catch a glimpse of his cheekbone in the mirror, impressed with the speed his burns were healing.

"Not looking too bad," Louis offered. "We're about an hour out."

Nodding, he checked his speed and eased up on the gas pedal.

The taste of Louis's blood clung to his tongue. The slight saltiness was unlike any of the thousands of pints he'd consumed over the decades. He ran his tongue over his fangs, cringing when he felt them regenerating faster than expected. "Louis?"

"Remember our little conversation about dismissing shit?" Louis asked, his jaw flexing. "It applies here."

Rolling his eyes, Jonathan shook his head. "I figured. I was going to ask how noticeable my fangs are right now."

Louis looked up from his phone. "Just don't smile and we'll be fine until Amarillo."

"Anything I need to know before we get there?" he asked, frowning when a text buzzed in, and Louis broke into a rare smile. "What? Good news?"

Tapping out a quick reply, Louis set his phone on the dash and leaned back. "Best news I've heard in months, actually. Dominic Kaius is engaged, and we're both invited to the bachelor party Mick is putting on once everything settles." He spiked his hair up and grinned. "You coming?"

"Damn right I am."

CHAPTER SEVENTEEN

Louis sauntered down the RV ramp to greet their hosts, jumping aside when Minks gunned the motorcycle's engine behind him. "Louis Forbes," he said, extending his hand to the elderly gentleman. "And the numbskull on the bike is my second-in-command, Jonathan Minks."

"Pleasure," the man replied, waving at Jonathan as he drove down the ramp and wove through the groups of vampires hanging around outside. "I'm Winston Stapleton, and this is my wife, Janet. I'm assuming you know most of our other guests?"

He looked around at the group and smirked. "Yeah, I know them. You've had your hands full."

Janet chuckled and led her husband toward the large house. "We have thirteen children of our own, all boys. I can handle an ornery vampire or two." She passed Christopher Chisholm, a vampire in his sixth century Louis knew well from his time in London and patted him on the arm. "All of you better be getting inside before you're nothing more than garden fertilizer."

Minks walked up behind him and lit a cigarette. "You want to bring out the kids, or should I?"

He nodded at another old vamp, a male in his eighth century who, according to Rhys, owed some serious favors. "I'll come with. We'll get them settled and discuss temporary custody once they're fed and in bed."

Turning to head back into the RV, he studied the burns on Jonathan's face. "You held up to that light like a fucking king."

"Or a fucking moron," Minks scoffed, gingerly touching the worst of the burns. "Okay, kids. Everybody out."

By the time the horde of young vamps were fed, hooked up with cots in the large basement living room, and divided among the elders in the outpost, Louis was done.

Done listening to the posturing of the oldest vamps as they discussed how many newbies they could safely lead.

Done seeing the wary eyes of the youngest vamps while they took in their new surroundings.

Done with the Deviant sightings Nichol was updating hourly.

Done with the questions.

Done with not having all the answers.

Most of all, he was done with seeing the healing wound on Jonathan's face. It was a tangible reminder of the beam which bore through his skin and into his cheekbone while he calmly lit a cigarette and took it without flinching.

Catching Jonathan's eye across the room, he nodded toward their room and excused himself from Christopher Chisholm's gleeful rant about plummeting global stock prices. The markets were only now feeling the hit as vampires moved centuries of wealth out of the system and squirreled it away amongst themselves.

Closing the door behind him, he thumped his head against the wood. "One more outpost," he chanted, his eyes closed. "Say it with me. One. More. Outpost."

When Minks didn't join in, he opened one eye. "Celebrate with me, dammit."

Jonathan grinned and ran his hand over his healing cheekbone. "We did it, Forbes. Eleven goddamn newbies, four hundred miles, two Vamp Div trucks. No one sludged, and each of those kids paired with a temporary sire." He held up his hand and wiggled his fingers. "Don't leave me hanging."

"High-fives are ridiculous," he stated, slapping Jonathan's hand as he spoke. "But yeah, we did it." His gaze fell to the spot where the UV light had held steady.

Minks tucked his hair behind his ears and gingerly touched the healing wound. "Small price, right? Besides, with your old-ass blood, it'll be gone by mor—"

Louis would freely admit he was a lot of things. Apathetic. Indifferent. Borderline rude.

Bought for the right price.

Sold on a better one.

Things happened around him but rarely to him.

It was, for the most part, a placid existence for a placid guy.

So it wasn't only Minks who was thrown off guard when Louis's arm shot out, and he yanked Jonathan to him by the collar, throwing the male off-balance as he kissed him hard, his regenerating fangs slicing his lower lip. Minks slammed his forearm against the door to steady himself, his feet inching forward slowly to catch up to his body.

He could taste his own blood on Jonathan's tongue when it slid into his mouth, snaked along his fangs, and sent his eyes rolling back in his head before his mind caught up with what was happening.

"Ah, damn," he grunted, releasing his grip on

Jonathan's stretched-out tee, and arching his head away from his lips. "We...uh..." A hot tongue was traveling across his throat, and a strong hand slid down his chest toward his jeans, making him second-guess his second-guessing.

Minks grazed his fangs along his ear. "We, uh, what?" he whispered, grinding his hips against him slowly and erasing all reservations from Louis's head.

Winding his fingers into Jonathan's hair, he tugged gently and ran his tongue over the Adam's apple that had caught his eye more than a dozen times over the past two weeks. "We, uh, nothing," he muttered against his skin. "Shut the fuck up."

Minks chuckled, his laughter morphing into a groan as Louis reached between them and snapped the button of his jeans open, his lust skyrocketing.

Until his phone buzzed.

"Ignore it," Jonathan murmured, his lips trailing along Louis's jaw while he pressed against him.

Wrestling his phone from his back pocket with one hand, he hooked his other in the band of Jonathan's jeans and ran his thumb along the taut skin as he opened the texts Mick had sent in rapid succession.

—*Woah, man. Felt that from here*—

—*What's the good word*—

—*Hey*—

—*Dude, what the fuck was that blast*—

—*Louis*—

—*Hey*—

Two more shoutouts buzzed in, and he locked his phone.

If Mickey felt the burst of lust from over four hundred miles away...

"Minks," he muttered, dislodging his hand from Jonathan's belt loops. "This isn't an...idea...right now."

Jonathan stepped back immediately, his eyes narrowing as he shoved his hands into his back pockets. "Not a good idea," he echoed flatly. "Fair enough, Forbes."

They froze in a silent standoff for a moment, interrupted intermittently by Louis's buzzing phone.

"You should probably answer that," Minks finally said, grabbing his cigarettes off of the dresser and lighting one as he walked over to his bunk bed and hopped up. "Might be an emergency."

"It's nothing," he replied, pushing away from the door.

Jonathan stretched out on the top bunk, exhaling a billowing cloud of smoke that swirled around him. "Shocker."

Tossing his bag onto the foot of the bottom bunk, he leaned on Jonathan's mattress and reached across him to take the burning cigarette from him. "I'm putting this out before you burn the place down."

"Janet gave me a tin can for the butts. It's on the shelf." Minks pushed himself up onto his elbows. "You sure you shouldn't be answering that?"

Crushing the burning ember out, he shrugged. "Yeah, I probably should, but I'm not going to."

"Who is it?"

"Mikhail Kaius." He walked back to the bunks and tugged his jacket off. "You know he's an empath, right?"

The hardness of Jonathan's eyes changed to curiosity. "Really? Not a lot of those make it out of their first decade with their lives. Or sanity."

"Yeah, well, Mickey's bullheaded." Needlessly

clearing his throat, he gave Minks a tight smile as he flicked off the lights and sat on his bed to unlace his shoes. "That's him buzzing in to check up." He could hear Jonathan shifting above him, and he scoffed when long brown hair and dark eyes appeared upside down in his periphery.

"He and I accidentally linked over a century ago during one of our less thought-out excursions which ended in some blood loss and a little splash-back. So he…" He trailed off, not sure where to go with it.

Minks disappeared back up top. "Can you sense him, too?"

"Not a lick. Thank fuck. He's a moody asshole."

There was a quiet chuckle above him. "So he can track you, but you can't track him?"

"Pretty much."

They lay in the stillness of the dark room for a moment before Jonathan spoke. "I don't remember him checking in on you at all over the past two weeks. Not even after those Deviants in Utah."

"Yeah, well, he probably got a weird spike," he muttered, running his thumb across his bottom lip. "Go to bed, Minks."

As Jonathan got comfortable above him, he pulled out his phone, opened up Mickey's texts, and tapped out a response.

—*Just stubbed my toe, Mick. All good*—

****

Jonathan stared at the ceiling, the sliver of light under the door providing enough illumination for him to count the pinholes in the tiles suspended above him.

He knew Louis was still awake, the small shifts in his position giving him away every hour or so while the day crept by at a snail's pace. And try as he might to clear his own head of what had gone on between them at dawn, he wasn't having any more luck sleeping than Louis.

Rapping his fingers lightly on the wall behind him, he attempted to forget the sensation of Louis's fangs grazing his throat by replacing the looping memory with a song from his human days. Focusing on the simplistic drum beat, he continued to tap along to the music in his mind until Louis snapped him out of his daze.

"I am going to fucking stake you if you don't stop."

His fingers stilled for a moment before resuming their rhythm at half speed.

"Minks."

"Yeah?"

There was a rustling of fabric below him, the faint squeaking of the mattress springs as Louis's weight shifted. "I have no problems removing your hands if you keep it up."

Increasing the song's tempo in challenge, he zeroed in on a manufacturing flaw in one of the ceiling tiles. "Not what you were saying a few hours ago."

The bed jarred as Louis kicked the base of the top bunk. "Yeah, you definitely need to shut the fuck up. Night, Minks."

"Night, Forbes."

CHAPTER EIGHTEEN

Louis hiked his new leather pants onto his hips, fumbling with the stiff zipper for a moment before tugging it up and squatting to test his mobility. "You know, I was expecting some tight-ass crap I couldn't sit in, but these aren't half bad," he stated, checking the fit in the mirror as he loaded his pockets with his phone and a king's ransom in blades. "How are yours fitting?"

Jonathan straightened the hem of his black tee and smoothed the fabric over his chest as he frowned and looked down. "Good?" He wrinkled his nose when Louis lifted another flap near his calf and shoved a stiletto knife into it. "Don't load those pockets up too heavy or those pants will be around your knees by the time you're halfway up the stairs."

Jumping up and down a few times to ensure Minks was wrong, he grinned. "I think I get why the Kaius guys are always in cargos instead of jeans. I can easily fit another six blades in here," he stated, shaking his leg out. "Big blades. Maybe even a stake or two."

Shrugging his leather jacket on, Jonathan came up behind him, humming while he ran his fingers through his hair and tucked the stray strands behind his ear.

"Minks."

"Yeah?"

"I'm going to be singing that song while I rip your vocal cords out."

Jonathan's brows lifted, and he smiled wide. "I look forward to it. Meet you topside."

Gathering his dirty socks and ripped jean coat off the floor, he shoved them into his bag and tossed his new jacket over his arm. He gave the room a final look before heading upstairs and out the back door, frowning when he picked up a familiar voice outside.

"...to start with unarmed combat limited to the established perimeter. Weapons can be added once participants demonstrate enough control to avoid causing severe damage to practice opponents."

Jagger?

Flinging the door open, he jogged into the yard, coming to a halt when his ears picked up the slight, tinny sound accompanying the computer speakers.

"You'll want to vary the ages and number of attackers, adjusting the fight limitations as required to ensure participants are challenged, not decimated."

Joining the group of vampires standing around a laptop on a worn picnic table, he watched while the camera panned over to a fight ring scuffed into a field he knew well. Rhys stood in the center, flexing, and whipping his shirt at Lis while she squealed and jumped onto the grass.

"For this live round, we're pitting a younger vampire against a much older one," Jagg's voice continued. "A blade has been planted in the ring, and Rhys will have five seconds to locate it before Nichol enters."

The videographer bounced the camera to the place where Nichol stood, his hazel eyes already locked on his target while Dominic's voice whispered in the background, reminding his fiancée Molly to keep the camera focused on the ring.

Louis smiled as Mickey wandered into the frame, tossing chunks of mud and snow at Rhys's bare back until Audra walked over to him, a single brow lifting. Mick grinned and made his final throw before chasing Audra with his filthy hands.

"Although sparring requires concentration, the goal is not to win but to learn," Jagger stated as Molly began the countdown. "Keep it amiable or—if your participants are like Nichol—cordial. Rhys? Go."

The young vampires inched closer to watch Rhys swipe the ground with his boot, catching sight of the small blade as Nichol launched into the circle. Louis stepped back, his attention on the action around the sparring ring. He could hear the soft murmurings of the older vampires around him while they broke down Nichol's attack form and Rhys's defenses, noting the moves their young adoptees could practice.

"They look like a good time," Minks said quietly behind him, elbowing him in the ribs gently. "Is that Mikhail?"

He nodded, rolling his eyes when Mickey began taunting Nichol. "Yeah, that's him. Dumbass probably forgot he's almost always next in the ring against Nic. I...ah, yeah. He just remembered." He laughed as Mick switched teams, tearing into Rhys instead.

They watched for a few more minutes, Louis pointing out who was who as they drifted on and off screen. Even Molly made it in front of the camera when she dropped it into the snow, her curses ringing through the air while she hurriedly cleaned off the lens and righted it.

"Okay," he finally said as Nichol took down Rhys,

his hand shoved deep into Rhys's jaw to stop the biting. "Let's head out."

Jonathan walked over to his bike and opened the hatch, pulling their riding gloves out and passing over Louis's helmet without a word. He shoved both bags into the cargo hold and got on, toeing the kickstand up as Louis joined him.

"Ready?"

Louis nodded, hesitating a moment before he grabbed on to Jonathan's waist. The motorcycle revved to life, and they tore out of the outpost in a flurry of dust.

****

Damn, it felt good to be back on the bike.

Jonathan glanced down at the speedometer and eased up on the gas, not willing to trade the thrill of riding fast for an unnecessary run-in with the local police.

The Deviant threat looming over the Oklahoma region for months had yet to rear its ugly head, so they tore along the secondary highways, nothing but the noise of the road in their ears for the past two hours.

Even Louis seemed more relaxed, his hands resting on Jonathan's hips instead of maintaining the death grip on his jacket he'd become accustomed to.

Flipping his visor up, he glanced back at his passenger, giving him a nod before he lowered it and returned his attention to the highway, the headset still silent as they drove through the night.

He was thrown by Louis's reaction to the Kaius haunt's live sparring demonstration, the deep lines creasing his face lessening while Rhys postured and Nichol glared. Mickey's antics drew a laugh, Molly's cursing drawing a flash of pride while she snarked back at Rhys's commentary about her videography skills. Bianca Schumann's name was whispered with a respectful awe when the dainty woman flashed across the screen, while Audra's name held a hint of fear. Even Nichol's mate, Simone—a spark of curls ducking out of view as quick as she'd entered—was named with an admiration Jonathan hadn't often heard from the male.

Every time Jagger spoke, quick commentaries describing the techniques of both Nichol and Rhys, Louis had leaned forward, listening intently. His eyes would narrow, flicking between the two fighters as he nodded slowly in agreement, muttering the odd comment about his own experiences in the ring with the old vampires.

Although Jonathan had called Louis out on his connection to the Kaius males nights earlier, it wasn't proven until he saw the hardened stress and wariness Louis naturally carried lessen the longer the video ran. Even his shoulders seemed to drop a fraction, as though the weight of their mission was lifted slightly by the virtual presence of the only haunt Louis had known.

"Forbes?"

An exasperated sigh came through his earbud, a deliberate statement of Louis's opinion on the break in their silent road trip. "Minks?"

He signaled, slowing into the turn onto the rural road. "You ever consider siring? Starting your own haunt?"

Louis snorted. "Think long and hard about what you know about me, then think longer and harder about why you even asked."

"I did," he replied, speeding up once he determined their new highway was deserted. "And I asked because I thought about it."

His passenger went quiet for a moment. "Never been my thing. How about you?"

Relaxing his hold on the handlebars, he scanned the dark terrain. "Can't say it ever interested me."

Louis tapped his thigh and pointed eastward at a solo Deviant stumbling toward the highway. "That may change as you age."

"Doubt it." He laughed, slowing to turn around and reaching back to balance Louis as the male pulled one of his blades from his leathers. "I have no desire to be tied to one place anytime soon. Want me to stop or do you want to practice your action shot?"

"Action shot," Louis called out as the bike circled back and he lined up his throw. "Did you know Kaius is the last sire in his line?"

The blade flew through the air and embedded cleanly between the eyes of the Deviant, sending it sprawling to the ground. "Yeah, what's up with that?" he asked, picking up speed. "Nichol's, what, a million years old?"

"Close." Louis chuckled, settling back in his seat and returning his hands to Jonathan's hips. "If none of them have spawned their own lines, I figure neither of us should have that pressure, right?"

With those wise words, they continued their trek through the dark highways winding toward Wichita, slowing only when the faint haze of city lights breached the horizon and Louis cleared his throat. "So before we get there…yesterday…"

Jonathan glanced down at his phone where the map to the outpost was lit up. "Yeah?"

"I said it wasn't an idea. Right now. Not that it wasn't a good idea."

CHAPTER NINETEEN

Louis shook Mr. A's hand when Jonathan reintroduced him and bit back a grin when Minks mouthed his surprise the human was still incapable of recollecting his existence. "Good to have you on board," he said, turning to Mr. B. "You as well, sir. We'll get this bike out of sight and head inside."

The men nodded solemnly and continued their patrol of the grounds surrounding the old motel outside Wichita, crossing the crumbling lot to update the other members of their group.

"That's just ridiculous," Jonathan scoffed, straddling the motorcycle and walking it along the side of the building. "I mean, come on. This is the third time in less than a week you've met them and neither remembered?"

"The humans I want to know remember me, like Molly and Bianca, so who cares?" He shrugged.

Jonathan toed the kickstand down and got off, slinging both helmets onto the handlebars and popping the hatch open. "Catch."

Snatching his bag out of the air, he tossed his gloves over and waited until his travel companion sauntered over to him. "Okay, Minks. One final outpost to survive."

"We got this." Jonathan grinned, throwing his arm over his shoulder. "Don't think of it as a place to survive.

Think of it as another place where our word is law."

"Our word backed by the Kaius haunt," he corrected, his end-of-mission tension tampered slightly by the muscled arm draped across his back.

Knocking on the only un-boarded entrance, Minks rolled his eyes. "Minor detail. I like my version better."

The door swung open to an ancient, grinning vampire. "Well, well, well. Louis Forbes. We've been expecting you, boy."

Stepping inside the dark lobby, he shook the male's hand. "Good to see you again, Vanito," he greeted, following the ancient and scanning the fortified interior. "This is Jonathan Minks, my second-in-command on this mission."

Vanito turned and flashed a fangy grin at Jonathan. "How old are you, boy?"

"In my sixth decade," Minks replied, removing his arm from Louis's shoulder to lift the cuff of his leather.

The ancient patted him roughly on the back and motioned down a narrow hall. "So this is the baby Minks your sire was keeping hidden all these years."

Louis bit the inside of his cheek as Jonathan scrunched his nose and yanked his cigarettes from his jacket. "Did you ever realize your creator was probably living a dual life?" he muttered, lighting up.

Vanito pushed a heavy wooden door open and laughed. "Most sires are. It's our responsibility to shield our young from our less noble sides."

Louis stepped aside, allowing Minks to walk in behind Vanito while he held back and perused the crowded meeting room.

There was a mix of young and old. Several new vampires were interspersed among older vamps, at least three he recognized as ancients closing in on their second millennia. Game systems were hooked to televisions lining the back wall, where a dozen males sat in deep concentration. Haunt leaders sat at the table in the center of the room, their discussions animated and light. Threadbare sofas were clustered along the east side, inhabited by vampires and...

"Does Rhys know there are Tenders on-site here?" he asked. "I was under the impression all human companions were evacuated by land into Denver."

Vanito's expression turned serious, and he gestured to the corner of the room. "Perhaps we should speak over there."

Swatting Minks on the arm to follow him, Louis nodded, waiting until Jonathan put out his cigarette on the rim of a garbage can, and they were sequestered in the dark corner before speaking. "Two humans on-site with twenty-eight vamps is a recipe for disaster."

"We encountered a minor issue when we attempted to separate the pairings," Vanito said quietly, looking over at the couple sitting across the room. "The males became more distraught the further their partners moved from our location." He dropped his voice. "We couldn't afford the weakening of two of our older fighters, so we made the executive decision to turn the women back. Rhys is aware of the situation and has advised we keep it somewhat quiet."

Louis frowned. "So are they counted in Nichol's numbers?"

"Ah, no," Vanito muttered. "I'm forbidden from contacting Nichol. And it is my understanding Rhys has kept the intel out of the database. Forgiveness over permission." His mood shifted and his smile returned as his attention shifted to Jonathan.

"Most of us will be retiring shortly. You two are in suite seven." He looked Minks up and down. "Would you be interested in a little nightcap to relax you before you turn in?"

Nichol.

An ancient.

An ancient Rhys forbade from contacting Nichol.

Louis stepped closer to Jonathan and shoved his hands into his back pockets. "We're going to find our room and prep for tomorrow night's debriefing. See you at dusk, Vanito."

Ushering Minks out, he left the vampire and his ancient blood in the meeting room, holding his tongue until they were secured in their room.

"Stay away from that guy," he ordered, flinging his bag onto the dusty dresser.

Jonathan gave him a perplexed look and nodded slowly. "Okay. Why?"

Sitting on the sagging mattress, he stared at the floor for a moment, deep in thought.

The Kaius haunt business was just that: Kaius haunt business. Through proximity alone, he was privy to some of the most sensitive information and secrets the haunt held tight to the chest. He knew sharing that intel with anyone outside of their small group could be dangerous.

Minks sat beside him and lit another cigarette. "Louis?"

Jonathan's first, and last, experience with a blood high shot to the front of his mind.

"Vanito's a blood peddler," he finally said, unlacing his boots. "Gets his kicks out of getting vamps stoned on his veins, getting them hooked, and making them pay.

This guy doesn't cut it with younger blood or human blood. It's pure ancient. A friend of mine…" Pausing to collect his thoughts, he hooked his thumbs in his boots and tossed them against the wall. "If Nichol can get hooked on that shit, a kid like you stands no chance. Got it?"

Blowing a perfect ring into the air, Jonathan's brows rose. "Nichol?" he echoed incredulously. "Nichol Kaius."

"That's the one." He looked over at Minks. "If you could keep it between us—"

Jonathan took another drag and gave him a lopsided smile. "Louis?"

"Yeah?"

Exhaling slowly, Minks got to his feet, disappeared into the bathroom, and ran the sink. "You've called me your second-in-command twice now," he stated, exiting the bathroom and standing in front of him, arms crossed. "We've been riding crotch to ass for over two weeks. I've watched you hypnotize vamps. And Louis?"

"Yeah?"

"I'd kind of like to make this idea," he said, gesturing between them as he crossed the room to the far bed, "a good idea. Pissing off Nichol Kaius and putting a bounty on my own head is kind of counter-productive to that." The mattress groaned when Minks hopped onto it and stretched out, tucking his hands behind his head. "Now I'm going to get rested up since some asshole kept me up drumming all last night."

Throwing a flat glare at the smartass vamp, Louis turned off the lights and lay back, listening to the comings and goings in the hallway and indulging in the ridiculous notion Minks might actually be a good idea after all.

****

Jonathan stood to Louis's left and hooked his thumbs in his belt loops. He watched the faces of the vampires around the table while they listened intently to the red-haired vamp at the head.

"With your runway being three miles away, you're going to need to get your hands on two more vehicles to transport a group this large. We don't need a breakdown causing any issues when word comes down to evacuate," Louis continued, glancing down at the notes on his phone. "Any last questions before I report back to the Kaius haunt?"

Vanito's hand rose. "Plan B," he stated, looking around the group. "Is there one? Should this evacuation fail?" With a smarmy expression gracing his face, he sat back in his chair and stretched his arms out. "This isn't the time for Nichol or the Kaius haunt to be putting all their eggs into one basket, is it now?"

Jonathan watched Louis contemplate the question, his eyes shifting from blue to a dark gray as the vampires chimed in their agreement with the question. "This is Plan B, gentlemen," he finally said. "If we want to get technical, this is Plan Z-Nine-Twenty. The Kaius haunt has coordinated evacuations, escapes, and routes for vampires across six continents for months. And for their companions," he added pointedly. "Plan A began when the first footage of vampires was released online fourteen years ago. I'm sure we all remember that night."

Every male nodded solemnly, several leaning forward as Louis continued.

"Human alliances were planted in governments, payoffs were made for intel, trades done for pushing the vampire agenda…all those were Plans A, B, C, and W. And we all benefited from them during that first decade."

Quiet murmurs of agreement rumbled through the room, and Louis shifted in his seat.

"The Deepfryer legislation delays, the research Jagger and Nichol conducted allowing us to know how long we could survive in them? Those were Plans A-Forty through to C-Ninety-one," Louis stated, his voice growing quieter as the mood in the room grew heavier.

"The rescue missions for those sentenced to the Deepfryer, the orphaned vamps, the haunt raids that came with the tattooing legislation? Plans R-Eighty-three to Q-Fifty-four. Now add in the first wave of evacuations. The second wave. The return wave in the past six months. All customized by territory, destination, vamp age, and haunt numbers. What are we at, Plan T-Four-Fifty-Five?"

Several of the vampires looked away, their eyes on the walls, on the floor.

"And now, here we are," Louis stated, pushing his chair back and standing. "Outposts. Weapons shipments. Blood transfers. Vehicles. Planes. Primary, secondary, tertiary routes for each and every one of you who arrived here. And from here, Denver. A goddamn sanctuary city with laws, housing, feeding protocols. All established and waiting for you." He straightened up and met each male's eye before speaking again. "This is it. All that's left is a thank-you email or two for the Kaius haunt."

He strode out the door, poking his head back in moments later. "Minks."

Giving the males at the table a quick salute, Jonathan jogged over to join Louis. "See you in Denver, gentlemen," he called before the door slammed shut behind them. "Sorry. I was too stupefied by your little speech there to move for a second."

Louis rolled out his shoulders and opened the door to their room. "I fucking hate talking. Especially to groups. Always have."

"You'd never know by how smooth you put those self-entitled ancients in their place." He grinned, kicked off his boots, and picked up the TV remote. "I'm going to catch up on local news for a bit. You rest, and I'll wake you when I get tired. Deal?"

Louis merely nodded and lay back, tossing his arm over his eyes. As the older vamp went completely still, Jonathan sat back, turned down the volume, and listened to the quiet murmurs of awe for Louis filtering through the thin walls.

CHAPTER TWENTY

Jonathan slowed the motorcycle and popped his visor up, adjusting his grip on the handlebars as he turned off the icy gravel road onto the narrow tree-lined path leading to the gates of the Stojanovski compound. "Still too early to say it?"

"Are we inside the gates? No? Then yes, too early," Louis snarled, glancing around while his hold on Jonathan's hips tightened.

The first three hours of the ride were downright pleasant, both males rested and alert and ready to take on whatever Deviants stumbled into their path.

But when the roads remained empty, and the drive continued uninterrupted, Louis grew more anxious. Jonathan's headset would flare up intermittently with mutterings of the calm before the storm, musings about what was over the next hill and how far off from sunrise they were.

At last count, it was well over a hundred and thirty minutes.

Leaning over to key in the lock code, he revved the engine and eased through the narrow gate, pulling up tight to the fence as the metal clanged behind them. "Now?"

Louis swung his leg over the seat and hopped off, scanning the quiet terrain. "Fine."

"Hey," he announced with exaggerated jubilance,

"we made it!"

Opening the storage hatch, Louis tossed both bags over his shoulder and slung his helmet over his wrist. "We did it. Hip hip hooray. Woo hoo. Party on. I'm going to text the guys and let them know we're here."

While Louis walked toward the main building with his head down, tapping message after message into his phone, Jonathan strolled along beside him, noting the absence of the hunt that made Stojanovski's compound famous among vampires.

"Louis?"

"Yeah?"

"What do you think will happen to this place once we evacuate?"

Louis looked up from his phone. "If we're lucky, it'll remain off the radar. The bunkers are a perfect outpost for down the road, so we—the Kaius haunt—will probably work out a deal with Jackson to ensure the property isn't forgotten in the shift."

He tossed his arm over Louis's shoulder, and they made their trek across the open field surrounding the building, stopping when Louis paused in the middle for a moment and looked around at the snow-covered ground before continuing.

The heavy wooden doors opened, and Stojanovski greeted them on the veranda as they reached the steps. "About time you two got back," he called out, jogging down the stairs to shake their hands. "Louis, your bunker is ready for you. Jonathan, I'll show you to your quarters on the way."

Following Jackson through the yard, they filled him in on the status of the other outposts, Louis throwing in the odd sly comment about some of the vampires they'd encountered and smirking when Stojanovski added his own observations about those who had passed through his compound.

"Here's your place," Stojanovski announced when they approached one of the small houses sitting atop the bunkers below. "You know the drill, Minks. See you at dusk."

Jackson continued on while Louis hesitated beside him. "I'll touch base with you in a bit, Minks," he said, glancing at their host. "Abuse his hot water tanks while you can."

"Please do," Jackson called over his shoulder. "Nichol Kaius is footing the bill, and I intend to gouge him for as much as he'll allow."

Jonathan gave Louis a tight smile and walked inside, shutting the door, and setting the first of two codes required for anyone to breach the secure underground bunker.

He descended the ladder and pulled the hatch closed, walking through the bachelor-style apartment that was an exact replica of every other single unit at Stojanovski's. The living area had a small fridge and microwave, an ashtray sitting on the rounded coffee table, and a single sofa separating the sleeping area from the rest of the space.

Opening the fridge, he gave the three carafes inside a quick sniff and selected the A-positive, deciding to drink it cold instead of going through the hassle of pouring it into one of the plastic-wrapped glasses and spinning it in the microwave. He wrinkled his nose as the first sip of cool blood hit his tongue. Flopping onto the sofa, he turned on the TV and checked his phone.

His brothers had pinged in throughout the night as

they always did, sharing photos of their perimeter patrol around Denver and texting snarky observations about the human protestors marching in heavily armed groups along the entrances to the city. Tapping play on a video, he rolled his eyes at the anti-vamp slogans being chanted, laughing when the camera swung to his oldest brother lounging against the barricade and chatting up a woman in a Species Purifier hat.

Armand rarely met a woman who wasn't drawn to him.

The noise of the television drowned out the stillness of the room as he finished his meal and stretched out on the sofa, tapping out his haunt leader's number.

"Jonathan, my boy! Have you arrived at Stojanovski's?"

"Got in an hour ago," he replied, lowering the volume on the television. "How's the patrol going?"

He could hear the protestors in the background as his sire moved closer to them. "The language being used is a little bourgeois for my tastes, but the creativity of the spelling on the signage provides a little entertainment. Has Xavier sent you any photos of his favorites?"

"Every night." He smiled. "Any rumors on when this evacuation is happening?"

Minks Silas called out to Armand and laughed before answering. "Your brother is attempting to sway the anti-vampers one woman at a time. No, we've heard nothing. Nichol Kaius issues nightly emails to every vamp in Denver to keep us apprised of the latest intel he and the others feel we need to know, but nothing yet on an expected date. Armand! Come say hi to Jonny!"

There was a rustling as Armand took the phone. "How's the bike holding up? That suspension work make any difference?"

"Smooth sailing, Arm," he replied, frowning when he overheard shouting. "Everything okay?"

"Just a Molotov being thrown over the barriers," his oldest brother huffed. "Caught one of the Landon vamps on the foot." The phone rustled again. "I better let you go. Talk tomorrow, Jonny."

The cell's screen went black, and he opened his cigarette pack, lighting one as he turned up the volume on the TV to mask the solitude.

****

Louis stretched his legs on the coffee table and waited until Rhys and Mickey stopped arguing. "Nichol," he called over the din on the other end of the video link, "any messages for Jackson?"

"Tell that asshole to confirm his numbers as of yesterday's influx," Nic instructed, swatting Rhys across the back when the male lunged over the table to smack at Mickey. "The Gregoire haunt should have fourteen, but they traveled up from Florida without contact for three weeks."

"Confirm. Will do," he replied, knowing how tough it was on Nichol to dwell on the dwindling vamp numbers. "Isn't tomorrow date night? I'll pass the info through Jagg."

The surly vamp's eyes softened slightly before he schooled his expression. "Go through Jagger and add me to the email. Don't forget to include names and ages. I don't want to be blindsided by another passel of brats again."

"No problem." He leaned forward in preparation of ending the conference. "Tell Simone hi for me. And Mick. Mick. Hey, Mick." Rhys tugged on Mickey's long blond hair and turned his head to the camera. "How are you holding up?"

Mickey struggled for a moment before grinning. "Better than you and your stubbed toe. You've had, what, two so far?"

"What the fuck's wrong with your footwear?" Nichol barked. "I can have a shipment placed today."

Rolling his eyes, he hovered his thumb over the end button. "I'm good. Talk to you idiots tomorrow."

He plugged his phone into the charger and swiped through the news, scanning the latest updates on the government's attempt to force Denver to open its roads to the FBI Vamp Division. When his mood was appropriately soured, he opened an article on the pro-vamp movement and followed the article's links until dawn's arrival shivered through his bones.

Setting his cell down, he lay back on the sofa and stared at the ceiling.

It was the most secure he'd felt since he'd left Stojanovski's weeks earlier. Armed gates, electrified fences, coded locks, daytime security. No territorial vampires in striking distance, no ancients with unknown grudges, no Deviants grunting and stumbling overhead.

He got to his feet and walked over to the bed, peeling his leather cargos off and tossing them into the corner of the room before falling face down on the bed.

Exhaustion was a bitch.

Rolling onto his back, he tucked his hands behind his head and closed his eyes, waiting patiently to fall asleep until his patience ran out and he stood back up again, thumping back to the coffee table to grab his phone. Swiping it to life, he scanned through his contacts.

—You up?—

Minks replied moments later.

—Yeah. You?—

He stared at his phone and tapped the phone icon. "Who is it?"

He rolled his eyes and stretched out. "What are you doing awake?"

"Watching reruns of some cop show from the nineties. It's weird seeing no vamp perps," Jonathan mused. "Did you touch base with the Kaius haunt?"

Relaxing into the expensive mattress, he nodded. "Mick and Rhys spent most of it beating each other over the table, but Jagg and Nichol shouted out a few orders over them." He chuckled. "They can be borderline feral when their partners aren't around."

"Sounds like my haunt," Minks replied. "We once had a contest to see who could eat the most hot dogs before throwing them up. Ever eat human food as a vamp?"

Louis snorted. "No. Is it as bad as they say?"

"Worse," Jonathan stated solemnly. "I swear I can still taste it. And this was three decades ago."

Reaching over to turn off his lamp, he lay back in the dark. "So, how many did you handle?"

"Eleven. But Gino beat me with thirteen. And I'm telling you, Louis, there is no feeling that can possibly top the sensation of losing *and* chucking up hot dogs on a basement floor."

The lilt of Jonathan's accent lulled him, and he closed his eyes. "How many of you are there, anyway?" he asked, trying to remember if he'd ever inquired about the Minks' bloodline.

There was a faint rustling of fabric over the phone

speaker. "Ten of us. Armand is the oldest at three centuries, followed by Xavier, Gino, Walter, Theo, Christoph, Frederick, Nero, Samuel, then me."

"I'm not getting any sleep anytime soon," Louis replied, tucking one hand behind his head. "Tell me about them."

Jonathan hesitated a moment before he spoke again. "Frederick introduced Xavier to the concept of the internet. Two years ago."

His brows lifted. "How did he go that long not knowing?"

"He knew it existed but not how to navigate it," Minks clarified. "But Frederick is kind of an ass, so he showed Xavier everything he could but didn't teach him any of those rules the rest of us just kind of learned on the way." There was a faint snick of a lighter and a deep breath.

"And, of course, Frederick made sure Xavier had his own email address and a link to every spam mail site he could find. You know all those forward-this-to-ten-of-your-friends emails? And those make-a-million-from-home ones? He forwarded all of them to us. Then he discovered memes. At one point, I was getting fifty emails a day from him."

Thinking back to Mickey's first forays into the internet world, Louis smirked. "I know a guy who used to do that."

"Yeah?" Minks said, exhaling loudly. "Did he fill your inbox with recipes and medical warnings? How about memes you'd seen a decade earlier? I'm telling you, Louis, by the time Nero stepped in and sat Xavier down, the rest of us had already created new email addresses Xavier still doesn't know about."

Holding back a laugh, he propped his pillow up. "Nichol would have staked him after the first spam page. What about the others?"

"All right, you asked for it. Christoph, Nero, and Walter's camping trip," Jonathan stated, taking another long drag of his cigarette. "Nero convinced the other two they needed to have a return to nature. Some shit about needing to unleash his artistic inspiration away from steel columns and the tainted molecules invading their bodies or something." He exhaled and chuckled.

"They spent two thousand on camping gear, strapped it to their backs, and made this huge deal of saying goodbye to all of us. I'm talking hugging, and promises to update us on their journey, and musings about the danger they would face. Then they marched up to the Hollywood sign in LA and sat there for three hours until Christoph got bored, Walter got hungry, and Nero became inspired to buy some neon paint. They actually had the nerve to call our sire and ask him to pick them up."

"Did he?" Louis asked, sitting up a little higher.

"Of course," Jonathan grunted. "Indulgence is his biggest fault."

Thinking about his own violent sire, he wrinkled his nose. "There are worse faults in a creator."

He could hear the smile on Jonathan's face when he responded. "Oh, I know. It's just fun to bust his balls once in a while. And to test how far he'll go."

The comment reminded him of Dominic, and he smirked. "Damn youngest hauntmates. Spoiled brats, all of them."

CHAPTER TWENTY-ONE

Jonathan exited the small house atop his bunker and crossed the yard toward the figure with the bright red hair standing in the middle of the field. "Sorry I slept in," he called out, jogging over. "I guess I was more tired than I thought."

"I just got here myself," Louis replied, shoving his hands into his back pockets. "Some blathering asshole kept me up past noon."

Grinning, he lit a cigarette and exhaled a puff of smoke into the crisp air. "Price you pay for asking me questions. I'll actually answer them, unlike, I don't know, you?"

Strolling toward the veranda, Louis looked up at the cloudless sky. "I'm a man of mystery."

"You're a sullen bastard, is what you are." He inhaled deep, coughing when Louis's elbow made contact with his ribs. "Truth hurts," he wheezed, pounding on his chest to clear the smoke. "What are the commands for tonight?"

Pushing the doors open, Louis grinned back at him. "Hang out. Nichol's orders."

"A vamp after my own heart."

They strode through the main hall, scanning the patrons milling around the various seating areas. Several of the compound's remaining humans sat in clusters on the stairs, one eye on the vamps while they chatted amongst themselves.

"Louis, Jonathan," Stojanovski called out, ushering them over to a small group of vampires perched on the sofas, ready for attack. "Gentlemen, these are the Kaius haunt representatives I was telling you about. Louis, this is the Gregoire haunt."

Seven males.

Louis stepped forward slowly and crouched down in front of them while Jonathan hung back, listening as Louis explained the evacuation plan, the housing setup in Denver, and reassured the vampires Nichol Kaius would not leave them behind.

"We can pay," the haunt leader stated, his dark eyes weighted. "Whatever Nichol wants is his."

"What Nichol wants," Louis stated quietly, "is as many vamps as possible on those planes when he gives the word. Wealth transfers are far down the list of issues requiring addressing right now. The Kaius haunt is prepared to finance all costs for up to a decade. Longer, if needed."

Gregoire stilled with the motionless of an ancient, the rest of his haunt looking to him for assurance. "We lost our seven youngest in the swamps of Arkansas. Deviants, dozens of them, lying in wait in the waters. I…we…cannot lose another."

Jonathan felt his stomach knot at the thought of seven of his brothers being ended at once.

He couldn't fathom surviving a hit like that.

Slapping Stojanovski on the knee, Louis rose to his feet. "This vamp here has been working with the Kaius haunt to ensure no vamp gets left behind. You will all have a place on the planes. Your job until then is to rest, feed, and rejuvenate. We don't promise an easy trip, and should anything go to hell, we'll need all the strength we can get."

Gregoire nodded. "With thanks."

Louis bumped past Jonathan, motioning to the clusters of sofas in the farthest corner. "Voice low," he whispered, glancing back while Stojanovski called several humans over to the Gregoires.

"That's an old-school ancient, closing in on twenty-five hundred." Waiting until the males stood and followed their meals up the stairs, he stretched his arms across the back of the couch and lolled his head back. "Do you have any idea how many Deviants it would take to get the better of a group like that?"

"That must've been the missing Oklahoma mob," he mused as Jackson joined them. "Evening, sir."

Stojanovski collapsed on the sofa next to him. "That puts our tally up to seventy-eight," he reported. "I have five planes on standby, so anything under an influx of forty more before we go is workable."

Louis pulled his phone out. "I'll update Jagger with the numbers." Shaking his head, he looked up, his face grim. "Another seven. Goddamn it."

"Jagger?" Jackson asked, grinning. "Ah, yes. It's Nichol's date night with my hybrid, isn't it?"

"Nichol's hybrid," Louis corrected, looking over at Jonathan. "You know anything about Simone?"

Shrugging, he wrinkled his nose. "Nichol's partner? Nothing except the curly hair."

Jackson sighed dramatically. "I paid Rhys a king's ransom for that little killer. His first Tender-Hunter hybrid."

"First and last," Louis corrected again, sliding his phone onto the table.

With feigned disappointment, Stojanovski looked over at him. "She truly was the purchase of the century. Unfortunately, when a Kaius male is connected to a female, those of us with scruples must step aside, allow the male the opportuni—"

"What Jackson's saying," Louis grinned, "is he was petrified Simone was going to make him her next target, so he used the connection as an excuse to trade her for my hypnosis services and here we are now, best frenemies."

Jonathan leaned forward, fascinated by the small tidbit of Kaius's haunt gossip. "So it's true then. Nichol Kaius is connected. To a Tender?"

"Not just any Tender," Stojanovski stated. "A vamp killer."

Louis cringed. "Technically, it was her job."

"How?" He hesitated, still dumbstruck at the idea one of the most influential Kaius males was connected to a vamp killer. "How many?"

As Stojanovski began counting names off quietly on his fingers, Louis swatted at his hands. "This conversation is over. Let's just say Simone's last kill was her finest and leave it at that."

Smirking, Jackson settled back on the sofa. "The Kaius males have a thing for dangerous women."

When neither he nor Louis expanded, Jonathan crossed his arms. "Don't leave me hanging."

Exchanging a quick look with Jackson, Louis cursed under his breath and flopped back in his seat. "Dominic's marrying a failed Tender with the impressive sniper skill that pierced the Deepfryer in L.A.—"

"Dominic's getting married?" Stojanovski interjected. "That poor kid."

Grinning, Louis continued. "Mickey's with Audra, who you saw on that training footage. She's insanely smart and more like Nichol than anyone I've ever met, which makes her terrifying. Jagg's with Bianca Schumann—"

"Ms. Schumann could serve as queen of the vamps if she wanted the title, even though she's human," Jonathan offered. "At least, that's what my sire always said."

"Precisely. There's Nichol and Simone. And then Rhys and Lis, and we all got to watch that unfold on network TV," Louis said, disdain in his voice. "Fucking media vultures still revisit that on the news every few weeks."

Whistling, he shook his head. "I suppose badass vamps attract badass wom—"

"Oh, my goodness! Louis! You're back!"

Jonathan's head whipped around as a woman called out from across the room. She ran toward them, her short hair spiked in a longer version of Louis's style.

She skidded to a stop at the sofas and wrapped her arms around Louis, smiling with excitement. "No one told me you were back! How did it go? Are you okay? Any word on the evacuation?"

Louis extricated himself from her grip and leaned back, completely at ease. "Just got in last night. It was fine."

"You must be starving," she breathed, shoving the sleeve of her shirt up and holding her wrist to his fangs. "You really need to keep your strength up, honey."

****

Louis glanced over at Jonathan, a strange wave of guilt hitting him as he unhooked his fangs from his meal.

"Thanks," he muttered, rolling her sleeve down. "It's been a while since I had a real bite."

His explanation for his uncontrolled snap into Dahlia's arm sounded weak, even to his own ears.

"Don't you dare apologize," Dahlia chastised, reaching behind him to run her thumb across the nape of his neck. "You know I'm here for you. How's Rhys doing? Molly?"

Stojanovski waved over another woman and introduced her to Jonathan, completely oblivious to the awkwardness filling the room. "Eat up, Minks. We must indulge while we still can."

Giving the woman a polite smile, Jonathan took the offered wrist and turned her arm over, kissing her hand once and placing it back to her side. "I'm afraid I overindulged already on the carafes you provided in my bunker," he replied. "But I thank you for the hospitality."

Jackson motioned for the woman to go. "In times like this, even my own Tender is sacrificing for the cause," he said, pointing at Dahlia. "Aren't you, dear?"

"Yes, of course." She laughed, squeezing Louis's hand.

His gaze lifted to Minks long enough to see the hardened dark eyes before returning his attention to the coffee table. "Much appreciated, both of you."

Jonathan's hand closed the gap between them. "I don't believe we've been introduced," he said, his Cockney accent completely replaced by the Queen's English. "Jonathan Minks."

"Dahlia." She smiled sweetly, shaking his hand and giggling when he kissed it. "Such a gentleman."

Jackson rose to his feet, taking Dahlia's hand with a flourish and a fangy smile. "While I'm not quite as smooth as young Minks, I do believe I'll be reclaiming my Tender for the evening. The grounds are yours, as are any of the humans on premises." Pulling Dahlia tight to him, he gave them both a stern glare. "Save this one."

"We'll catch up later!" Dahlia smiled as she walked off with Jackson, leaving him and Minks in a strained silence until Jonathan broke it.

"So that's a Rhys-trained Tender in action, is it?"

Louis nodded and leaned back, giving Minks a tight smile. "It is. She knows me from the Kaius haunt."

"I figured as much." He stood and stretched, rolling his shoulders out. "I need a cigarette."

Louis watched him walk away, his meal sitting like lead in his gut.

It was just a feeding.

The rationalization was sound.

And true.

But it didn't erase the guilt he felt over the look that flashed across Jonathan's face when Dahlia's arm draped over his shoulder.

Pushing himself to his feet, he strolled out the door after Minks.

CHAPTER TWENTY-TWO

"Minks."

Jonathan exhaled slowly into the air, watching the smoke dissipate as he took another drag. "Yeah?"

Louis stopped at his side. "Dahlia is—"

"Not any of my business, Louis," he stated, frowning when his attempt at a smoke ring failed.

Spiking his hair up, Louis stepped in front of him. "My business has been turning into your business a hell of a lot over the past few weeks, so yeah, it is, Minks."

Tossing his cigarette over the balcony into the snow, he crossed his arms and leaned on the ornately carved banister, pulling another from his pack. "There's a line between need to know, want to know, and don't have any business knowing, Louis. Dahlia falls into the last category here."

They stood in stony silence, stepping out of the way when the Gregoire haunt exited the hall and passed them, nodding respectfully at Louis on their way by.

He was caught off guard by the way the woman hadn't hesitated to squeeze in tight to Louis, twirling her fingers in his hair as he fed and skimming her thumb along the collar of his tee while she chatted amiably.

But what really threw him for a loop was Louis's reaction.

Or lack thereof.

There was no hint of hesitation when Dahlia jumped

onto the sofa beside him, none when he took her offered wrist, none when she ran her hands on him with the familiarity of a lover who had done it hundreds of times.

"She's sweet," Louis said, breaking the silence. "She put up with me, I guess." He glared at the swampy quadrant of the grounds. "I'm not a likable guy, and I don't particularly care that I'm not. And Dahl? She didn't really care that I didn't care, you know? I was part of her job, and it worked." Running his tongue over his fangs, his back hunched slightly. "I fucking hate talking, so I'm going to shut up."

Jonathan tossed his second cigarette butt over the balcony, making a mental note to gather them up before dawn. He walked down the stairs, shoving his hands into his back pockets as he began to make his way across the field. "Coming?"

There was a pause before he could hear Louis's boots crunching in the snow, falling into step with his own. They clomped through the field, passing the swampland to their right as they made their way to the fence where his motorcycle stood.

"The grounds are ours, right?" he asked, pulling his keys from his pocket and passing them to Louis. "Let's make the most of it. Get on."

Louis scoffed and tossed the keys back. "I'm good riding in back."

"Well, I'm not," he stated, grabbing Louis's hand and shoving the keys back in. "I don't know how the hell you've survived this long being unable to drive, but it ends tonight."

Louis frowned, his eyes narrowing at the bike. "I ran. Or hitchhiked. We don't have helmets."

"And we won't be going fast," he replied. "On."

Mounting the bike gingerly, Louis toed up the kickstand and put the key in the ignition. "You're getting on too, right?"

Waiting until the motorcycle was balanced, he swung his leg over and got as comfortable as he could on the back lip of the seat. "Move up a bit."

Louis adjusted his position and Jonathan did the same, putting his hands on Louis's hips. "Okay. Start her up. How much attention did you pay to me when I was driving this thing?"

"I can't win on that answer," Louis grumbled. "If I say lots, you'll expect lots. If I say none, you'll see if I sink or swim."

Grinning, he put his feet on the bars. "Off we go, Forbes."

****

Louis cringed as they walked through the shredded field. "Stojanovski is going to lose his shit when he sees the yard."

"He said the grounds were ours, so we'll feign ignorance," Minks replied, tossing his arm over Louis's shoulders. "You did pretty damn good, Grandma."

Scuffing some mud into one of the deep ruts in the turf, he glanced at the closed door of the main building. "Slow and steady wins races."

"Only in children's tales, turtle."

They walked over the snow-covered grass, slowing when they reached Jonathan's bunker.

"Are you touching base with Jagger again tonight?" Minks asked, keying in his code and opening the door to the small house.

Louis shrugged. "Probably not. I filled him in on numbers earlier, and with Nichol occupied until sundown, there won't be any new orders coming in until then." He rocked back on his heels.

"So I guess enjoy the calm. I'll text you when I get up." Pursing his lips, he looked toward his own bunker. "And thanks for the driving lesson. I'll show off to Rhys and Dominic when we get to Denver."

Jonathan stepped inside and turned, grabbing the top of the doorframe. "My pleasure. Night, Louis."

He gave Minks a tight smile and started to walk away, his feet strangely heavy.

"Forbes?"

Looking back, he stopped. "Yeah?"

"Come in?"

A thousand thoughts ripped through his head.

Deviants crawling across the continent. Vamp hunters gunning for them. Deepfryers powering up. Khthonios still on the loose.

Without a word, he crossed back to the house, passed Jonathan, and stomped the mud and snow from his boots before entering. Minks knelt at the hatch in the floor and keyed in the code, leaning back so Louis could memorize it.

"Got it?" Jonathan asked as he popped the heavy wooden cover open and descended the ladder.

"Yup."

He dropped into the bunker and looked around, kneeling to remove his boots while Minks sat on the sofa and grabbed the remote. "Are we going for a legal drama, a movie, or are you in the mood for some reality TV?"

"Screw reality TV," he scoffed, sitting beside Jonathan and snatching the remote away. "How about this?"

"A shark documentary? All right then."

Setting the remote on the table, he leaned back and watched the underwater footage, quickly becoming enthralled with the clarity of the film. When the program broke for a commercial, he glanced over and grinned. "Humans are dicks, but they create some amazing stuff, don't they?"

Jonathan chuckled and pulled his cigarette pack from his pocket, his nose wrinkling when he popped the top open and looked inside. "I'm doing a smoke run tomorrow night."

"I'll be going with you," he muttered as the show resumed.

Mesmerized by a diver's descent into the water with nothing more than steel bars between him and the enormous hunters swimming past, he jolted when a heavy hand dropped to his thigh.

"Sorry," Jonathan apologized, snatching it away.

Without hesitation, he grabbed the hand and put it back. "Nothing more than an eating machine," he said in awe. "I mean, people like to make up stories that they're thoughtful and planning out their attacks, but they aren't. It's just what they were created to do. Eat. Fuck. Die. Like, I don't know, ID personified." As a great white slammed against the diver's cage, he grinned. "I wonder who would win, vamp or shark."

"We'll give it a try some time," Minks laughed beside him, his thumb drawing circles on Louis's inner thigh.

Nodding, he put his hand on top of Jonathan's. "That would be cool."

****

As the second documentary wrapped up, Jonathan reached forward and grabbed the remote. "It's a week-long marathon. We can watch more tomorrow."

Louis leaned back and looked at him, his chameleon eyes a bright green. "That underwater shit is just…wow. Whatever Nichol has us doing tomorrow, I want to get back in time for the hammerhead doc."

"I'll set a timer on my phone." He chuckled, standing up. "Speaking of, my cell's charged up if you need to plug yours in over there." When Louis got to his feet and crouched beside the bed to feel around for the cord, he looked between the bed and the sofa. "I don't know if Stojanovski has extra blankets or anything down here."

"I'm good," Louis replied, grabbing one of the pillows and tossing it over the back of the couch. "But I'm annexing this for the day."

His fingers were itching to grab the last cigarette in his pack as Louis squeezed past him, the bunker suddenly feeling cramped. "Yeah, no problem," he agreed, giving him a tight smile and heading over to his bed as Louis flopped onto the sofa. "Night."

"Night."

He turned off the lamp and lay back in the dark, listening to the sofa springs creak while Louis got as comfortable as he was going to get.

Room for two on here.

The thought pulsed at the back of his head.

Sure, he could make the move. He'd done it before, after all.

But now the idea of a possible rejection warred with the growing need to be close to Louis. What had started as a crush had rocketed to a whole other level, and he wasn't certain he wanted to risk being shot down and then trapped in the same room until sunset.

Cringing internally when his mind jumped to his overreaction to Dahlia's presence, he rolled onto his stomach, decision made.

****

Louis pushed his heels against the arm of the sofa, willing it to stretch another inch or two before giving up and dropping one foot to the ground.

The subtle movements on the bed let him know Jonathan was still awake as well, the faint rustling of the sheets every time he adjusted his arms giving him away.

If he's awake...

Shoving the idea aside, he removed the sofa's back cushion beside his leg and let his knee rest against the wooden frame.

At some point in the next week or two, evacuation orders would come in, and he'd be back in Denver—back in his room in the Kaius haunt—and Jonathan would settle in with his own haunt.

The false seclusion of their mission would be a forgotten memory, and the reality of being informally tied to the Kaius name would take hold once again.

Informally.

Glaring at the ceiling, he adjusted his hips on the cushions.

Mickey's email was still sitting on his phone, a constant reminder of the decision he'd been putting off for weeks. And until he made up his mind on that, he had no business getting involved with Minks.

He'd seen how the mates of the Kaius haunt were brought in, equal partners in the unending loop of missions, requests, emergencies, and meetings. Their lives became completely enveloped by the pressures the Kaius name brought with it, and Jonathan was too young, too laid back to be shoved into that existence.

Just once...

Sitting up, he looked over at the motionless lump on the bed, at the foot hanging off the edge.

He wasn't fool enough to think once would satisfy him.

"Everything okay?" Minks muttered.

"All good," he replied, tossing his arm over his eyes and wondering how much longer he could tell Mickey the surge he was getting off him was a stubbed toe.

Three times was probably pushing it.

CHAPTER TWENTY-THREE

Jonathan stepped out of the shower, wrapped a towel around his hips, and walked into the main room to grab his brush. "Are you driving, or am I?"

Louis looked up from his phone, his eyes raking over his bare chest before they snapped back to his cell, and he continued to tap away. "You."

Smirking, he started the process of untangling his hair, using his foot to open the fridge door and prop it open. "Want anything? There's a B-negative and half an O-positive left."

In his peripheral, he could see Louis's head turn slightly, his gaze traveling down the length of his back before his lips drew into a tight line. "I'm good, thanks."

Although neither of them said a word about it, both had been awake all day. The shower did little to rejuvenate his tired mind, but the glint of desire in Louis's darkening eyes was more than making up for it.

Pouring a glass of the O-positive, he downed it quickly and resumed brushing out his hair, tucking it behind his ears as he tossed his bag over his shoulder and returned to the bathroom to dress.

He could hear Louis walking around the room, followed by a sharp knock on the door. "I'm heading back to my place to rinse off," Louis called out. "I'll be back in fifteen, and then we'll head out."

Buttoning his jeans, he opened the door and leaned

against the frame. "Are you going to let Stojanovski know we're heading out, or should I?"

"Damn," Louis muttered, kneeling to do up his boots. "Let's meet in the main hall so we can touch base with him first. I should probably do a check on the Gregoire haunt, too. Make sure they're holding up okay."

As Louis climbed the ladder and entered the code, Jonathan watched him until the hatch slammed shut, the lock activating.

Pulling his shirt over his head, he grabbed his phone and swiped it to life, hoping to catch his sire or brothers before they went out on patrol.

—*Just checking in*—

The senior Minks responded immediately.

—*You kept me up half the day with whatever was going on there, kid. Who's the lucky guy?*—

Wrinkling his nose when he remembered his sire's ability to sense him, he straightened the blankets on his bed with one hand while typing with the other.

—*I'll introduce you if things go well*—

There was a lag as the haunt leader typed and deleted before the final message came in.

—*I'll be waiting. Impatiently.*—

Shoving his phone into his back pocket, he shrugged his leather jacket on and laced his boots, grabbing his helmet on the way up the ladder.

Stojanovski was barking orders to the humans on-site when he entered the hall, the Gregoire haunt sitting huddled in the corner of the room.

"Minks," Jackson called over. "Hungry?"

"Still good," he replied, nodding politely when Dahlia bounced past him with a smile. "Louis and I are heading into town right away. Anywhere in the vicinity where we won't be staked on sight?"

Stojanovski nodded, crossing the floor with the swagger that defined the swarthy vamp. "There's a little place in the valley called Winker's. Put it in your GPS and it'll lead you right there. Betty Winker owns it, and she and I have come to a very amicable agreement over the years. Tell her Jackson says hi and"—he reached into his front pocket and pulled out a wad of cash—"tell her thank you for treating my patrons well."

"Save your cash for a jacket that fits," Louis called out behind him. "I loaded up from my bunker stash. Betty, is it?"

Stojanovski nodded, adjusting the lapel of his obviously expensive and tailored suit. "I'll take that under advisement." He chuckled. "A round trip should take no longer than an hour and a half. Any longer, and I'll be sending assistance. Yes?"

Louis nodded and walked over to the Gregoires, crouching at the haunt leader's side.

"Minks," Stojanovski said, pulling him from his blank stare. "I don't believe I've introduced Andy to you."

A young vampire joined them, his wary eyes downcast and shoulders hunched, dirty blond hair falling into his face. He inched his arm forward. "Nice to meet you."

Jonathan shook his hand, moving slowly to avoid spooking him. "Hey, Andy. Jonathan Minks. Jackson taking good care of you?"

"Yes, sir."

"Andy," Stojanovski murmured softly. "Why don't you head upstairs with Dahlia and find a movie we can watch later?"

The skittish vampire nodded, skulking up the staircase with the Tender at his side.

"Did Louis tell you about him?" Jackson asked, watching as Andy walked away.

Recalling the name from one of their drives, he nodded. "How's he holding up?"

"He's surviving," Stojanovski replied, a sad smile crossing his face before he schooled his expression. "Be careful out there, Minks. I don't want to be the one giving your final death details to your haunt."

Louis sauntered up to them. "I got him," he stated. "Ready?"

****

"I'm not coming back for you if you fall off," Minks warned. "Hold. On."

Louis tightened his grip on Jonathan's hips and turned his head away from the broad back in front of him, which brought up images he definitely didn't need to be focusing on while they drove through hostile territory. "Better?"

Revving the engine for emphasis, Minks sped up down the deserted road. "Much."

He scanned the darkness for Deviants, desperate to keep his thoughts off the visuals burned into his mind.

He knew Minks was a big guy, the span of his shoulders a dead giveaway to even the most unobservant, but to see the cut of his abs and the defined muscles across his back without the fabric of a shirt to hide the view?

Hot. Damn.

The body a human was turned with was the one they had for eternity as a vamp, and Jonathan was apparently in peak condition when his sire selected him.

He, on the other hand, looked as lean and hungry now as he did over two centuries ago when he was lean and hungry on the streets of London.

"That's gotta be it," Minks called through the headset, slowing when they approached a small storefront on the side of the road. "Are we good to pull over?"

Examining the dark terrain and finding nothing but a coyote peering at them from the bush, he nodded. "Good to go."

Jonathan eased off the road and into the gravel parking lot, looping around so the bike faced their exit before he killed the engine. He flipped his visor up and unsnapped his helmet, sliding it onto the handlebars and holding his hand out for Louis's. "I'm going to grab a carton."

Louis led the way into the store, where a woman watched them from behind the counter. "Excuse me, ma'am? Are you Betty?"

"Who's asking?"

Easing his money from his back pocket, he laid a wad of twenties next to the till. "Jackson says hello."

Her leery demeanor evaporated, a smile breaking out across her face. "That little rascal. You tell him to keep that money for a suit that fits." She laughed and leaned her elbows on the counter. "He's so vain, it'll drive him nuts. What can I get for you boys?"

Minks chuckled behind him and approached the woman, hand extended. "Pleasure to meet you, Betty. I'll get two cartons of…those…light and tall."

Betty turned around to grab the cigarettes. "So, where are you boys from? Europe somewhere?"

"England, ma'am," Jonathan replied, placing another stack of cash on the counter. "Appreciate the hospitality."

Ringing in the sale, Betty shook her head. "Not at all," she huffed. "So tell me, is young Andy still around? I haven't seen him in a few weeks."

"He is," Louis said, shaking his head when Betty attempted to hand him the extra money. "Th—"

"Goddamn it, Betty," a growled voice yelled from the entrance. "How many times I gotta tell you to stop serving these things?"

Louis stepped between the man and Jonathan, his eyes flicking between the man's hands and the store windows.

"You just mind your business and watch that mouth of yours, William," Betty barked back. "These gentlemen here are customers. Paying customers. And unless you're itching to buy something, I'll thank you to walk right on out that door and go home."

The man glared at them for a moment before he stormed to the magazine rack and grabbed one, shouldering Minks as he passed them.

"William!"

Jonathan gave the woman a fangy grin. "I'm fine, ma'am. Have a good night, and thank you."

They walked out, listening to the man complaining about the price of the magazine he was rage-buying.

"Circle around back," Louis murmured while they did up their helmets and slid the cartons into the cargo hatch. "We'll hold off until he leaves."

Nodding, Minks drove to the far end of the parking lot before he eased toward the back of the building. He turned the engine off until the sound of the man's truck filled the quiet night and disappeared to the south.

"I'm going to touch base with Stojanovski," he muttered, typing out a quick message. "I don't want to leave here until we know Betty won't have any issues with that guy." As Jackson's reply buzzed in, he chuckled. "William is Betty's husband, and that guy is about to get a tongue-lashing from hell. We're good to go."

Jonathan tore onto the road, waiting until they were close to the Stojanovski compound before he pulled over. "Your turn."

Louis moved up and gripped the handlebars, steadying the bike until Minks was on, his hands resting on Louis's hips. "Hold tight," he instructed, his focus wholly on keeping upright and not on the gentle pressure of Jonathan's fingers.

"I will, but I don't need to at this speed, Grandma."

Ignoring the slight, he wove them to the gates of the compound, going so far as to maneuver through the treed path at a speed just slightly below that Jonathan had driven.

"Not bad, Forbes," Minks stated. "Why don't you park it behind my bunker?"

He locked his focus across the yard and sped up, feeling somewhat cocky, until two cold hands slid up his shirt and across his chest. His foot jerked forward on the gas, sending the bike skidding sideways.

Before he could react, Minks was on top of him, his hands grasping the brake levers while he angled his weight, bringing them to a stop along the electric fence.

"What the hell!" he gasped, flipping his visor up and looking back at Minks. "You could've fucking killed us."

Jonathan's laughter echoed against his own visor. "At fourteen miles an hour? Not likely. Okay, you have three hundred yards to go."

"No. Way," he stated, dismounting and slinging his helmet onto the handlebars. "I'm walking."

Minks moved forward, his helmet dangling from his arm as he crept along beside Louis. "I didn't think you'd freak out." He grinned and sped up enough to do a quick circle around him.

"I didn't freak out," he argued. "Your hands are fucking cold. It was a shock to the system."

Looping along the grounds, Minks finally parked beside his bunker house, tossing both helmets inside before joining Louis. "Ready for shark week?"

Louis glared at him for a moment before nodding. "My place this time. I have a bigger TV."

CHAPTER TWENTY-FOUR

Louis arched his head back to look up at Jonathan. "Last one. This place is getting hazy."

"Sorry," he muttered, pinching the cherry off of his cigarette and dropping it into the glass of yellowing water where his discarded butts were floating. "I rarely chain them like this."

Louis returned his attention to the shark movie he'd found after the hammerhead documentary, stretched his legs out across the floor and hiked his elbows back onto the sofa where Jonathan was lying. "Yeah, it's a pretty intense scene. I saw this a dozen times in the theater. Need to know the ending?"

Biting his lip to keep from laughing, he shook his head. "I like the suspense."

While Louis continued to mouth along to the film, Jonathan tucked one hand behind his head and continued to watch Louis.

The red-haired vamp was completely engrossed in the movie, a rare moment when his guard wasn't up, and his posture wasn't hunched in preparation for attack. Even the color of his eyes was brighter as he ran his tongue over one fang before mimicking the facial expressions of the lead actor.

A small bubble of guilt wormed through his head as he thought back to the moment he'd put his ice-cold hands against Louis's chest.

It wasn't even an intentional act.

Knowing Louis was so intensely focused on safety had relaxed him to the point he'd been daydreaming, zoning out while the scenery slowly passed by.

The next thing he knew, the ass end of the bike was skidding out.

Tilting his head, he watched Louis sit up straighter, eyes locked on the screen.

He was a rough-looking guy, the deep lines on his face accenting his sharp features while his hollow cheeks stood out against the cut of his jaw and cheekbones.

There wasn't an ounce of fat on him, either. Every muscle looked like it was built from a life of hardship, not the intentional bulking of targeted workouts and exercise.

A lean, mean fighting machine.

He grinned as the thought flashed through his mind.

"Hey," he said, sitting up and putting his hand on Louis's shoulder. "We should spar tomorrow. I'm out of practice."

Louis nodded absently, ignoring the physical contact completely. "I'll request Stojanovski's gym at sundown. Can't stand fighting in the snow. Goddamn ice getting in the boxers? No thanks." He shifted a fraction closer to Jonathan's knee. "You're gonna love this part."

Tracing Louis's shirt collar with his thumb, he turned his attention to the movie until the scene ended, and Louis relaxed against the sofa, muttering under his breath about the goddamn humans and their inflated sense of superiority.

Which, coming from a species with no qualms touting their own supremacy, struck Jonathan as rather humorous.

He remained still until the closing credits ran and Louis grabbed the remote, flipping through the channels and settling on a documentary he immediately deemed "old" and "outdated."

Inching his hand along the back of Louis's neck, Jonathan leaned into him, hoping his intent was very fucking clear.

And hoping Louis was at least on the same novel, if not on the same page yet, as him.

****

Jonathan hesitated, inches from Louis's lips.

"Are you fucking kidding me?" Louis huffed, tangling his fingers in Jonathan's long hair and pulling him in for a kiss he felt down to his toes. "You almost got us killed, and now you're stopping long enough to think about consequences?"

Minks smiled against his lips. "That was a pretty wild fourteen-mile-an-hour ride. The grass stains would've been a bitch to get out."

"Damn right they would have," he murmured, nipping at Jonathan's bottom lip before going back for a leisurely kiss that wove a strange warmth through his veins.

All thoughts of sharks and divers evaporated as he pushed himself off the floor with one hand, his refusal to break their kiss making his movements awkward and clumsy until he made it onto the sofa. He stroked his tongue down the back of Jonathan's left fang, repeating the motion on the other when the fingers trailing along the back of his neck dug in, and Jonathan's hips bucked up.

"Ahh, woah," Minks gasped, his head falling back while Louis dragged his tongue along his jaw. "That was a cool trick."

Untangling his fingers from Jonathan's hair, he slithered his hand up his shirt, indulging in the sensation of the solid muscles flexing against him while he went in for another kiss. When he felt a tongue flick against the back of his own fangs, a shiver traveled through him. "Fast learner," he groaned, pressing into Jonathan when that incredible tongue picked up speed, sending electrified jolts along every nerve ending in his body.

"I'm a pretty smart guy when I'm not being a dumbass," Minks murmured against his lips, tugging at the hem of Louis's shirt. "Off."

Balancing one arm on the back of the sofa, he got up on his knees and yanked his tee over the back of his head, letting it drop to one wrist while Jonathan pulled his own off. He splayed his hand across the muscled chest, sitting back to admire the closeup view of the image seared into his memory earlier.

His fingers twitched against the cool skin. "Minks?"

"Yeah?"

"Are you breathing?"

Jonathan swallowed and nodded; his dark eyes locked onto Louis's fangs. "Still got those newbie reflexes when I'm distracted."

Minks tracked his movements while he slung his leg over him and straddled him, his knee digging almost painfully into the wooden sofa frame as he bent down for another deep kiss. "You taste like a goddamn ashtray," he muttered, the rhythmic rise and fall of Jonathan's chest strangely comforting.

"I'll quit tomorrow."

Grinding his hips against Minks, he swiped his tongue across his lips before trailing his fangs along his throat. "Don't. Makes it easier for me to find you in the dark."

One of Jonathan's hands gripped his hip, the other spreading across the back of his neck as Minks ran his tongue along the shell of his ear, his ragged breathing ratcheting Louis's libido to dangerous levels.

He wanted this. Bad.

But he wanted Jonathan more, and drowning in the lust barreling through him could set a tone he wasn't sure he wanted for them.

For them.

"Them" had never included him before.

"Minks."

"Yeah?"

The breathy response was nearly enough to change his mind.

"We, uh…" He swallowed as Jonathan's thumb slid along his inner thigh, inches from his hardened length. "Maybe we should dial back a bit," he finally choked out, his will eroding fast.

Jonathan's hands stilled, and he leaned against the back of the sofa, his dark eyes confused. "Yeah. Yeah, of course. I…yeah." He pushed his hair back and tucked it behind his ears. "We good?"

"Fuck yeah," Louis replied, leaning down for a final kiss before he stood up and shoved his hands into his pockets. "I…we…" His shoulders hunched slightly, and he knew his eyes were narrowing as he tried to explain himself while Jonathan watched him with a growing wariness. "I don't want to set a precedent…" He trailed off, craving a cigarette himself.

Jonathan's expression morphed into mild amusement, and he grabbed the remote, turning off the television. "Pass me a pillow and I'll crash on the couch today."

"I'd rather you maybe didn't," he grumbled, grateful for the easy out Minks had given him. "Stojanovski went for style over comfort on those sofas, and I don't need to listen to you shifting around all day." He flicked off the lights in the small bunker, motioning toward the bed in the darkness. "There might be more comfortable."

He tracked Jonathan's footsteps to the bed, swallowing hard when he heard jeans being kicked into the corner of the room. He followed suit and crossed his arms. "This is my side."

Minks chuckled, the mattress springs creaking faintly as he stretched out. "Already staking out your territory?"

With a grunt, he adjusted the band of his boxers and flung the blanket back before getting in, apprehension setting in as he tried to get comfortable without infringing on Jonathan's assigned side.

"Louis?"

"Yeah?"

The entire bed moved as Minks rolled over and slung his arm across Louis's ribs. "I can feel you freaking out from here. And judging by how many times your phone has buzzed over the past hour, so can Mikhail Kaius."

****

Jonathan opened one eye and tightened his hold on Louis's sleeping form, inching a little closer before getting comfortable again.

It had taken a good forty-five minutes, but Louis had finally relaxed enough beside him to drift off, the slight twitches of his tense muscles eventually stopping as he fell into a deep sleep.

He had no idea if Louis had woken throughout the day as he had. Every hour or so, Jonathan had roused to a content consciousness, nodding off again only after he'd checked Louis remained close by.

Although his body sure as hell wasn't on board with Louis's idea to dial it back, his head was. At least, it was once it caught up with Louis's inelegant explanation.

He had ample experience with relationships rooted in sex, and this was one time he wasn't willing to risk the complications that always arose. They had enough issues pushing against them. They definitely didn't need to add any more.

Louis shifted under his arm, one hand feeling along Jonathan's bicep before he sat up, turned around, and flopped onto his stomach.

"Put it back," Louis mumbled, his movements stilling almost immediately when Jonathan draped his arm across his hips.

CHAPTER TWENTY-FIVE

Louis smirked as Jonathan pulled his shirt over his head, tossed it at Stojanovski, and flexed. "I'm taking this red-headed devil down."

Jackson scoffed and passed the shirt to one of the humans hunched over a mess of electrical cords. "Even I would be hesitant to make such a claim without having seen him in action."

Folding his own tee, he set it on the bench beside the warmer holding two carafes of blood. "I'll play nice for the first round. Maybe even let you pin me like lions do for their cubs."

Wrapping an elastic around his hair, Minks began circling the ring. "I'll take it as long as you yowl when I do." He straightened up and cocked his head. "I forgot you had tattoos."

Looking down at the faded crude sketches trailing down his arms, he shrugged. "I spent some time on a ship in my human years. I'm probably lucky these didn't kill me."

Jonathan leaned in closer. "They suit you." Clearing his throat, he threw a few jabs into the air and frowned, turning to Stojanovski. "You calling the rounds?"

"Ah, no," Jackson replied, lifting his hands in feigned regret. "Recent experience has taught me I make a lousy referee. I believe Jagger Kaius will run this session."

Jonathan's brows shot up, and Louis grinned. "Everything almost ready to go?" he called to the human. "I figure we're both probably rustier than we should be, so why not invite the master?"

All cockiness drained from Minks as he eyed the video camera being mounted in the corner. Feeling a little bad about springing it on him, Louis walked over and stood close enough to keep their hushed conversation unheard by the vamp helping run cords.

"Jagg can tweak form better than anyone," he said quietly. "I'd like the reassurance my second-in-command can walk away from anything we come up against over the next few weeks. Yeah?"

Nodding, Jonathan glanced over his shoulder at the TV as it crackled to life. "Not gonna lie," he muttered. "This is very fucking intimidating."

"Don't I know it." He gave Jonathan's arm a light squeeze and leaned in to whisper a quick reminder before the video feed snapped on. "Make sure Jagg can see your mouth when you talk."

"Louis!" Jagger greeted with a smile, his ice eyes filling the screen as he pushed his hoodie off his head. "And Jonathan Minks. How old are you?"

Lifting the hem of his jeans, Jonathan gave Louis a quick look. "Sixth decade, sir."

Mickey's blue eyes came into view, the laptop's camera bobbing and jostling as it was moved further away from the Kaius males. "Don't 'sir' this asshole," he ordered, wrapping his arm tight around Jagger's throat. "Call him a baby-fanged, small-dic—"

With the side of Jagger's hand shoving deep against Mick's mouth, Dominic's laughter could be heard in the background.

Louis scanned what he could see of the room behind Jagg, ensuring he was facing the camera as he spoke. "Are you guys in the sparring room?"

Wrestling his way out of Jagger's grip, Mickey bent down. "Me and Dominic are your demos tonight."

Jagg crossed his arms and sat back in his swivel chair. "We have relatively the same age gap to work with here, so we're going to start with a free-for-all round and narrow our focus from there. Stojanovski, you staying?"

Jackson stepped into view of the camera and nodded. "I have someone joining me in a moment. We'll be nothing more than spectators."

"Andy?" Mickey asked, sitting back on his haunches when Stojanovski nodded. "Good."

"Okay, boys," Jagger announced, slamming his hands on the table and giving the camera a fangy grin. "Let's get this party started."

****

Jonathan accepted the carafe of blood and downed it ravenously. He wiped his mouth with the back of his hand and cringed at the number of gashes streaking his arm and the blackened UV burns slashing across his chest.

"Ready?" Jagger called out through the speakers while Stojanovski drew a chalk circle in the middle of the room. "Back to fists and fangs for the last round. Jackson, could you put those flashlights away? They're distracting the combatants."

Louis slid both lights to Stojanovski and stepped in close, blocking their faces from the camera. "You okay?"

Pushing his hair from his eyes, he nodded, glaring at the UV flashlights being hung on the wall. "I can't believe those things are part of standard training for you lunatics."

Reaching up to tuck a stubborn stray strand behind Jonathan's ear, Louis smirked. "I gave you the first round, didn't I?"

"Doesn't count if you don't yowl for me," he huffed in response, the intense pain of his burns easing slightly as his meal boosted the healing.

Louis shrugged and turned to face the camera. "We'll work on that later. Jagg, any instructions?"

Jagger launched into a detailed list of areas he and Louis needed to focus on, interspersed with remarks about improvements they'd made over the past four hours. Mickey and Dominic were in the background, both looking as rough as he and Louis did, their good humor from earlier replaced with a narrowed concentration.

"Jackson," Jagg called out, waiting until Stojanovski and Andy were in sight. "I'm going to need this round to be between us and them. You okay with that?"

Bowing, Jackson led Andy from the room. "We'll return in an hour to supervise the tear down."

The sparring room door slammed shut, and he glanced over at Louis. "What's going on?"

"Battle of abilities," Louis murmured when Jagger turned his back to the screen and spoke quietly with Mickey and Dominic. "You don't have to reveal if you don't want to."

His stomach knotted when he remembered Louis's skill. "Fuck."

He knew the moment Louis realized it himself. His expression hardened, his eyes darkening to a deep gray as Jagger returned to the helm.

"Final round, skills," the Kaius male announced as Mickey and Dominic sat against the far wall, wiping down their arms and chests. "If you don't want to participate, we'll switch it up. However, most vamps don't utilize their abilities during sparring sessions and therefore don't learn how to wield them in a controlled, effective manner."

Louis took a step toward the camera. "We'll forgo—"

"Strength," Jonathan stated, hooking his thumbs in his belt loops. "I've been holding back."

Louis looked over at him, brows raised. Jagger sat back and crossed his arms. "You're aware of what Louis can do, based on mission reports. You sure you want to go head-to-head on this?"

"Positive." He took his place in the ring and squared off with Louis, stretching his arms over his head and smirking when Louis's dark gray eyes traveled the length of his torso. "You gonna make me cluck like a chicken?"

Although his tone was light, the idea of losing control over his own mind was more terrifying than the flashlights hanging to his left.

"Say it's okay," Louis replied, his expression locked down. "Or I won't do it."

Arching his neck to release the building tension, he nodded. "It's okay. Do your worst."

"Feet on the line," Jagger instructed. "Three. Two. One. Go."

Louis had the speed and strength of age, but it was nothing when pitted against the power Jonathan had kept contained. Within seconds, he had Louis pinned to the mat, keeping his head ducked to avoid making eye contact.

Until Louis relaxed under him and growled. "Fucking. Hot."

Caught off guard, he looked down.

"Let me up."

Shaking his head, he tried to close his eyes, snarling when he couldn't. "No."

Louis's eyes shifted to a light blue, and he felt his hold release a fraction. "Let me up, Minks."

His body rose off Louis reluctantly, his muscles going slack as his conscious and subconscious mind warred. He stepped away, still shaking his head. "No."

Jagger called the round, and he felt his control return in full force.

"Minks."

Backing out of the circle, he held one hand up and turned his back. "Just give me a second."

He caught sight of Louis approaching him slowly from behind and he yanked the elastic from his hair, running his hands through it to steady himself until he could light up outside.

"I'm sorry," Louis said quietly, wrapping one arm around his shoulder and resting his forehead against the back of Jonathan's head. "But if you ever feel that sensation, at least now you know what it is and to get the hell out of there. We can maybe practice blocking me if you want."

He closed his eyes to center his mind, the sensation of being unable to control his own thoughts and actions still worming through his head. He flexed his hands to reassure himself he still could. "Good plan, Forbes." Kaius haunt long forgotten, he reached back to ensure Louis remained tight to him and hooked his thumb in the band of Louis's jeans as a voice hollered through the speakers.

"Oh, fuck!"

His eyes snapped open, and Louis jumped back, looking almost sheepish when Mickey's grinning face filled the screen. "That, my man, is no stubbed toe."

****

Louis crossed his arms and shook his head, motioning back to the humans hanging around on the hall staircase. "First you eat, then we watch sharks."

As Jonathan rolled his eyes and sauntered off, he pulled out his phone to read the wall of texts coming in from Mickey since they'd ended the sparring session.

He ran his thumb along his bottom lip.

Ended the video portion of the sparring session, to be more precise.

The make out portion had taken a little longer, hence the bombardment of messages.

He caught Jonathan's eye and nodded, watching while Minks led an overeager guy down the stairs and into the alcove beneath where they had a modicum of privacy.

—*Yeah, I'll bring him around once things settle if he wants*—

Jonathan's fangs sunk into the man's wrist, and he looked over, his nose wrinkling as he removed the guy's other hand from his ass.

Louis's phone buzzed again, a series of emojis spelling out a crude message filling the screen.

—*You're an idiot. Text me tomorrow and stay outta my bubble tonight*—

Mickey replied almost immediately.

—*Not touching your bubble when I'm anywhere near Audra or your influence will have me banging her into next week—*

Brows raised, he shoved his phone into his back pocket and scanned the room, nodding at the leader of the Gregoire haunt who sat with the rest of his quiet brood, their eyes staring blankly at the walls.

Having no haunt had its drawbacks, but having half your haunt wiped out in a single day was infinitely worse than any amount of isolation could ever be.

His skin crawled as his mind flashed to the battle the Kaius haunt had faced against Khthonios. Nothing in his existence could compare to the helplessness he felt as he sat with Jagger, Mickey, and Dominic and watched while the rest of their brethren went head-to-head against the ancient female vampire who sired Kaius and, as they discovered that night, a mute vamp named Boy who was long thought to be a straggler, an orphan like himself.

Except Boy was no orphan. He was the creation of the most powerful female vampire in existence, an ancient in his own right who was the original sire of Kaius. But when Kaius's turning went Deviant, it was Khthonios who saved him, her strong blood filling his veins and completing Kaius's transition to pure vampire and relegating Boy to nothing more than a guard dog for what Khthonios viewed as hers.

Louis thought his creator was a jerk, but Boy and Kaius's sire took jerkdom to a whole new level. Violent and manipulative, Khthonios pitted her line against Kaius's, forcing Kaius to fight against the very vampires he sired.

Kaius's bloodline won, but the price they paid was high. Nichol's haunt-saving arrow had pierced Kaius's heart, eliminating Khthonios's blood from his body and leaving Boy's running through his veins.

The illustrious leader of the Kaius haunt, the namesake, was now nothing more than a Deviant hidden somewhere north under the staying hand of Boy and far from the terrifying gaze of Khthonios.

He looked behind him quickly, reassuring himself said female vamp wasn't standing at his back.

"There," Minks huffed, giving a tight smile and a wave to the man winking at him from across the room. "Happy now? I think I'm engaged."

Biting back a smile, he motioned to the exit. "Don't let it go to your head. Any tie to the Kaius haunt, no matter how distant, seems to be an aphrodisiac around here."

Jonathan smoothed his hands down his chest and tugged his cigarette pack from his jacket pocket. "And here I was thinking Franco there was drawn to my animal magnetism." He inhaled as he lit up. "Seriously, though. A fresh meal isn't worth the bruises on my ass from his groping little hands."

A flash of anger barreled through Louis, and he shoved it aside roughly. "I could go kill him if you want," he offered with a grin, half-kidding. "Let me see those burns."

Minks pulled the hem of his shirt up to expose the light red streaks crisscrossing his abs. "Better."

"And that's the benefit of a fresh meal," Louis stated, tilting his head to get a better look before Jonathan dropped the shirt and exhaled a cloud of smoke into the air.

They walked in silence across the yard until they reached Jonathan's bunker.

"Coming in?" Minks asked, his eyes looking tired in spite the influx of blood to his system.

Louis shoved his hands in his pockets and glanced across the field to his own bunk. "This my place/your place stuff is stupid. Why don't you grab your stuff and just, I don't know, put it in the same bunker I'm staying in until we evacuate?"

Within the hour, Jonathan lay sprawled out on Louis's bed, out cold.

Louis lowered the volume on the reef shark documentary he was watching and pushed himself off the sofa, gathering the clothing piled in the corners of the room and bringing it up into the house above his bunk where Dahlia would be by at sunrise to collect their laundry.

Before sundown, she'd be back with a cooler of carafes and a stack of folded clothes.

Scrawling a quick thank-you note to her on the back of the order card Stojanovski left out for his guests, he locked up tight and returned to the sofa, checking on Minks every half hour until he finally turned off the television and stripped down to his boxers.

Nudging Jonathan's knee out of the way, he climbed into bed and closed his eyes, relaxing only when a heavy arm swung out and settled across his chest.

CHAPTER TWENTY-SIX

Jonathan rolled onto his side and read the text Louis was holding out for him. "I was wondering when one of the humans would make their way that deep into the field." A second message popped up, and he winced. "Probably a good thing we'll be long gone by the time the snow melts and Stojanovski sees just how torn up this area actually is."

Louis snorted and fired off a quick reply before setting his phone down and stretching out beside him. "We'll have Jagg slide in an extra payment approval in spring. I'm not getting out of bed to stomp dirt back into place."

Humming in agreement, he flopped onto his back and tossed his arm over his eyes.

Although the monotony of stomping down divots and ruts held no appeal, the time they'd spent ripping around the yard over the past three nights was totally worth it.

Sometimes he drove, staying tight to the frozen swamplands and practicing a few tricks that inevitably ended with Louis hopping off and swearing never to get on again. Other times Louis drove, winding along the perimeter of the compound at speeds slow enough they could leave their helmets in their bunker and just enjoy the solitude of the night.

It was the only time their phones were tucked out of

sight. The only time Louis's cell wasn't buzzing with updates as the pressures to evacuate mounted.

Deviant mobs had gone underground around the outposts where infighting among the vampires was taking hold, the uncertainty of the Deviant whereabouts adding to the strain of confinement.

Vamps continued to battle their way to the safe houses, trickling in under the Kaius haunt's watchful eyes and meticulous plans. Their dwindling numbers were a stark reminder of the belated urgency of the evacuation.

The military was mobilized, moving in on Denver and clashing with the pro-vamp supporters who descended on the city in numbers too large for Nichol to house.

A winter storm was moving toward the central states, threatening to ground planes and close roads.

And for the past three nights, as they settled into bed, Louis would scan through his emails, his thumb hovering over the Kaius haunt contract before he would slide his phone onto the nightstand and roll onto his back, tossing and turning until Jonathan draped his arm over him, stilling him.

Nightly sparring sessions were fast becoming a ritual, a way to pass the time far from the haunted eyes of the Gregoires and the orphans who sat sullenly in the hall. Hiding in the basement of the Stojanovski Hall, they worked on Jagger's suggestions, with Louis focusing on his offense techniques and Jonathan learning to read the subtle cues of his attacker.

And although Louis insisted Jonathan spar with his full strength, he hadn't pushed the hypnosis issue again.

For that, he was grateful.

"Minks?"

He lifted his arm and opened one eye. "Yeah?"

"I'm not leaving the bunker tonight."

Rolling over to face Louis, he pushed his hair out of his eyes. "Do we even get to claim sick days?"

Louis arched up enough to kiss him lightly. "I figure if Nichol can get a twenty-four-hour sabbatical, we can, too." He ran his fingers through Jonathan's hair, letting it fall into his face again. "I can't believe it's still wet."

He crawled on top of Louis and shook his hair out like a dog, his fangs elongating when Louis splayed his hands across his chest. Louis's fingers trailed along his shoulder blades and pulled him down, kissing him hard and doing that little tongue trick along his fang that nearly sent him over the edge every time.

With Louis's determination to avoid "setting precedent," their languid make out sessions had become an excruciating exercise in control.

An addicting, excruciating exercise in control.

He was in a constant state of craving for the torturously slow movements of Louis's fingers along his ribs. For the leisurely swipes of his tongue across his chest and the unhurried scraping of fangs over his throat. For a guy accustomed to charged, frantic groping in the back rooms of bars or motel rooms, the languid pace Louis set kept him in a state of arousal for days.

Fangs scraped across his shoulder, and he groaned, his hips grinding involuntarily against Louis. "I'm fucking dying here," he murmured into Louis's ear, smirking when the male beneath him shuddered.

For as hot as Louis made him, he was quickly figuring out he had the same effect.

"Like that?" he whispered, flicking his tongue along

Louis's lobe before he nipped at it. "How ab...hot damn," he muttered, dropping his head into the crook of Louis's neck when Louis reached between them and gripped him through his boxers. "I...uh...fuck."

Nights of being kept on the edge weren't going to do him any favors in the lasting department.

He dropped to one forearm and made the mistake of looking down when Louis slid his hand under his boxers and wrapped his cool fingers around him. "Motherf...goddamn," he grunted, digging his fingers into Louis's shoulder, his other arm shaking from the effort to maintain control. "Louis...I..."

"Stop. Talking." Louis grinned and nipped his lower lip before slipping his tongue into his mouth and swiping it along Jonathan's fangs.

He couldn't even argue if he wanted to at that point.

Louis worked him at the same leisurely pace he set every time they kissed, a pace out of sync with Jonathan's rapid panting, while he tried in vain to hold back the orgasm building up to the point of no return. After being kept back from the brink for so long, his body was thrumming, hyper-aware of every lick of Louis's tongue, every graze of his hands along his spine, every slight shift in Louis's grip, which kept him right on the precipice but refused to shove him over the edge.

It was simultaneously too much and not enough. Louis, with his expert hands and tongue, held all the control, and he was unable to do anything more than thrust into his fist and pray nothing would interrupt them.

Because he would definitely be the first case of spontaneous vampire combustion if this ended before he finished.

Louis's fingers threaded gently through his hair, and

he was downright close to purring before Louis wrapped the hair in his fist and gave it a sharp yank, the sudden movement breaking their kiss and shifting the charge in the room. "Give it to me, Minks. Now."

"God*damn*," he snarled as his release barreled through him and his blunt nails drew blood from Louis's shoulder blade, the scent only amplifying the sensation overload. Every muscle in his body contracted and flexed, every nerve ending ignited almost to the point of pain until he began to come down.

When his unnecessary breathing slowed, he rolled onto his back and pushed his hair from his face, still panting when Louis leaned over him with a smirk. "Damn, Forbes. Just…damn."

****

Louis strode over to the coffee table and grabbed the remote, ducking his head to check out the television mounting brackets before he tilted it to face the bed where Jonathan lay sprawled out, a lazy smile still on his face.

And he couldn't help but feel a little proud of the fact he was the one who put it there.

"Hungry?" he asked, popping the fridge door open and frowning at the selection. "We have cold A-positives and a cold AB-negative."

Minks walked across the room with footsteps more weighted than usual. "I'm good," he murmured in Louis's ear from behind, and he slid his hands up his chest while Louis opened one A-positive and sniffed it.

"You gotta eat something." He checked the freshness of the AB-negative. "Maybe we'll order in fresh."

Judging from the fingers ghosting down his stomach

toward his boxers, Jonathan's mind wasn't on eating.

When lips descended on the nape of his neck, he nudged the fridge door shut and closed his eyes, covering Jonathan's hands with his own while they skimmed across his skin, creeping along the band of his boxers.

Screw precedent, he thought when Minks pressed tight against him, hot, hard, and ready.

They had precedent.

Shark documentaries and riding were more than enough precedent at this point, especially when Jonathan's chest was rising and falling with unneeded breaths hushing into his ear and traveling straight to his dick.

"Hey," Minks whispered, sliding one hand under the band of his boxers and gripping his cock. "Do you have any idea what I want to do t—"

CHAPTER TWENTY-SEVEN

Jonathan blocked out the blaring alarm as he yanked his shirt over his head and kept one eye on Louis while he tugged his jeans over his hips, his shoulder holding his phone to his ear.

"Fuck if I know, Jagg," Louis growled, snatching his bag from the floor and dumping his blades out of it before he shoved his meager belongings inside. "Stojanovski just sent out the alert."

Tossing anything he could find into his own satchel, Jonathan grabbed both leather jackets and helmets and climbed up the ladder, keying in the code and holding the hatch open for Louis.

"Yeah, fill Nichol in and maybe ask him to be on standby. We're heading to the hall now," Louis called over the shrill scream of the compound's alarm system. He pushed past Jonathan and scanned the darkness outside the front door. "This better be good."

They ran across the field, Louis's head swiveling from side to side as the other guests stepped out of their bunkers, their arms loaded with their belongings.

"Nichol didn't call the evacuation, did he?" he asked while they vaulted up the veranda stairs.

Louis flung the door open, phone in hand. "Jagg said the storm system crossing over the Midwest is too severe to risk it, so I don't know what...what the fuck?"

Stojanovski stood in the middle of the room. The

few vampires who had already made it on-site were flattened to the walls while a short woman in tall stiletto boots sauntered through. Her long black braid swung as she stopped and turned to them, smiling with long viper fangs on full display.

Vamp.

Female. Vamp.

What. The. Fuck.

Her delicate nose twitched, and she frowned, her fangs lying over her bottom lip. "These?" she sneered, gesturing toward them. "These infants are the Kaius haunt envoys?"

He took an instinctual step closer to Louis as his mind caught up with what he was seeing.

Stojanovski nodded. His phone was clutched in his hand.

The female vamp crossed her arms. "You," she called out. "With the red hair, who reeks of mongrel blood. Do you speak for the Kaius haunt?"

Louis stepped in front of Jonathan. "Under their orders," he stated, slowly easing his phone into his back pocket to keep the light of a placed call concealed from the female.

Her heels clicked on the hardwood floor as she approached them, and her onyx eyes zeroed in on Louis. "Do you think they would be interested in a little game? A challenge, perhaps?" Glancing back, she smiled. "One without the need for spineless referees?"

Stojanovski paled visibly while Louis held his silent ground.

"All these beautifully prepared chess moves played by the Kaius mutts have been entertaining to track. Perhaps it's time I make another little move of my own on the board," she continued, her gaze moving past Louis's shoulder to Jonathan. "Wouldn't you agree, child?"

Certain he was as white as Stojanovski was, he stared at the floor until her perfectly painted nails cupped his chin.

"Well, aren't you a pretty boy?" she cooed, giving his face a light tap. "My first was a pretty thing like you. Stunning, really. Blond and beautiful, like a wild horse. But he turned out to be such a disappointment."

With feigned sadness, she pursed her lips, her fangs lengthening. "Are you a disappointment to your sire? Does he lay awake all day cursing you for aligning yourself with the bastard Kaius bloodline?" She stepped closer to him and looked up, her eyes completely black. "Does he rue the day he created you?"

"I hope not, ma'am," he ground out, caught between confusion and a rising fear.

Her gaze moved back to Louis, her hand resting on Jonathan's neck with a gentleness belying the speed with which she could snap it. "Which of those filthy beasts did you exchange blood with, Red? The *Medico della Peste*? The impudent Russian? No, wait, don't tell me. Let me guess." She looked at the ceiling for a moment, her nose twitching. "It was the empath!"

The female vampire appeared giddy while she awaited Louis's response, her fingers skimming across Jonathan's throat.

Louis swallowed. His gaze locked on her hand as it moved down Jonathan's chest. "Correct."

Squealing with delight, she spun around to Stojanovski. "Remember what I said earlier? Games are the only thing worth living for. Especially when you're good at them." Without waiting for a response, she turned back to Louis. "This is so exciting, isn't it? You and your mongrel leaders placing your pieces, me placi—"

Jonathan was still looking in the spot the female had stood when he heard a strangled howl from across the room, the sound of cracking bones hitting his ears moments later.

"Impulsive decisions are the downfall of so many players," she sighed, her delicate fingers tightening around the neck of a vampire who dangled in the air, his arms and legs hanging at unnatural angles.

"Your assessment of me was rushed and incomplete. Now look at you." She gave the vamp a shake, holding a blade up to his eye. "What did you think this silly little knife would do? Maim me? Your sire failed in your education."

Lowering her arm, she strode calmly around the room, dragging the injured vampire behind her. "The greatest trick my child's bastard bloodline ever played was convincing our species they could win without me." Slowing to give every vamp in the room a good look at the broken body in her hands, she examined her lipstick in a mirrored frame. "Raise your hand if you're here because the Kaius line told you to come."

One by one, arms rose into the air.

"Hands down," she ordered, closing one eye and running her pinky along her lashes. "Now raise your hand if you know who I am."

Stojanovski's arm lifted, and she smiled before glancing over at Louis and leveling him with a look of disappointment until he followed suit.

"Well," she huffed. "Introduce me, envoy."

Louis stepped directly between him, and the female's and Jonathan's eyes dropped to the faint light still glowing in Louis's back pocket.

"Khthonios," Louis stated, his shoulders squared and voice steady. "Sire of Kaius Khthonios."

Her nose wrinkled in disdain. "I'll thank you not to remind me of that mutt." Her expression brightened, and she gave a little curtsy. "But yes, my blood runs through those you've put your faith in. Anyone care to share why that was a silly idea?" When no one spoke, she made a production of lifting one finger to her fangs and scoring it, turning slowly to show the beads of blood forming before she shoved it into the mouth of the injured vampire in her other hand.

"Voilà!" she exclaimed, clamping the vampire's mouth closed and dropping him to the floor. "And now for the finale."

The vamp's arms and legs healed at a rapid rate, and he struggled to his feet, scrambling away once he was able.

Khthonios clapped her hands and smiled wide, taking in the shocked expressions of her audience. "If you think that was impressive, watch this."

All humor vanished from her face as she concentrated on the healing vampire, a satisfied smirk appearing when the male pitched forward onto his hands and knees and vomited up a horrific mixture of blood and what looked to be organs.

"Fuck," Louis whispered as he reached back to Jonathan and tried to nudge him closer to the exit.

"Fuck is right," Khthonios laughed when the vampire collapsed, his slow disintegration holding the attention of every male in the room. "We all have our

little quirks. Blood manipulation happens to be mine."
Her dark eyes met Louis's. "All it takes is a few drops
and a hint of vengeance. Are we ready to play now?"

****

Louis stood his ground, hoping against hope that
Nichol and the rest of the Kaius haunt had picked up the
call and were listening in. "Why play?" he asked, buying
as many precious seconds as he could while the body of
the decomposing vampire on the floor seeped into the
expensive Persian rug. "Why not just take them out? The
Kaius haunt? You can do it, right?"

Khthonios sauntered across the room and looked up
at him, her tiny stature unnerving against the power she
held. "Where's the fun in that?"

"The ultimate display of superiority has to hold
some entertainment value," he pressed.

"I'm a selfish, competitive creature by nature. I
prefer to play." She licked her lips and smiled sweetly.
"Besides, isn't the ultimate display of power the ability
to remove existence on a whim? To grant the mirage of
security and then rip it away?" Arching her neck, she
looked past him to Jonathan. "Anticipation is a powerful
tool, is it not?"

Louis moved between them again and she laughed.

"Raise your hand if you've had the blood of a male
who has ingested Kaius blood. If you're a member of the
small, intimate group whose blood I can track and
control," Khthonios demanded, scanning the room
before her gaze returned to Jonathan. "Raise it higher,
child."

He felt his heart contract in his chest, all thoughts
zeroing in on her words.

Raise it higher, child.

He fought past the rising panic in his head. "What's the game?"

With a satisfied hum, Khthonios crossed her arms. "Survival, as it always is," she replied. "The Kaius haunt has moved their pieces into place. Now let's see if they anticipated where I placed mine. You have fifteen minutes."

Fifteen minutes.

Fifteen…

"Fifteen minutes for what?" he growled, taking a step forward and regretting it when Khthonios sent him flying against the wall with the tap of her hand on his chest while she strode by.

"Jackson, dear," she called out as she pushed the heavy doors open. "You may want to pack anything you cherish. This place won't be standing much longer."

CHAPTER TWENTY-EIGHT

Louis grabbed Jonathan's arm and dragged him up the hall staircase, booting in doors until he found a room overlooking Khthonios as she sauntered across the field in the snowfall, her long braid swaying against her back. He yanked his phone from his pocket as he slouched against the window frame and tracked her until she disappeared over the fence.

"Nichol?"

"Nichol's a bit busy," Rhys snarled through the speaker. "Where is that bitch?" There was a clatter of metal in the background. "Could we maybe get a countdown timer we can all fucking see?"

He could hear Nichol barking orders to his hauntmates, and he turned to Jonathan. "Minks."

When he was met with silence, he stepped in front of him. "Hey. Minks. Look at me."

Jonathan's dark eyes snapped out of their daze, and he nodded. "Yeah. All good, right?"

"Not at all," he said quietly, leaning his forehead against Jonathan's. "But we made it this far with our heads intact, okay?"

The young vamp relaxed a fraction. "I can't wait to tell my brothers I survived a run-in with a female vampire."

"Call them now."

Giving his hand a squeeze, he returned his attention

to the activity blaring through his phone and led Minks back downstairs, where the Stojanovski inhabitants stood silent. "I need orders, and I need them now, Rhys. Fill me in on anything else once I mobilize the ground."

While Rhys began reciting a litany of instructions, Louis relayed commands to the vampires eyeing him warily.

"Stojanovski, begin evacuation procedures," he called out, keeping Jonathan tight to him as he walked toward the exit. "We have twelve minutes to be in those planes and airborne. Minks and I will do the final sweep of the grounds on the bike. Keep numbers updated so we aren't chasing phantoms, and I'll text you the extent of the threat once we're en route to the runway."

Jackson nodded and straightened his lapel before he took control of the room; Andy stood quietly in his shadow.

Louis and Jonathan pushed through the doors and into the night, and he put his phone to his ear. "Okay, Rhys, what do you know on your end?" he asked, jogging toward the motorcycle and scanning through the blowing snow for Khthonios as he put the cell on speaker so Jonathan could hear over the wind.

There was a muddle of cursing voices on the other end before Nichol took over. "Every airport in the Midwest has shut down operation with the storm. Visibility is shit, and none of the planes we've contracted are meant to withstand the wind speeds we're dealing with," Nic growled, his voice barely audible once Stojanovski's evacuation vehicles revved to life. "There isn't a plane in existence guaranteed to survive the winds."

Jonathan hopped on the bike and gunned the engine,

already walking it forward as Louis got on. "So we're the only ones hauling ass."

"You think I'm going through this shitstorm twice?" Nichol barked. "Working theory is our missing Deviants are being activated in nine minutes on Khthonios's orders. Which fucking sucks because six minutes ago, someone put in a call to the FBI Vamp Div headquarters giving GPS coordinates for the eight outposts." His voice muffled for a moment. "I'm emailing updated flight paths and alternatives to the pilots to compensate for the winds, along with an app to assist in any last-minute changes. But it's in beta form." The sound of a fist hitting a table echoed through the phone, followed by a long exhale from Nichol. "Goddamn beta form."

"Beta's better than nothing," he said as they approached a cluster of bunkers. Louis jumped off the bike and slammed on doors before firing off a confirmation to Stojanovski. "Three from the southeast quadrant are MIA," he called to Jonathan, getting back on and grabbing Minks around the waist with one hand while balancing his phone with the other. "I…Nichol. You're cutting out."

The call crackled in his ear once more and went silent.

"Goddamn it," he snarled as the bike slung out to the right, skidding across the fresh snow before it righted and he spotted his missing vamps walking toward the main hall. "Get your asses to the SUVs," he hollered, glancing down when his phone buzzed. "Compound's accounted for," he reported to Nichol the moment he picked up the call.

Rhys's voice answered, low and tense. "Louis, do you know how to read a flight map?"

"What the fuck do you think?" he growled. "No."

"Learn," Rhys stated. "We have nineteen planes hitting the air in the next seven…six and a half minutes. Nichol and I are on crisis management, Jagger's on evacuation updates, and Mick and Dominic are monitoring the Deviant and FBI threats. With five planes there, we need someone coordinating the takeoffs in real time."

"I can do it," Minks called over his shoulder, herding the last of the vampires toward the escape vehicles. "One more tour past the hall?"

Louis nodded. "You heard him, Rhys. We'll be able to do it once we're on the tarmac."

The motorcycle tore across the yard, circling the main building a final time as Jonathan hollered out to him over the storm. "It's going to take at least ten minutes for those planes to be prepped for flight."

Tightening his hold on Minks, Louis fired off another message to Stojanovski. "They're almost on-site. I…okay. Jackson and the oldest Gregoire are going to help me hold off whatever comes at us until we can take off." They sped off toward the exit, and he squinted against the blasts of snow hitting his face. "How are you doing?"

"Half of me is excited to see my new room in Denver," Jonathan called back. "The other half is dreading sharing it with Armand because he moans in his sleep. Hold tight. This will hurt."

Louis clung to Minks as the bike blasted out of the compound. They ripped into the unkempt forest surrounding it, and he inched his hands up Jonathan's chest to his heart.

Wayward branches could stake a vamp faster than

he wanted to think about.

They wove along the ruts created by the evacuation vehicles, Jonathan's legs shooting out to balance them every so often when the wheels jolted askew. "We have a lot of shit to discuss when we land," Minks yelled, speeding up when the runway came into sight. "Just giving you a heads-up that we're going to be having a we-need-to-talk moment."

Louis eased up on his grip and checked his phone. "About Khthonios?"

"What the hell else would I be freaking out over?"

One by one, the lights of the five planes pierced through the storm as they approached, a swarm of humans and vampires racing out of the SUVs and across the tarmac. Jonathan skidded to a stop, balancing the bike while Louis hopped off. Hesitating for a moment before he dismounted, Minks toed down the kickstand and gave the motorcycle a quick pat.

"Jackson," Louis hollered, texting Rhys as he ran. "What's the ETA for takeoff?"

Herding a group of orphaned vamps toward the third plane, Stojanovski scanned the perimeter. "Seven minutes. What's our countdown?"

"Two minutes. Those of us remaining on the ground will hop into that plane there."

Jackson nodded tersely and continued to direct the vampires while Louis jumped into the first plane and beelined to the cockpit. "We set?"

The human pilot and copilot gave him the thumbs-up. "Everyone will be ready for takeoff in six minutes."

"Hold for my word," Louis stated, backing out of the cramped space. "There will be a few of us on the ground until the last plane rolls. And I'm deeming this the last plane, got it?" Peering out the window into the whiteout storm, he pursed his lips. "If it becomes an issue of go without us or die waiting, go."

Another reluctant thumbs-up, and he jumped out, checking the grounds for Jonathan.

"Minks!" he called out, only to be met with the barked orders of Stojanovski loading the final plane.

Running past the noses of the aircraft, he scanned the shadowed strips between them, a rising panic building in his chest until he caught sight of broad shoulders hefting the last of the human females aboard the second plane.

"Seal them up," he commanded to the eldest vamp before hollering into the night. "One minute."

He jogged to the back of the runway, Jonathan at his heels. "Minks?"

"Yeah?"

"Get on a damn plane."

Jonathan smirked at him. "You first."

The whirr of engines was the only sound remaining as Stojanovski and Gregoire approached them. Their eyes scoured the darkness while they adjusted the lapels of their suit jackets.

"Which one is Andy on?" Louis asked when the thirty-second countdown began.

Jackson looked over at the planes. "Five."

"He'll be first out," he said quietly, motioning toward the corners of the tarmac. Gregoire and Stojanovski sprinted to their position while he stepped between Jonathan and whatever lay beyond his view. Glancing back at Minks, he gave him a tight smile. "Ready?"

****

"Three, two, one…"

Stojanovski's count ended, and Jonathan looked over Louis's shoulder, seeing nothing but a tangled mess of trees and brush.

The four vampires remained motionless in the blizzard, stretching their senses past the sounds of the airplane engines while the snow obscured their vision.

"Five minutes, thirty seconds," Louis whispered, starting the next countdown until the aircraft would begin their flights. "Where the hell is whatever we're waiting on?"

He continued to scan the tree line. "Maybe Khthonios forgot." When Louis glanced back at him and grinned, he shrugged. "Possible, right?"

Another minute ticked by with excruciating slowness.

And another.

"Deviants to the northeast!" Stojanovski suddenly called out.

He turned toward the invasion, his arm yanked back by Louis.

"Coming at us from the southwest," Louis yelled, pointing his blade into the snow-covered forest. "Twenty and counting."

The horde advanced, their numbers multiplying through the snowfall.

"Louis?" he said slowly as he got a good look at the mob.

"Yeah?"

"Why are they dressed like extras from a Wild West movie?"

Louis adjusted his stance and lifted his blades. "I have the feeling Khthonios set the chessboard up a long time ago."

Keeping his back to the planes, Jonathan gripped his own knives and held position until Louis made a move, striking cleanly through the throat of the first Deviant to breech the makeshift tarmac.

He was slashing through the spine of his fifth attacker when Louis swung the body of an injured Deviant across the ground.

"You expecting company, Jackson?" Louis yelled. "Because we got over two dozen sets of lights coming this way from the south, and they sure as hell don't look friendly."

A single gunshot blasted through the air, and Louis grabbed him, running toward the planes. "Get in!"

"I'm no—"

Louis hefted him up and shoved him on his ass onto the airplane floor, the heavy door heaving shut. He jumped to his feet and slammed his hand against it, tracking Louis until he disappeared toward the front of the aircraft with a wave of lurching Deviants stumbling onto the tarmac behind him.

He flung the cockpit door open, wedged himself between the humans, and grabbed the com system mic. "ETA until takeoff," he growled, wincing as bullets pinged off of the metal body of the plane.

The four other pilots chimed in immediately. "Two minutes, sir."

With the timing in his head, he launched himself at the door, flinging it open and jumping down atop a Deviant outweighing him by fifty pounds.

"Get the fuck inside!" Louis bellowed as the lights of the vehicles breached the tree line.

"Not a chance in hell," he called back, yanking a

Deviant off the wing of the third plane and burying his blade in its heart before he made his way to the southern threat. "Ninety seconds."

Stojanovski and Gregoire were behind him, slicing a swatch through the Deviant mob and tossing bodies out of the paths of the planes as the incoming vehicles came to a stop.

Dozens of doors opened at once, the unmistakable sound of weapons being cocked stilling both the vampires in their sights and the Deviant horde.

For a moment, time froze.

"Louis," Stojanovski said quietly, Gregoire at his side. "The Kaius haunt will care for the orphans, yes? We have your word?"

Confusion flashed across Louis's face. "Uh, yeah. Of course. We discussed that nights ago."

The swarthy vamp flattened his lapel. "Go."

Louis hesitated for a moment before nodding. "You've got this. We've got Andy." Looking to Gregoire, he bowed his head. "Your haunt will survive. I give you my word."

Jonathan opened his mouth to argue as Louis grabbed his arm and dragged him to the planes, the wheels of the first one starting to roll.

"What the fuck?" he hollered when the door opened and Louis pushed him inside, jumping in as gunfire echoed through the night.

Louis hefted the door shut, stumbling as the aircraft lurched forward. "Plane one is airborne," he stated, watching while Jackson and Gregoire led the Deviant mob toward the gunmen, hands tucked into their jacket pockets as they calmly sauntered into a hail of bullets.

Jonathan swallowed. His eyes locked on the carnage

outside while Louis pulled out his phone.
"Tell Nichol we're up."

CHAPTER TWENTY-NINE

Jonathan sat in the cramped plane and stared blankly out the window while Louis muttered to himself, turning his phone from side to side.

Grateful for the distraction, he pointed to the map on Louis's cell. "That cluster is us. If you tap that, it'll give you the real-time data."

Frowning at the screen, Louis ran one hand through his snow-dampened hair and wiped it on his damp jeans. "How do you know this shit?"

"Sibling rivalry," he replied. "Theo was into it for a while, and since Minks Sr. was so impressed, I had to show him I could do it, too." Reaching over to tap on a few more features, he hummed in appreciation. "Completely customized. Nichol created this app?"

"The vamp's a genius. A complete asshole, but a genius."

He glanced back at the rest of the vamps and lowered his voice. "Any word on the Gregoires?"

Louis nodded, tilting his phone and pulling up the texts coming in from the fourth plane, where the remaining Gregoire males were being subdued after one leaped from the plane shortly after takeoff. "The ancients on board are guarding the exit to prevent another from jumping," he whispered back. "I've already updated Mickey and Audra. They have a team of psychologists on standby at the airport."

"What about Andy?"

Shaking his head, Louis fired off a reply to a text from the second plane. "We'll be telling him once we land. Audra and Bianca are compiling a list of established vampires who may be a good match for him."

He returned his attention to the window, inching his hand over Louis's as the sounds of hundreds of rounds of ammo being unloaded at Stojanovski and Gregoire continued to ring in his ears. "They just walked into it."

Louis gave his fingers a squeeze. "More of a strut, I think."

Remembering the cocky tilt to Jackson's head when the first shots went off, the corner of his mouth turned up a fraction. "Once an arrogant bastard, hey?"

The phone buzzed in Louis's hand. "Rhys. Update."

"Two planes downed before takeoff in Utah. Wichita's gone offline somewhere just outside the city," Rhys stated without emotion, his voice just loud enough to be heard by every vamp in the aircraft. "The pilot in Dubois delayed takeoff until Nichol deposited an extra fifty grand into his account, but they're en route as of eleven minutes ago."

Louis lowered the volume on his phone and leaned close to Jonathan to let him listen in. "How are the skies? Because this thing is shaking like a goddamn vibrator."

"You'll make it," Rhys replied tersely.

"Why? Because failure isn't an option?" Louis scoffed, elbowing Jonathan lightly in the ribs.

"Because I'm not telling Mickey his best friend went down over Nebraska, dumbass."

He elbowed Louis back and was met with a flat glare as Rhys disconnected and the phone went black. "Just sign the damn contract already," he hushed. "It sounds like it's nothing more than a formality at this point, anyway."

Louis's lips drew into a thin line as he looked around at the somber vampires staring absently out the windows. "The idea of having hauntmates to lose isn't all that appealing right now." His gray eyes darkened a fraction. "Speaking of which…when I give you an order to stay put, you fucking stay put."

"What can I say?" he said with a shrug. "I suck at obeying. Comes with the youngest-in-the-haunt territory. Kind of like withholding information about an ancient female vamp with a hate-on for everything Kaius-related comes with the loner-rogue territory."

When Louis responded with nothing more than a snort, he leaned back and looked out the window into the darkness, wondering how many more would die before dawn.

****

Louis propped the cockpit door open with his bag and returned to his seat. "All good."

Jonathan attempted to stretch his legs out, bumping the seat ahead of him before he lolled his head back and flopped his knees apart. "Are you up for that talk I warned you we were going to have?"

Wrinkling his nose, he spiked his hair up and nodded. "Might as well get it over with before we go down in flames." Several vamps glanced over at him, and he cringed. "Kidding."

Minks smirked, waiting until they were no longer the center of attention before leaning in close. "Khthonios," he stated. "Explain."

"Gimme a second."

Opening the notes app on his phone, he typed out a

quick rundown of Khthonios and her tie to the Kaius haunt then angled it toward Jonathan.

—*Khthonios is Kaius's sire. Obvs, Kaius Khthonios. Also Dovidas's, Chen's, and Boy's.*—

Chen and Dovidas were familiar names, an ancient and a traitor to the species.

Jonathan pointed to Boy's name. "How come I'm only recently hearing about a whole other member of the haunt?"

—*Long story short, Boy is a scary-ass mute vamp who's always been a Kaius haunt hang-on. Always there, no one knew why. Different blood scent, whole nine yards. Shit hit the fan last spring, and we found out Boy was Kaius's first sire. Turning went bad, and Kaius went Deviant. Khthonios re-turned him with success. Last summer, Nichol, Boy, and Rhys killed Dovidas and Chen at Stojanovski's. Nichol staked Kai. Kai reverted to Deviant. Boy took off with him and left the country. Khthonios is pissed.*—

Eyebrows shooting up, Minks sat back in his seat and stared at the headrest in front of him. "Discussion over. I can't even start to wrap my head around that."

Deleting the message, he shrugged. "Probably one of those things you had to be there for." Peering out the cockpit window, he fired off a check-in to Rhys. "We should be landing in under two hours."

Jonathan drummed his fingers on the armrest. "Two hours. If I was still human, the nic fit would be killing me right about now."

Tapping the no smoking sign above their heads, he grinned and put his hand on Jonathan's knee. "You can light up the moment we land."

"I intend to…oh hell, what now?" Minks groaned as

Louis's phone buzzed with a slew of messages cut short by a call from a Kaius line.

"Louis here," he said, standing up to take the call as far from the rest of the vamps as he could in the small plane.

"Rhys is in charge," Nichol stated, ending the call immediately.

He looked at Jonathan and motioned for him to follow as he dialed back, cursing when the call went to voicemail. "Minks?"

"Yeah?"

"I think we have a problem."

"Just one, hey?" Jonathan grumbled, leveling him with a flat stare as the cell buzzed, Rhys's number popping up on the screen.

"Louis here," he said as he tapped the copilot on the shoulder and nodded to the cab.

"You better fucking be," Rhys barked. "Nichol's out, and we need you to take over your end completely."

He stepped aside to let the human copilot out while trying to tune out the raised voices behind Rhys. "Say that again?"

Jonathan wedged in beside him, crouching down between the seats and leaning close to the pilot to whisper instructions.

"You and Minks are bringing your five into Denver," Rhys repeated, his voice strained. "I'm covering the others with Mickey while Nichol...what the fuck do you mean you don't have aerial on that location? Louis, hold tight."

Minks looked over at him. "Whatever it is, the three of us can coordinate. Open the app and pull up our flight paths."

"We're still flying blind in this storm," the pilot offered, going silent when Louis glanced at him.

Rhys's voice came back over the mayhem in the Kaius haunt com room. "The good news is Simone isn't dead. Bad news is Nic—"

"What do you mean Simone isn't dead?" he demanded, sitting in the copilot's seat and keeping his knees as far from the multitudes of buttons and lights on the dash as he could. "Why the fuck would she be dead?"

"I just said she isn't dead," Rhys barked. "Nichol called you, grabbed Dominic to drive him into Denver, and put me in charge on his way out the door. Dom just texted in, and all he's gotten from Nic is Simone is hurt bad, and Nichol is barely keeping it together. They're thirty miles off her patrol site."

Jonathan's gaze snapped to him.

"We'll get the planes down," he said, looking out into the darkness briefly before leaning closer to Minks. "What's happening on the ground?"

Rhys was hollering orders to the remaining hauntmates, the stress in his voice carrying through the speaker. "Nothing much. Just around twelve hundred Deviants and, I don't know, five thousand armed troops with a shoot-on-sight order breaching the city."

The phone clanged, and the sound muffled as Rhys snarled another round of orders before returning to the call. "Mickey and the mayor are in talks with the Vamp Division now. If we can get a pullback on that front, we can focus on eliminating the Deviants before our perimeter lines fall."

"Keep us posted." He turned his attention to Jonathan as he sat back on the floor and hunched over his knees, staring at the unanswered texts on his phone.

"Anything?"

Minks shook his head. "No news is good news, right?" he muttered, sending another message. "Do you have the flight app open?" Looking over at Louis's cell, he tapped the aerial map. "The only planes in the sky are ours. That looks like the Wichita group there. If timings remain steady, the westbound flight will land twenty minutes before the eastbound ones. South should be on the runways in half an hour. North will touch down thirty behind that."

Committing the timings to memory, Louis reached over Jonathan to the pilot. "Louis Forbes."

"Adam Demmers," the man replied, shaking his hand. "Former Air Force. We all are." He flipped a switch and sat back, completely at ease. "We'll get you there, sir."

Louis nodded and draped one arm over Jonathan's shoulder, watching the texts from the Kaius haunt light up his phone while Jonathan's remained silent. "Minks?"

"Yeah?"

"We got this, okay?"

CHAPTER THIRTY

Louis tucked Jonathan's hair behind his ear and smoothed it down, a slight tremor in his hand as he tried to remain calm. "Almost there," he murmured while Minks rocked slowly on the floor, his arms wrapped tight around his knees. Looking between his buzzing phone and the pilot, Louis scanned his messages. "Runways are prepped for landing, and a ceasefire has finally been called between the FBI Vamp Division and the remaining city perimeter patrols."

Thirty minutes too late.

Jonathan's shoulders heaved against his leg as he took another deep breath. Clearing his throat to ease the tightness in it, he answered Rhys's call.

"Louis here."

"How is he?" Rhys asked quietly, the mayhem constantly present in the Kaius haunt com room now little more than hushed voices coordinating the final stretches of the evacuation.

Placing a staying hand on Jonathan's back, he stared out the window. "Is Nichol back on-site?"

Respecting his refusal to respond, Rhys shifted gears immediately. "Audra, Lis, and Molly are en route to the hospital now to sit with Simone during the day. Nic will hole up in her quarters in the city until sundown, but she's stable and apparently pissed, so we expect him to be reachable and controlled by tomorrow night."

The plane began its slow descent, and Jonathan's head lifted for a moment, giving Louis a glimpse of his empty eyes before he dropped his head back to his knees, and his hair fell forward again to hide the dried blood streaking his face.

"Plane five has touchdown," Adam reported. "Two is circling until they have a clear visual."

Rhys muttered something to someone in the room and returned to the phone. "Louis, Jagg, and Bianca are waiting at the airport to bring you and Jonathan home. See you soon, brother."

The call ended, and Minks exhaled, his shoulders trembling as he tightened his hold on his knees and resumed the slow rocking he had been doing since he took the hits of his hauntmates 'deaths thirty minutes earlier.

Louis stroked Jonathan's hair gently and stared at the ice building on the nose of the plane, oblivious to the turbulence shaking the aircraft while they dipped below the clouds.

Jonathan would never hear the word *brother* spoken to him again. Would never return home from his travels to hauntmates who simultaneously coddled and tortured him. Would never read a chastising text from his sire that made him roll his eyes before firing off a cheeky reply.

Louis hadn't needed Mickey's frantic call reporting the blast taking out the entire southwestern perimeter patrol. The moment the homemade bomb detonated, Jonathan had pitched forward, clutching his chest as his forehead smacked off of the plane's console.

He'd been unable to speak as he drew fast, deep breaths, the blood running down his face only adding to the confusion in the cockpit while Louis tried frantically to figure out what the hell was happening.

When tremors akin to death rattles shook Jonathan's body in nine convulsing waves, Louis's chest seized.

Mickey's words minutes later only confirmed what he already knew.

—Reports are saying no survivors from the Minks line, but I'm looking through the footage and aerials now, Louis. If any made it, we'll find them and get them out.—

He was unable to respond, unable to tell Mick not to bother looking because there wasn't a single member of the Minks line who survived the night.

Except the orphan currently huddled at his knees.

"Planes two and three are on the ground," Adam reported, and the aircraft angled to the right as the voices of the other pilots cracked through the radio. "I'll circle once while plane four lands before I go in."

Nodding, Louis texted Rhys with the update.

Jonathan hadn't spoken a word. When the tremors subsided, he'd merely stilled, save for a slight rhythmic rocking and deep, shaking breaths.

The passengers had gone just as quiet, the soft murmurings filling the plane silencing.

Adam began flipping switches and pressing buttons with a meticulously practiced cadence. "We're going in."

Louis sat up and looked out the window, keeping one hand on Jonathan's back. "You can see the runway?"

The man gave him a tight smile and tapped his radar. "Combination of this, skill, and instinct are landing the plane tonight."

Running his thumb along the collar of Jonathan's jacket, he braced himself for the evacuation mission's final landing.

And the aftermath.

****

Louis slung their bags over his shoulder and knelt at Jonathan's side. "Time to go," he said quietly, easing one hand under the male's arm.

Minks allowed Louis to help him to his feet, his movements sluggish, while Louis guided him to the plane's exit and down the stairs pushed alongside the aircraft. Adam stood at attention at the bottom, giving Louis a nod as they passed, his eyes tracking Jonathan with solemn respect.

Bianca and Jagger stood beside their SUV, where Jagg was attempting to shield Bee from the heavy snowfall while she shooed him off, her tiny form scurrying across the tarmac when she saw them.

She was at Jonathan's side in an instant, taking his hand and clutching it silently between both of hers while Jagger jogged toward the last of the taxis rushing the evacuated vamps to their new homes.

"Let's get you two in here and warm," Bianca cooed as she ushered them into the back seat before she rushed around to sit in the passenger seat. She held her hand out to Louis. "There's plenty of room for those bags up here."

He passed her the satchels, knowing better than to argue with the Former Tender. "Thanks, Bee. What time is it?"

"Two hours until sunrise," she replied, rifling through her purse and handing him a packet of wet napkins. "Jonathan, honey? I'm Bianca Schumann. Bee, for short. You just sit tight, and we'll get you a meal and a warm bed the moment we get to the haunt."

Minks swallowed hard and lifted his head slightly, his eyes not quite looking at her through his damp, tangled hair. "Pleasure to meet you, ma'am," he mumbled. "If it's not too much trouble, could I be dropped off at my...my home?"

Bee glanced at Louis as Jagger got in the driver's seat, concern in her bright eyes.

Shoving the package of wipes into his pocket, Louis leaned in close to Minks and clasped his hand. "Maybe we can head over to the Kaius haunt tonight and go there tomorrow."

Jonathan continued to stare unseeing at his feet while Jagger drove them off the tarmac.

"Louis, honey?" Bee said, turning in her seat to face him. "Once you two are settled, we'll need to have a quick debrief before you retire for the day."

He grunted in agreement, his attention on Jonathan. "Hey," he whispered, looking up at Bianca for a second before giving his hand a squeeze. "If you want to go home, we'll get you there, okay?"

While Bee mouthed the possible change in plans to Jagger and eased her phone from her purse, Minks took a deep, stuttering breath, one finger hooking over Louis's.

Jagg adjusted the rearview mirror to see him. "Bianca has the address pulled up. We can be there in twenty minutes."

Sliding closer to Minks, Louis reached over and tucked his hair behind his ear. "Yeah?"

Jonathan merely nodded, his shoulders hunching a fraction more.

They drove through the quiet streets, the odd emergency vehicle passing them at dangerous speeds on the icy roads. Louis looked away from Jonathan every few minutes, tracking their location to ensure he had a good idea where the Minks haunt was housed.

When they passed a familiar apartment block, he tapped Bianca's arm. "That's Simone's place, isn't it? How is she?"

"The surgeons managed to repair the perforated lung, and Nic's blood is assisting with the surface damage. As of an hour ago, Simone is stable," Bee stated quietly, keeping her head angled toward Jagger while her gaze flicked to Jonathan. "Nichol, however…"

"Isn't," Jagger finished for her, lacing his fingers with hers. "He's still at the hospital researching alternative treatments and driving the nurses up the wall with his reassessment timeline recommendations." He eased onto a narrow side street and came to a stop in front of a row of townhouses. "Number fourteen."

Louis watched Jonathan raise his head and look out the window, pausing before he lifted the door handle and heaved it open slowly. As he got out, he hesitated again and turned toward Bianca's unrolled window. "Thank you for the ride."

Bee's eyes watered, and she reached out to him, patting his arm. "If you need anything, day or night, Louis will make sure you have all our numbers. Don't you dare wait to call."

Louis jogged around the SUV, slowing when Jonathan shoved his hands into his jacket pockets, trudged up the un-shoveled walkway, and stopped at the door.

"I don't know the code to get inside."

Louis looked back at Bianca helplessly. "Does anyone have the code? Nichol, maybe?"

She turned to Jagger, both of them huddling over their phones while Jonathan continued to stand in front of his door until Jagg hopped out of the car and ran up the walk.

"Rhys sent me a reset," he stated as he tapped on the keypad. "You're in. You can set whatever code you want once you're inside, okay?"

Jonathan nodded and opened the door, his knuckles white on the knob. "Louis?"

"Yeah?"

"Could you..." His head bowed. "Could you maybe call me tomorrow?"

****

Louis accepted his and Jonathan's backpacks and exited Jagger's SUV as Audra pulled to a stop in front of Simone's apartment complex. Nichol sat motionless in the front seat, and she gave a small smile when Nic flung the door open and jumped out.

"Hourly updates," Nichol barked out, storming toward the apartments.

"Of course," Audra replied calmly before she looked back at him and held out her cell. "If you give me Jonathan's address, I'll drive by there a few times today. The hospital's only a couple miles away."

He entered the address and passed the phone back. "I appreciate it. I didn't want to leave him there but—"

"I know," she said softly. "Go inside, keep your phone charged, and try to get some rest."

Waving as she pulled away, he followed Nichol into the hall, standing back while the miserable vamp keyed in the code and flung the door open.

"Boots on the mat," Nic grunted, unlacing his and setting them on the black rubber mat beside the door.

"Hang your jacket in the closet."

Obeying without a word, he set his boots in place and grabbed a wire hanger.

"The shower takes eighty seconds to reach optimum temperature. Anything over ten minutes affects tank rebound."

Side-eyeing Nichol, he set the bags down, carefully ensuring Jonathan's was closed tight before rifling through his own for a phone charger.

"If you play any of the gaming systems today, sign in under your own profile. The ones already on there are off-limits."

Louis dropped onto the sofa, elbows on his knees and head in his hands. "Nichol? Could we maybe curb the commands for the day? I'm—" He squeezed his eyes shut, not knowing how to explain the misery swirling in his mind.

The couch bounced as Nichol joined him and Louis shoved his hands through his hair, leaning back while the old vamp studied the coffee table, a blue game controller in his hand. "She's high as a fucking kite right now."

He looked over at Nichol. "You can feel that?"

Nic hunched forward, turning the controller over and over. "I felt everything. I was...not as controlled as I should have been."

"No one's going to blame you for going to your connected mate when she's injured." Louis grabbed the remote and passed it to Nichol when his hazel eyes narrowed. "Pick whatever, but I'm not really in the mood for a comedy."

Grunting, Nichol flipped through the channels, settling on a medical drama. "Studying procedures," he stated when Louis's nose wrinkled. "Medicine has changed since I required it." They watched in silence until a commercial came on and Nic turned down the volume.

"I didn't anticipate it," he said quietly, the subtle grinding of his molars subsiding when he spoke. "Seventeen vamps, six humans. And I didn't...I was unprepared for the possibility of suicide bombers inside the perimeter."

Swallowing a lump that refused to leave his throat, Louis reached over to his phone and unplugged it from the charger, opening and closing his messaging app a few times to ensure he hadn't missed a text. "How many vampires were successfully evacuated?"

"Two hundred and thirty-one. Forty-eight didn't make it to the Denver tarmac."

What happened to those forty-eight didn't need to be spoken.

He sat back as Nichol turned the volume up and stared at the TV. The old vampire's jaw flexed rhythmically while he ground his teeth. The muscles in his arms twitched with tension as his phone buzzed incessantly.

Swiping his own cell to life, Louis tapped on Jonathan's number and fired off a quick text.

—*Minks?*—

As the minutes ticked by and the message went unanswered, he settled into the sofa to wait for sundown.

CHAPTER THIRTY-ONE

Jonathan sat with his back against the door, his arms draped over his knees as he took another drag of his cigarette. He listened to Louis's voice calling to him softly from outside while the rapping of knuckles against the heavy wood reverberated along his spine.

Exhaling a cloud of smoke into the darkness, he continued to stare at the grains in the wood flooring, the only place in the room that didn't hold any reminders of his brothers or his sire.

The open closet to his left was off-limits. Even if he ignored the empty hangers on the rod, the jumble of shoes piled on the bottom racks were too easily identifiable, too easily matched to each brother.

Samuel's cowboy boots to give him the extra inch he needed to break the six-foot barrier.

Theo's metallic-trimmed sneakers Gino teased him about mercilessly.

Frederick's flip-flops, the ones he deemed to be the greatest invention of humankind ever.

The cigarette in his fingers burned down to the filter, and the stench competed with the smell of stale smoke in the room as he butted it out on the floor and added the crushed filter to the stack of others.

Louis's knocking ceased, his voice falling to a whisper while a woman spoke in hushed tones.

"Jonathan?" Louis called out, and the rustling of a

plastic bag filtered through the heavy door. "I'm just going to leave this here, okay? There's a phone charger and a carton of cigarettes." The knob rattled while Louis hung the bag. "I'll be in the city all night. Just a few blocks away. And I'll try calling again in a bit."

He could hear them walk away, their shoes crunching in the snow as the woman spoke quietly.

"Give him time, sweetie. We'll come by again later, before dawn."

He lit another cigarette to mask the scents of the room.

The drugstore cologne Walter always overdid.

The incense Christoph burned while he read.

Give him time.

Taking a long drag, he dropped his forehead to his knees.

He had yet to make it past the doorframe.

****

Audra reached over and patted Louis's knee while she pulled into the hospital parking lot. "We alerted Jonathan's neighbors of the situation. They'll let us know the moment they hear or see anything."

"Thanks," he muttered, the numbness that had settled over him the previous night refusing to lift. "What's going on over there?"

Audra undid her seat belt, got out of the car, and waved at the cluster of humans standing at the entrance. The group was singing with candles in hand while photographers snapped pictures and reporters stood to the side, scribbling notes on their tablets. "Candlelight vigil," she replied, shooing him away from the hubbub. "We'll go in the side doors."

He followed her through the maze of hallways,

keeping his head bowed to hide his eyes and fangs from the nurses and doctors strolling past them.

"Louis?" Audra said quietly as she pressed the elevator button and stepped back to wait. "You're allowed to be here."

Shoving his hands in the pockets of his leather jacket, he lifted his head, his shoulders hunching forward as he did.

They rode to the fifth floor, and Audra placed her hand on his back, guiding him to the nurse's station. "Hi, Mel. This is Louis Forbes. He's with us. Louis, Mel is the queen of the ward, and you'll do well to remember that."

The woman looked up from her computer and gave him a bright smile. "Nice to meet you, Louis. We have a selection of meals available for you in the cooler over there. The waiting room to the left has a TV, and make sure you connect to the Wi-Fi," she said, handing him a card with the password.

He took the card and pocketed it, shaking her hand. "Pleasure to meet you, ma'am," he replied, wincing as Jonathan's words channeled through him.

Audra stepped up to the counter. "Has Nichol gone to the conference room yet, or do I dare go into Simone's room and remind him?"

Mel chuckled, swinging back and forth in her chair. "He was just out here offering fifty thousand dollars to any of us willing to sit with Simone until he returned. He seemed to calm down when I showed him Alicia's rotation and assured him she was scheduled to remain in Simone's room for the night. He's gone back in to assess her before he heads over to the conference room."

Rolling her eyes, Audra glanced down the hall. "I'll

get him out of Alicia's hair. Thanks, Mel."

Trailing behind Audra, Louis paused in the doorway of Simone's room.

"If she doesn't put a stake through that dead heart, I sure as hell will," Simone snarled, and Louis peeked in, brows raising when he caught sight of Nichol standing in the far corner of the room, arms crossed and eyes blackening while he clutched a medical chart. "Audra, tell me you brought my crossbow."

Audra walked over to Simone's bedside and fluffed her pillows. "You're going to pop your stitches and give him an actual reason to be obsessive," she warned, helping Simone recline back on the bed before she turned to Nic. "And you are not helping her recovery if you're causing her stress. Let Alicia do her job, and you do yours. You and Louis head over to the conference room, and I'll join you in a minute."

Hesitating a moment, Nichol slammed the chart on the equipment stand and stomped across the room, stopping at Simone's bed long enough to give her a kiss that caused her heart rate monitor to beep out a warning.

As they left the room, Louis could hear Audra speaking softly to Simone about the increased death tolls which came in throughout the day.

Two of the humans in the bomb blast had succumbed to their injuries hours earlier.

Three others weren't expected to survive the night.

The youngest of the Gregoire haunt had overpowered their daytime security and walked into the sun at noon.

Jonathan's vacant eyes barreled through Louis's head, and his steps stuttered.

"Louis," Nichol grunted, giving his back a

surprisingly gentle pat as they entered the conference room. "Let's get this meeting done so you can check in on Minks, and I can see how far I can push my luck with Simone."

Rhys was lounging in an executive chair, arms behind his head and feet on the table as a doctor perched beside his boots, her fingers sliding along her stethoscope while she smiled demurely at him.

"Welcome back, you red-headed devil," Rhys called over. He ran his tongue over one fang and smirked when the woman leaned a fraction closer to him. "We'll do a quick debrief tonight, go over a few pressing details, and then I'll be heading home to bang the hell outta Lis before we have to prepare for whatever shitstorm comes next."

The doctor's eyes narrowed, and she stood, giving Rhys a final once-over before striding past Louis and Nichol and stopping to whisper with Mel and Audra at the nurse's station.

Nic glanced down the hall and swung a chair around for himself. "If you could perhaps avoid distracting or aggravating Simone's pulmonary specialist until she's discharged, I'd appreciate it."

"I warned her I was involved." Rhys grinned. "Just wanted to drive the point home."

The clicking of Audra's high heels was a welcome sound for Louis as she came up behind him and temporarily pulled him from the numbness, easing him back into the familiarity of haunt life.

"Seriously, Rhys?" Audra huffed, her catlike eyes locked on him as she sat beside him. "*Bang the hell outta Lis*? Could you at least try to be decent for a few minutes? We're in a hospital."

Rhys cocked his head and winked at someone outside the conference room. "I wasn't the one flashing a hot-pink thong at a strange vamp, sweetheart."

Louis slipped over to the table and sat beside Nichol, leaning over to see what had the cranky vampire's rapt attention.

"Audra," Nichol barked, and she took the deep breath that always preceded a lecture. "Does this visual calm you?"

She blinked slowly and looked at Nic's phone. "Sure. Rhys, we're guests here, and we need to—"

"Is this color soothing?"

Exhaling loudly, Audra humored Nichol and nodded. "Yes. Blue is proven to be calmative. Rhys, we need to be aware of perception, especi—"

Nichol scooted his chair closer to her and pushed his phone directly into her line of sight. "But red is believed to alleviate anxiety. Would Simone's current mental state be classified as anxious or stressed?"

She closed her eyes for a moment and turned her back to him. "Especially when anything we say can be warped on social me—"

Nichol didn't miss a beat, his rapt attention on his cell. "Given the choice between lavender and vanilla, which would you recommend to promote relaxation? What about classical music or nature sounds? Rhythmic waves seem optimal, but I have concerns over the auditory processing issues presented in this journal."

"Oh my god, Nichol," Audra groaned, facing him. "What are you going on about?"

Tapping away on his notes app, Nic showed her. "We all know I'm not going to back off Simone anytime soon, so I'm going to create as relaxing an environment as I can to counter all the negative effects my presence causes."

Audra's eyes softened, and she pulled up tight to Nichol, Rhys's indiscretions forgotten. "If you order a scent diffuser, you can pick up a variety to see which she prefers."

While Audra and Nichol hunched over his phone, Dominic and Molly thumped through the hall. They called out loudly to Mel and Simone, their voices dropping to whispers when the nurse chastised them.

"Sorry, everyone," Dom hushed, pulling the door shut. "We got hung up at the vigil downstairs."

Molly was already halfway across the room, her arms wrapping around Louis's neck. "It is so good to have you back," she mumbled into his jacket. "I'm so, so sorry about the Minks haunt. How's Jonathan?"

Knowing it was better to remain still and let Molly get her sniffling out, he kept his hands where the young, connected Dominic could see them and hugged her back. The contact brought on a wave of sadness he struggled to shove aside. "Not good. I…he's not answering his phone."

She released him and rolled a chair to his side, her dark eyes tearing up. "Aww fuck. We'll be quick, okay?"

Shaking off the heaviness settling in his chest, he looked over at Dominic. "About time I got to say congratulations to you two." Molly switched gears instantly, her face lighting up as she held her hand out to show off her ring. His brows shot up, and he leaned in closer to examine it. "Is that a black diamond?"

Dominic grinned. "Pretty cool, isn't it?"

A fleeting thought flashed through his mind, and he cleared his throat. "Very."

"Happy Sunshine Mellow Time is fucking over," Rhys announced, thumping his feet to the floor and effectively bringing the meeting to order. "Jagg and Bee are holding down the fort, and Mickey's sitting in with the mayor to deal with the details of the ceasefire, so let's get this over with." The room went quiet, and he rocked back in his chair, crossing his arms. "First order of business, we fucking did it."

The statement was met with somber nods, and Louis glanced over at Nichol, surprised the de facto leader of the Kaius haunt was sitting back while the wild card ran the meeting.

Rhys looked down at the table for a moment before licking his lips. "As you all know, we took heavy losses. Final tallies won't be known for a few more days, but the price was high." His eyes drifted to Louis. "Jagger is drawing up new rotations to ensure hauntmates are no longer working alongside each other, with the exception of mates."

"Any update on who organized the bombs?" Audra asked. "Neither Mickey nor I caught any uprising chatter on any of the platforms we were monitoring."

Rhys shook his head. "We have a few names, but nothing written in stone. Jagger is coordinating with human law enforcement, so we'll know what they know and vice versa. Moving on to the second bullet on the outline Nichol texted me ten minutes ago: the media."

Dominic and Molly groaned, and Audra's face mimicked Nichol's expression of disgust.

"Shut the fuck up and listen," Rhys groused. "According to today's talk shows, the vampire will to live was victorious last night and some other flowery bullshit I didn't pay much attention to. Basically, the

251

presidential election frontrunner has grabbed hold of that bandwagon and is currently rallying for us. The other side's rallying for our immediate executions, but whatever. As of now, vampires are the defining platforms for both sides."

Nichol snorted and set his phone down. "Which, as history has taught us, should go over real fucking well."

Rhys flipped him off. "I'm in charge tonight, dumbass. So yeah, what Nichol said. We'll draw up a media campaign aligning with the pro-vampers tomorrow. More pressing right now is issue three. Orphaned vamps."

All eyes flicked to Louis, and he sunk down slightly in his chair while Molly wrapped her arm around his shoulder.

"Orphan numbers are up, elder numbers are down," Rhys continued. "Wolfgang Vicente has offered to house twenty in a dorm-style setup, thanks to Audra's smooth tongue, which Mickey is usually the sole benefactor of." When she reached over and swatted his knee, he grinned. "It's a compliment."

Nichol's teeth ground for a moment before he muttered under his breath. "Stojanovski was slated to take on nine on top of the one he'd already snatched up."

"Andy," Louis interjected quietly. "Where is he?"

"In the motel we converted on the north end," Rhys replied. "Same as the Gregoires and ninety-three others."

Ninety-three.

Louis tuned out the rest of the discussion, his mind unable to move past the image of Jonathan it drug up from the depths of his worst memories. The moment Jonathan's hauntmates were ended.

Over and over, it looped in his head. The jolts

rippling through his body. The blood running from the gash on his forehead. The agony in his eyes before the emptiness settled in.

"Louis."

He snapped back to the table and straightened in his seat, forcing his attention to Rhys. "Sorry, what?"

Rhys studied him, his eyes moving between Louis and Nichol until he waved his hand. "Nichol, go harass Simone. We can email you the rest later. Louis, same thing. Take the SUV Audra was driving and head out. Mickey will pick her up on his way by."

He muttered his thanks and stood, catching the keys when Audra tossed them his way.

"And Louis?" Rhys called out as he walked out the door. "Sign the fucking contract already."

CHAPTER THIRTY-TWO

Louis flattened his palm against the door one last time and got to his feet, brushing the ice from his jeans as he rested his forehead on the wood. "I'm just a few blocks away for the day," he said softly. "Anything you need. Anything, and I can get it done, okay?"

The plastic bag still hung on the knob, untouched. "Minks?"

When he was met with nothing more than the snick of a lighter, he turned and jogged to the car, the light of day threatening to break before he made it to Simone's apartment.

Signaling his intent on the empty road, he eased into his lane and crept through the icy streets until he reached the apartment parking lot and aimed for a spot in the empty quadrant at the side of the property.

The sun crested as he hit the safety of the sheltered halls and knocked on Simone's door, grateful for the return of the numbness settling in his bones when Nichol ushered him in.

"How is he?" Nic demanded, entering the lock code and claiming his spot on the sofa.

"Wouldn't know." He placed his boots beside Nichol's and hung his jacket in the closet. "Not a word." Joining Nic on the sofa, he passed the remote over. "And Simone?"

Nic's jaw twitched. "My blood appears to be

assisting the healing. If she takes it."

"If? Why wouldn't she?" Louis asked, not expecting the old vamp to answer such a personal question.

Settling on a war documentary, Nichol sat back and crossed his arms, the tendons in his neck strained. "Simone's under the incorrect assumption that the more she takes, the more I experience her discomfort. I've enlisted Lis and Molly to deal with the misinformation throughout today and am hoping to resume her recovery schedule by midnight."

Louis glanced over at him. "She wants to protect you."

"I'm over fourteen hundred years old."

And with that, all discussion was over while they waited out the sun for the second day in a row.

****

Jonathan butted out the last of his cigarettes on the hardwood floor and dropped his chin back to his arms, his limbs heavy from exhaustion as the sun rose higher in the sky.

He'd wanted to call out to Louis, wanted Louis to sit with him on this side of the door until he steeled himself to go further into the house his hauntmates had called home.

But he was unable to speak, unable to build the will to do anything more than stare at the floor for the hours Louis sat inches away from him on the other side of the door with only his quiet voice periodically breaking through the silence to remind him he was there.

The faint scent of Nero's oil paints broke through the haze of cigarette smoke hanging in the air and he squeezed his eyes shut, burying his face in his arm to block the memories the smell carried with it.

He fought off the assault to his senses for hours until he broke and got to his knees sluggishly. He put one hand on the doorknob, turned his face away from the sun, and opened it to retrieve the bag Louis had left for him. The pain was instantaneous as his skin was seared by the afternoon rays, and he fumbled the door shut as the plastic tangled in the knob and ripped, sending the contents clunking onto the hardwood.

Crawling back to his position on the floor, he tore the carton opened, lit a cigarette, and collapsed against the door. The blisters on his sun-exposed arm were worth the stench of smoke covering the scents of his brothers, giving him something to focus on outside of his own head.

****

Louis's feet left the floor as Nichol yanked him back down to the sofa and held him there. "He'll survive eight seconds of sun exposure. Now sit your ass down, stop watching that goddamn video, and keep talking."

After attempting to shake out of the old vampire's hold for a moment, Louis relented and sat back, turning his phone over to avoid the temptation to re-watch the footage of the Minks house the human patrol team had sent in to the Kaius haunt. "Sorry." He peeked at his cell to glance at the time. "What was the question?"

"The Deviant clothing," Nic stated, his laptop open to the document he was working on. "What exactly qualifies as 'old' for you?"

Jonathan's words played in his ears. "They were dressed like extras from a Wild West movie," he recalled. "Eighteen-fifties kind of garb."

Snorting, Nichol entered it in and glared at him. "We need to tighten up your definition of 'old,' Forbes."

"Jonathan's words, not mine," he qualified.

"Then it's an apt description aligning with the reports we received from the ground elsewhere." Closing the document out, Nichol opened his email account. "We've received information about Deviants in clothing dating them as far back as the seventeen-hundreds."

He tilted his phone up again, growling when Nic pushed it flat against his leg. "Just checking the time," he argued weakly.

"It's been eighty-three seconds since your last check. Do the math."

Flopping back, he ran his hands through his damp hair. "What the fuck else am I supposed to do for the next forty-two minutes?"

Nichol continued to fire off emails, his phone buzzing nonstop on the coffee table. "Finish your laundry so I don't have to look at your half-naked ass anymore."

Laundry.

Right.

He wandered over to the small closet housing the washer and dryer, flinging the metal door of the dryer open with enough force to receive a barked insult from Nic.

"I'm emailing you my laundry document now," Nichol called over and Louis's phone vibrated on the table. "It contains a chart of proper folding techniques."

Carrying the clothes back to the sofa, he dropped them onto the floor so he could sort them, acutely aware the miserable vampire beside him was watching his every movement.

He opened the email and scrolled down to the section on folding. "Since when do you do laundry?" he asked, lifting one of Jonathan's shirts and carefully smoothing it out on the coffee table.

"Since Simone and Audra met up for coffee and my traitor of a best friend informed my mate, I had *outdated preconceived notions of household responsibility division*," Nichol sneered, badly mimicking Audra's voice. "One of these nights, I'm going to gorge myself on that woman's veins and leave her body for the coyotes."

Aligning the seams of Jonathan's jeans, Louis folded them up and set them on top of the shirt before reaching down for his own and standing, tugging them up over his boxers. "Did you tell Audra of your plans?"

"Do I look stupid to you?" Nichol snarled, glancing over his texts before returning to his computer and opening an intimidating spreadsheet. "Once I finish these funds transfers, we can get ready to go."

Yanking a clean shirt over his head, he got to work on the socks. "What was with those wills you were printing off earlier? I didn't know haunts did those up."

"They don't," Nichol grumbled, flipping between four accounts. "With media attention on the death toll, I'm anticipating questions from the financial branch regarding the transfer of wealth between deceased haunt leaders and their surviving offspring." He frowned, hunching over the laptop. "Mickey scanned and emailed every vampire signature we had in Rhys's files over the centuries, so now we have authorized documentation to ensure the smooth transfer of asset control to the affected orphans."

Adding Jonathan's socks and boxers to his pile, Louis slid the stack into his bag. "So Minks…"

Nichol stopped what he was doing and looked up.

"Jonathan's was the first to be completed. When the time is right for him, we'll make the necessary filings. Sun sets in twenty-seven seconds. Don't forget to grab that cooler when you go."

Louis slung Jonathan's bag over his shoulder and snatched the cooler off the floor, yanking his boots on while he fumbled through the lock code. "Thanks, Nichol. Tell Simone I say hi."

Nichol's grumbled response went in one ear and out the other as he jogged down the hall and stepped into the darkness as the last of the sun's rays disappeared.

The SUV sat across the parking lot, and he wrinkled his nose, playing with the keys in his pocket and glaring at the icy pavement before deciding it was faster, and safer, to run.

Six minutes later, he was right.

He gave a quick wave to the humans wrapping up their daytime patrol on the quiet street and walked up to Jonathan's door, knocking softly on the wood. "Minks?"

Met with silence again, he cleared the skiff of snow off the entranceway and sat, setting the cooler beside him and Jonathan's bag onto his lap.

"Got a cooler of A-negative," he finally said into the silence. "And your bag if you want it. Everything's washed. By me. In a washing machine. I used the dryer, too, but some of the socks didn't get completely dry because I forgot to un-bunch them." He flattened one hand against the door. "Nichol has this document he put together for doing laundry, and it's probably the most anal-retentive thing I've ever seen. Color-coordinated headings, pictures, bullet points with asterisks leading to notes about different stains…"

****

Jonathan stared at the woodgrain pattern in the floor and listened to Louis's smooth baritone go on and on about Nichol Kaius's quirks, the soft rumble of his voice lulling him into an almost tranquil daze despite the intermittent spikes of pain accompanying the slow healing of his burns.

A small part of his mind knew he needed to feed. That small part also recognized he couldn't sit on the floor forever.

But that small part held no weight against the heaviness pulling down the rest of him.

The thought of getting to his feet was met with an internal resistance he had neither the strength nor the inclination to fight. Even the lighting up of a cigarette was becoming harder, his gaze falling on the open pack long before he could make the effort to pull one out.

"Minks? I'm here, okay?"

Every hour, Louis would call out his name, and every hour, he tried to respond. The minutes would tick by, and his weak determination would waver before he would listen to Louis settle back against the door and continue to talk to him, promising himself that next time he would answer.

CHAPTER THIRTY-THREE

Nichol's arm remained firmly fastened around Simone's waist while he typed out a text to Louis, his posture noticeably relaxed since he'd arrived at Jonathan's doorstep with his mate. "That code will get you into the apartment. The rest of the information is a general list of things you can and can't touch, as well as drawers you're forbidden to open."

Louis got to his feet and pulled his phone out to read the list over, biting the inside of his cheek at Nichol's frequent use of the word *unmentionables*. "I appreciate this, Simone," he said, shoving his cell back into his pocket. "Good luck bunking in Nichol's room for the next few nights."

She smiled at him, her skin still paler than usual. "If he acts up, he'll sleep in the common room," she stated, lowering her voice as she stepped closer to him. "Keep us posted, okay? And make sure Jonathan knows, had it not been for his hauntmates, we would've lost dozens more."

Nodding, he watched them walk to the SUV parked on the street.

The footage of the explosion was something the Kaius haunt was guarding rabidly, refusing to allow him or anyone else to view it. All he knew was Minks Sr. had detected the faint ticking of the bombs' countdown clocks moments before they detonated and had ordered the brothers to form a barrier between the two armed cars and the rest of their rotation.

Waiting until they drove off, he resumed his position in front of Jonathan's door, the cooler and bag left untouched from the night before.

"Minks?" He leaned his head against the wood and scoured the dark sky for one of the two constellations he knew.

"Yeah?"

He jumped to his feet and grabbed the doorknob. "Hey," he called back, resting his forehead on the frame and closing his eyes as a surge of relief shot through him. "Hey. Open up?"

There was a long pause before he heard the code being punched in slowly and the knob turned in his hand.

He was prepared to see Jonathan's vacant eyes, prepared to see him looking rough, maybe disheveled.

But he wasn't expecting Minks to be dressed in the same filthy clothes he'd worn the night of the evacuation, his boots still laced on his feet. The shoulder-length hair that always held touchable shine was hanging in limp tangles around his blood-streaked face, his hunched back bringing his height down to Louis's five-foot-eleven.

"That bad?" Jonathan asked, his voice gruff as his eyes remained locked on the ground.

"Yeah, that bad," he confirmed while he unhooked Jonathan's bag from the doorknob and hefted the small cooler up. "Can I come in?"

Minks stepped aside silently, and Louis walked into the dark foyer, catching sight of dozens of cigarette butts piled on the burn-pocked floor. He set the cooler down and knelt to untie his shoes before reaching over to undo Jonathan's as well.

"Up," he ordered softly, tapping on Jonathan's foot and pulling his boot off when the leg lifted on command. "Jacket, too."

With sluggish movements, Minks shoved his leather jacket from his shoulders, not resisting when Louis reached up to tug it off from the cuffs. Louis nudged his other foot and removed Jonathan's second boot, setting it all in a pile to deal with later.

Along with the cigarette butts.

"All right," he said, getting to his feet. "Let's get the lights on an—"

"No lights," Jonathan mumbled. "Please."

Nodding, he started toward the staircase, stopping at the bottom when he realized Minks wasn't coming. "Minks?"

Jonathan shook his head, his eyes locked on the dark hallway at the top of the stairs. "I need…a minute."

Frowning, Louis glanced over at the mud-caked boots beside the door, his eyes traveling over the dried chunks of dirt around the front door, realization dawning on him when he noticed the tracks didn't lead past the foyer.

He walked back to Jonathan's side and held out his hand. "We don't have to do this," he offered. "We can head over to Simone's. Give you a night or two to clear your head."

Minks shook his head and took a step toward the staircase.

****

Jonathan felt around the tiled shower walls for the shampoo and squeezed some into his hand, inhaling sharply when the scent of Xavier's preferred salon brand hit him full force.

"Minks?" Louis called out to him from the countertop where he had promised to remain.

Lathering up his hair, he exhaled slowly and focused on the heat of the water. "Fine," he replied, his voice echoing against the tile. "I'm fine."

Louis responded with a quiet grunt in the pitch black of the bathroom but didn't argue.

Although he was hesitant when Louis had coaxed him toward the shower, he had to admit the heat and water felt good as it pummeled his muscles and washed away the dried blood and mud from his skin.

And although the initial hit of the shampoo's scent had thrown him, the faint smell of it as it rinsed from his hair was almost soothing.

Almost.

Until his mind started flashing the loop of images it had been replaying night after night, memories of stupid, trivial moments he'd spent with his sire and brothers.

"I'm tossing a towel over the rod," Louis said, his voice keeping Jonathan from getting too deep into his head. "Take your time. I'm not going anywhere."

I'm not going anywhere.

Louis had said it a few times while they made their way up the stairs and down the hall, taking Jonathan's constant hesitation in stride and patiently waiting him out. Louis had led the way through the upper hallway of the house, letting Jonathan set the pace in the darkness.

Angling into the spray, he gave his face a final rinse and turned it off, feeling around for the towel.

"Ah, hell," Louis suddenly huffed, his feet thumping to the ground. "I forgot your bag downstairs. Hold tight."

When the door opened, he froze. "Wait," he called out, the idea of being by himself pressing on his chest.

"I…"

"No rush. I'm not going anywhere. We'll grab it together later."

Drying off as quick as he could, Jonathan wrapped the towel around his hips and got out of the shower. He followed Louis back down the hall, his eyes on the floor to avoid the morbid temptation to open his brothers ' bedroom doors.

There was no way in hell he was ready for that.

Louis snatched up his bag and slung it over his shoulder as he grabbed the small cooler he'd brought. "Minks?"

"Yeah?"

"No decision is final here," Louis said slowly, stopping at the base of the stairs. "You can change your mind any time. Stay, go, sit, stand. Whatever you want. But you need to feed, and you need to rest. Neither of those are an option. Where you do it is up to you, though."

He glanced up the stairs and pushed his tangled mess of hair out of his eyes. "The kitchen, I guess."

Louis passed him his backpack. "I'm going to heat one of these bags up while you get dressed, okay? I'll be right there."

Nodding, he watched Louis's shadowed form disappear into the darkness, the sound of his footsteps giving him something to focus on while he dressed quickly and tossed his wet towel next to the stairs.

"Bring your bag in," Louis ordered. The sound of clinking glass preceding the whirr of the microwave, its light guiding Jonathan to the table and providing enough illumination for him to notice the orange paint on the kitchen walls.

As Louis set a glass of warmed A-negative in front of him, he pulled the glass closer. "It's a Minks Sr. thing." He tried to see the walls through the blackness of the room but refused to turn the light on. "Every fucking kitchen is orange. I'd put money on the plates and bowls being orange, too."

"They are," Louis confirmed. "Bag?"

Passing the backpack over, he lifted the cup to his lips. "What color is this?"

"The cup?" Louis asked. "What color do you think it is?"

"Lime green."

He could feel Louis's hand graze over his hair. "You got it. Not going to lie, blood looks a little nasty in a green glass. Drink up while I get this rat's nest under control."

Part of him wanted to protest, to insist he could brush his own fucking hair.

But a bigger part didn't have the energy to fight it. And that part was compounded by the fact he didn't want to fight it.

****

Louis dragged the brush slowly through the length of Jonathan's hair, returning to a stubborn knot at the ends and gently working it loose.

"You don't suck at this," Minks mumbled, taking another quick sip of his meal. "I'm impressed."

"Yeah, well, Mikhail Kaius is my closest friend, and that guy's hair is a good four inches longer."

He turned his attention to the tangled mess on the left side, holding Jonathan's hair in one hand while he started at the tips and worked his way up.

"You play hairdresser for Mickey a lot?"

Frowning at the hoarseness still present in Jonathan's voice, he carefully used his fingers to ease out the worst of the snarl. "I've known him for almost two centuries," he said slowly, choosing his words deliberately to avoid revealing more than Mick would be comfortable with. "You know how empaths rarely make it past their first decade before they succumb to the stress of the constant emotional bombardment from the rest of their haunt? Mickey was blessed with a skill that drives most vamps to walk into the sun. Add in the strong Kaius blood amplifying skills, and he was hit with a double whammy."

With the toughest knots gone, he dragged the brush through every strand.

"But he had his moments," he continued. "Still does, to be honest. Sometimes I was the only one around when Mick would hit one of his lows, and he needed someone to be there until he came out of it, so I learned how to brush out long hair and shove muscled assholes into showers." He set the brush on the table. "Done?"

"Yeah," Minks said, sliding his chair back and standing. "Now what?"

Louis put one hand on Jonathan's hunched shoulder. "Now you need to rest. And it's up to you where." When the muscles under his fingers tensed, he softened his voice. "We can go to Simone's if you want."

Jonathan shook his head. "I don't want to leave. I just…"

"There's a sofa in the living room. Three, actually," he offered. "Why don't we try that for the day?"

Minks took a deep breath and exhaled loudly. "I can do that."

CHAPTER THIRTY-FOUR

Jonathan opened his eyes and stared into the darkness, reminding himself not to breathe in when the scents of his hauntmates assaulted him. "Louis?"

"Yeah?"

Adjusting his position on the sofa, he turned his head toward Louis's voice. "How long was I out?"

The couch across the room creaked as Louis moved around. "Eighteen hours."

Eighteen hours.

He hadn't slept that long since he was human.

Louis's bare feet padded toward him in the darkness. "Can I get you anything?"

A flash of anger ricocheted through him before he could bite it back. "My fucking hauntmates back would be a nice start."

When Louis responded with nothing more than a quiet "I know," his temper rose.

"Do you?" he demanded, getting to his feet, and feeling his way through the pitch black until he found a lamp, his fingers hovering over the switch. "Do you really fucking know? You may know how goddamn painful the death hit is, but does it count when you're the sire-killer?"

He could hear his accusations booming through the house, his voice growing louder with every word he was unable to hold back.

"You know what fucking sucks, Louis? What really fucking sucks?" he snarled, snapping the lamp to life and wincing when the light hit his retinas. "At some point, I'm going to have to clean out Gino and Theo's room. All that shit they've hoarded for years is going to take a month to go through. And Walter's closet. Holy fuck, Walter's closet. He probably has clothes in there from the eighteen-hundreds, complete with the moths that came with them."

He stormed to the foyer closet, threw the door off of its hinges, and yanked all the ball caps from the top shelf. "And what the fuck am I going to do with seventy hats? Who the fuck even needs that many? Aside from Xavier, of course."

In the back of his mind—the piece still clinging to rationality—he knew he was being unfair, that he was raging at Louis solely because he knew he could. Because he knew Louis wouldn't stake him.

Or worse, leave.

Stalking through the living room, he slammed his hand against the light switch and the place lit up the crowded collection of sofas and armchairs. "Nice to know the place is set up for those fucking haunt meetings we had to have every single fucking time I wanted to go on a trip. Because heaven knows I couldn't make the decision myself, right? Everyone had to have their say about the where and the how and the why. Maybe I wasn't the one they should've been keeping in check. Maybe they should've been busier watching their own asses."

A flash of anger in Louis's eyes was tampered as quick as it appeared, raring his own rage up.

"You want to say something, Louis? You want to

tell me all about how that's how haunts work? Lie through your fucking teeth about how lucky I was to have them looking out for me?" Shoving one of the armchairs over, he stormed around the sofas. "What, no words of wisdom? Not even a little jab to remind me just how little you think of haunt life? Nothing?"

His tirade was met with silence as Louis shoved his hands into his back pockets.

Slamming his hand against the banister, he tore up the stairs, knocking pictures off the walls and flinging the first bedroom door open, acutely aware of Louis's quiet footsteps behind him.

Samuel's CD tower stood in the corner of the room, the carefully alphabetized collection in perfect rows, until he grabbed the top and brought it crashing down. "Two hundred country albums," he hissed, kicking at the cases scattered on the floor. "On a constant rotation, day and fucking night. In the car. In his room. Even his fucking ringtone." Turning to Louis, he threw his hands in the air. "Of course, Samuel was fucking whiny. Look at this shit. I don't know how the fuck Frederick could stand it. Probably because he was too busy sitting on his fucking computer playing games to notice."

He pushed past Louis and booted in the next door, the scent of oil paint and incense causing him to recoil and take a step back into the hall.

"You know what's fucked up?" he asked, staring at the blank canvas on Nero's easel. "Christoph and Nero? They're...they were like twins born decades apart. Always together, always with their little secrets and jokes none of us were allowed to know. One would say something stupid and the other would fall over laughing and no one else thought it was funny," he sneered, yanking the door closed and cursing when the broken lock didn't catch.

Louis leaned against the wall, his arms crossed and chameleon eyes a dark gray.

Jonathan mimicked his pose, his rage burning down as the overwhelming numbness returned. "The room at the end is probably Minks Sr.'s," he stated flatly. "Which would make the one on the right mine and Armand's."

Louis finally spoke, his voice calm and unaffected. "Do you want to go over there?"

"I don't have to," he grunted. "I already know what they look like. Senior's is five shades of red. And not the vamp red, either. More like circus red. All bright and stupidly cheerful for a guy who would remove your fangs for insolence and place them in a jar beside your bed as a reminder." Shaking his head, he looked long and hard at the door he deemed his own. "That one's the darkest room in the house. Grays and blacks. Armand's side probably has the mirrored furniture he was going on about a few months ago, which means I'll have that shiny black and chrome shit he used to like." A web link Armand sent him last year came into his mind and he rolled his eyes. "And padded headboards."

The memory hung in his head for a moment before he shoved it aside, unwilling to remember the inane argument he'd had with his eldest brother over whether the beds were sexy or cheesy.

They stood silently while he tried to convince his feet to move ahead, to walk the final length of the hall to his bedroom.

"Louis?"

"Yeah?"

"Can we go back downstairs?"

****

Louis ran his hands through his hair, glanced over at Jonathan to ensure he was still sleeping, and replied to Mickey's text.

—I'm here until he doesn't want me to be—

When Mick responded with a thumbs-up emoji, he set his phone down and looked around.

The light of the upstairs hall was still on, providing enough illumination on the main floor to see the wreckage remaining from earlier. The ball caps were strewn around the room, cigarette butts scattered across the burn marks dotting the hardwood. He didn't have to look up the stairs with its broken banister to know the fallen artwork remained on the floor or that pieces of broken CD cases still littered Samuel's bedroom.

Jonathan's anger evaporated as swiftly as it rose, all energy draining from his hunched shoulders. His gaze had returned to the floor, his fingers twitching at his sides until Louis passed him his cigarettes and a lighter. The rote motion of smoking appearing to be more soothing than anything.

Getting to his feet, he picked up the ashtray and walked to the kitchen, dumping it out before setting it in the sink to rinse later.

There was nothing he could say to Jonathan, nothing to combat the hurt and rage erupting in his snarled rants and destructive swipes of his hands.

Everything that came to his mind sounded wrong. Coddling or condescending, thoughtless or deceptive. He wanted to fix what couldn't be fixed. To come to a rational conclusion Jonathan could accept.

Neither was possible.

So he stayed silent.

He shoved a plastic bag into his back pocket, walked into the foyer to pick up the ball caps, and stacked them back onto the top shelf of the closet before turning his attention to the butts scattered at his feet. One by one, he deposited them into the plastic bag, wrinkling his nose when he noticed the tips of his fingers blackening from the ash.

—Tell me this is about him, not you—

Jonathan was resting for a solid hour when Mickey's first text of the day rolled in, letting Louis know Mick had felt the surge of helplessness he'd attempted to tamper down.

He'd failed miserably.

Slipping past Jonathan's sleeping form, he padded up the stairs and into Samuel's bedroom, adding shards of broken plastic cases to his garbage bag before righting the CD tower and inching it back into place as snippets of Mickey's texts filtered through his mind.

—Can't make it right. No one can—

—Anything either of you need, name it—

Pausing to ensure Jonathan was still resting, he began alphabetizing the CDs.

The last time he experienced desperation, his creator was opening the door to their shack. The blood from his most recent kill—a child Louis knew was no older than ten—was still fresh on his breath.

Louis hadn't hesitated when he drove a sharpened branch through his sire's ribs and into his heart, not caring if the older, stronger vampire killed him in the process.

But even that didn't compare to the desperation he felt when Jonathan stood in the hallway, his dark eyes locked on the closed door of his bedroom.

He'd wanted to grab him and go. Throw their bags into the SUV and drive as far from the house and the memories as they could. Drown Minks in ancient blood until he forgot the past week.

—*If you want me to drain you, let me know*—

Mickey's offer looped in his head as he wandered through the house, hanging art and returning the furniture to rights.

The empath's ability to drain the strongest of emotions from his hauntmates was one Louis rarely experienced or required. It was his flatness, his apathy, which Mickey hid in when his brethren became too much, when their lust and anger and frustrations threatened to consume him. Over the decades, Mick needed him to remain calm as much as Jonathan needed it right now.

Setting the garbage by the door, he turned off the lights and stretched out on the sofa, closing his eyes to center his thoughts.

"Louis?"

Jonathan's voice was strained, the gruffness from earlier amplified by his exhaustion.

Getting back up, Louis crept over to him and crouched at his side. "Yeah?"

"I didn't mean it," Minks murmured. "Any of it."

He put his hand on Jonathan's and got comfortable on the floor, knowing he wasn't going to be going anywhere soon. "I know. And so do they."

CHAPTER THIRTY-FIVE

Jonathan sat on the sofa he'd claimed as his own for the past four nights, lighting his first cigarette of the evening while he listened to Louis whisper on his phone in the kitchen.

"Yeah. I might swing by there to pick up a few things, but I don't want to be gone long. I...sure, yeah. I'll drive by and check when I head to the store in a few. No. No, we're good. Keep me posted, and I'll text when I'm mobile."

Exhaling a puff of smoke into the air, he locked his eyes on the repaired closet door while Louis entered the living room.

"Okay, Minks. I'm heading out to pick up another carton of those disgusting things," Louis called over his shoulder as he grabbed his jacket off the back of an armchair and slid it on. "Might be about two hours since I'm also going to head out to the Kaius haunt and restock our blood supply." Opening the closet, he frowned at the faint squeak in the door and ran his fingers along the track. "Anything else you can think of before I go?"

He flicked his ashes into the tray Louis had left out for him and ran one hand through his stringy hair. "Could I come?"

There was no missing Louis's moment of stunned silence while he froze, his sneaker half-tied. "Come? I...yeah, of course. Hell, I'll let you drive if you want."

Nodding, he got to his feet and ventured out of the living room for the first time since his rampage through the house, hesitating when he got to the base of the stairs. "Do I have time to shower?"

"We've got all night," Louis replied, walking up behind him. "I was going to head up there and check my hair before I leave anyway, so move."

Bullshit.

Jonathan stepped aside to allow Louis by, then followed him up the stairs and into the bathroom.

"Remind me to pick up some grease for the doors," Louis ordered as he leaned into the mirror and added a little more styling wax to his red spikes before angling his head to check his style. "I'm going to test the rest of them up here while you shower." Striding past him, he walked out into the hall, leaving the door slightly ajar. "Squeaking is a pet peeve of mine."

Jonathan stripped down and started the water, tracking Louis's movements as he stepped under the spray.

It was easy, given how frequently doors were being opened and closed for his benefit.

"Just grabbing that laundry," Louis called out to him when a blast of cool air wafted in. "There's fresh clothes on the counter. And you're coming downstairs with me before we go so I can show you how to use the washing machine."

Louis had kept up a casual one-sided conversation with him for the past two nights, narrating his movements through the house while Jonathan sat in the living room and smoked, grunting single-word responses periodically. Monologues about dishes and emails were interspersed with the odd commentary on the movies

Louis played on the big television. Most of them shark themed. Or, at the very least, ocean themed.

He'd wanted to join in, to let Louis know he was listening to every word, that he was grateful for the semblance of normalcy Louis was attempting to bring into the quiet house.

But what he wanted and what his mind would allow were two separate things.

Turning off the shower, he grabbed a towel and squeezed the excess water from his hair while Louis's footsteps stilled.

"We have a line on a fresh meal if you want," Louis called into the bathroom. "Nichol and Mickey set up a third donor clinic in the north end that has a massive influx of volunteers. We'd be doing them a favor by partaking."

Dressing slowly, he wiped his hand across the mirror to clear the steam.

He looked like hell.

His eyes were sunken and bloodshot despite the inordinate number of hours he'd spent sleeping over the past four days and nights. But the bagged blood he and Louis were subsisting on was aged, the potency of the oxygenation weak.

A fresh meal would probably do him some good.

Yanking out the last of the knots in his hair, he opened the door. "Yeah. I'd be up for that."

Louis passed him his leather jacket. "Dinner date?"

****

Jonathan turned into the blood donor parking lot and eased smoothly into a spot. "You have more room than you think," he said, his voice sounding a fraction better than it had since they hit Denver. "No need to be parking

277

way off in no-man's-land."

Louis glanced out his window. "I like my method."

When Minks scoffed and got out of the SUV, a small rush of hope ran through him.

Driving was the first thing Jonathan had done without any cajoling. His hunched shoulders straightened as he buckled his seat belt and turned on the engine. His vacant eyes were alert, flicking between the road and the storefronts while he played with the vehicle's brakes and handling.

At least, that's what Minks called the erratic movements.

Louis wasn't fully buying it.

The volunteer lot was full of people milling around and laughing. Their phones lit up their faces under the LED lamplights ringing the building. Several took notice of him and Jonathan as they walked toward the entrance, waving them over with eager smiles.

"What the hell?" Minks whispered under his breath.

Scanning the area for protestors and finding none, he opened the door and held it for Jonathan. "It's like Denver entered a wormhole and became some kind of alternate universe."

The receptionist greeted them with a smile. "Name?"

Minks looked at him and went silent.

"Louis Forbes," Louis answered, his trust in Nichol's hand in the operation the only thing keeping him from turning and walking out.

But Jonathan needed a fresh meal. A safe one.

And he was going to get one.

The receptionist's smile grew wider. "Pleasure to meet you, Louis. Mikhail Kaius said you might be dropping by." She looked over at Jonathan. "And who's your companion?"

When Minks shrunk back a fraction, Louis stepped between him and the counter. "Jonathan Minks."

Her eyes lit up with recognition, the elation on her face disappearing. "Oh, angel," she breathed as she got out of her chair and walked around the counter, her arms outstretched until they wrapped around a stunned Jonathan. "Your family is the reason my brother walked away that night. I'm so sorry." Her voice became muffled as she spoke into his shirt. "And forever grateful."

Minks was rooted to the spot, his dark eyes fixed on the floor until the woman released him and stepped back, waving her hands in front of her face, and promising to get them into a private room immediately.

Louis stepped up tight to Jonathan, keeping his voice low. "We can go."

Minks shook his head slowly. "No, I'm fine. Just caught off guard."

"This way, dears," the receptionist called over to them, motioning them down a hall and into a small room. "Two volunteers will be with you shortly." She paused long enough to give Jonathan another hug as he squeezed past her. "If you need anything, you let me know."

They sat in silence for a few minutes and listened to the increasing whispers outside the doors, the Minks name being spoken from dozens of lips.

"Say the word," Louis reminded him. "We don't need to be here."

Jonathan nodded and continued to gaze at the floor. "Did you ever think you'd see the night when random women would hug you and thank you for being a vamp?

In the middle of a species war?"

Scoffing, he shook his head. "Not in a million years." He reached over and put his hand on Jonathan's knee. "Are you listening to all that out there?"

"Every word."

While the awed murmurs continued outside the room, they sat back and waited for dinner.

****

Jonathan flashed his fangs at the patrolling officer and waited while their photos were uploaded to the Kaius haunt perimeter security server, giving the man a polite nod before continuing down the highway.

"Maybe don't speed along this stretch," Louis suggested as he glanced at the passenger-side mirror. "I don't know how the whole ticket thing works here."

He looked down at the speedometer.

Twenty under the limit.

"How far out are we?" he asked, ignoring Louis's cautious advice and bringing the SUV up to speed.

"Five miles up, then hang a left. I'll tell you when."

When Louis sat up straighter and focused on the dark road ahead, Jonathan eased off the gas a little.

It was amazing the difference a fresh meal had made for him. Some of the pain in his gut he'd attributed to the loss of his hauntmates was gone. The twinges in his back began to wane. And while it did nothing for the tightness in his throat or the dull ache in his chest, the overwhelming exhaustion and weakness subsided enough for him to move without thought.

Even his mind felt clearer. The daze he'd quickly grown accustomed to lifted slightly. His ability to end the looping thoughts in his head gave him a mild relief from the crushing pain and pressure in his mind.

"I should probably warn you about them," Louis suddenly announced. "Not saying they aren't…they just…they all have some weirdness I should maybe give you a heads-up about."

Images of his own hauntmates flashed through his head, bringing a wave of guilt along with it. "Oh, yeah?"

Louis hunched forward, elbows on his knees. "Dominic might growl at me, but it's nothing. Remember when I told you about being linked to Molly? He's still a little sore about that. And Molly doesn't help because she's a hugger, and hugging and connected males are always a bad combination."

Jonathan scanned the sides of the road for wildlife.

None of his brothers were connected. Although Armand was actively searching.

"Mick is cool, which you already knew. But Audra is scary. She gives you these looks when Rhys says shit and you laugh. And it's like every person you ever disappointed channeling through her."

He felt his lip turn up a fraction.

Minks Sr. was a master of guilt manipulation. Audra would be manageable.

Pointing out their turn, Louis straightened up. "Remember, Jagg's deaf, so you'll want to make sure he can see you when you talk to him."

He nodded and eased into a turn.

"The guy can read lips in something like eight languages." Louis smirked and looked at him. "Because of that, he hears more than any of us, I think."

Xavier's limited eyesight came to mind, and he nodded, thinking back to how strong his brother's other senses were.

"And then there's his mate, Bianca," Louis said with

a huff. "The whole Former Tender thing is kind of a minefield because she still goes full-on Tender with us when she's worried or thinks we need it. But her terrifying mate is like *right there*, watching you while she's folding your boxers and fixing your shirt collar. So don't fight her, but...yeah. Pull over here for a minute."

He slowed and parked along the snow-covered dirt road, a vague memory of Bianca at the airport flitting through his mind.

Louis clasped his hands together tight and looked down at them. "And you know Rhys, so I won't even touch that disaster. But his mate, Lis? From the news? Sweetest thing on the planet, aside from the whole master-killer issue. Total opposite of Rhys. And I know you have that whole chivalry thing going on, but don't get involved if Rhys acts up with her. I guarantee you she's got him by the balls and can bring him to his knees in a heartbeat when she wants."

The idea of Rhys Kaius being brought to the ground by the pixie he'd seen on TV gave Jonathan an amusing image. One he was hoping to see while they were there.

"Nichol."

He looked expectantly at Louis, finally motioning for him to continue.

"Nichol is the most intimidating bastard in existence," Louis stated. "And his mate, Simone? She's terrifying in her own right. And probably just as lethal. If you piss off either of them, you're on your own because I'm sure as hell not getting in the way when they're on the warpath. Okay, keep going. Nichol probably has our arrival time charted out already, and if we deviate from it, he'll be asking questions."

"What about Kaius?" he asked, easing back onto the

road.

Louis's lips drew into a tight line. "Not a topic to bring up there right now," he replied. "Kai and Boy are holed up in the Canadian north. Remember the whole Kaius-turned-Deviant thing? Last I heard, there was no change, so Kaius is a pretty touchy subject."

If there was anything he could empathize with in that moment, it was the loss of a sire.

Shoving the reminder aside, he pulled up to a gate, impressed when it swung open before he could roll his window down. "Nichol's probably watching us now, isn't he?"

"Guaranteed he's had eyes on us since we turned off the highway. Everything here is wired, recorded, watched, and noted," Louis replied. "Park in front of the garage there, and we'll take the side entrance. Watch the trip wires and motion sensors."

Pocketing the keys, he got out and looked around at the serene landscape, trying to find the cameras and wires completely hidden from view.

"Just wipe your shoes here," Louis called over his shoulder, scuffing his feet briefly on a floral welcome mat. "If it looks like you made an effort, Bee won't come after you too bad for making a mess."

With as much snow and dirt cleaned from his shoes as he could manage, he followed Louis down a stairwell, momentarily thrown by how dark and dungeon-esque the place was.

"The Kaius haunt really bought into the whole underground tomb thing, didn't they?" he murmured, doing his best to avoid moving his lips in case Jagger was on monitoring duty.

Louis flicked a sconce on the wall. "Wait until you

see the rest of the place. Now that the women have moved in, there's a lot more pillows and carpets." His phone buzzed, and he tugged it from his pocket, cringing as he read it over. "Ah, hell. Nichol saw me do that. And he wants you to know the pillows and carpets were voted on and approved by a six to four ratio."

Glancing furtively around the hallway, he tried to see where the cameras were embedded. "It's kind of unnerving to know we're being watched." His own phone vibrated, his nose wrinkling as he scanned the message. "It's even more unnerving when the guy watching you sends you a picture of you in real time."

A barking laugh echoed down the hall, followed by the sound of bodies hitting the floor and a chorus of female chastisements.

Louis gave him an amused look and picked up his pace. "Welcome to the Kaius haunt."

CHAPTER THIRTY-SIX

Louis stood in front of the bathroom mirror and draped his tie around his neck, frowning when the video moved too fast for him to keep up. "Maybe we should have a code word in case you want to head out early," he called downstairs. "Something easy to remember. Like, 'Screw this, I'm out.' "

Met with the same silence Jonathan had sunk back into upon their return to the Minks haunt a week ago, he backed the video up and leaned down to watch the guy go through the steps to tying a Windsor knot.

"Vampires don't do funerals."

Nichol's statement had hung in the air as an argument brewed in the com room over whether a memorial was needed for the vamps lost during the evacuation.

Molly, Lis, and Bianca abducted minks shortly after their arrival. The women yelled out promises to return him in one piece after Louis finished up with the evening's discussions.

Within an hour, Louis was up to date on the issues bearing down on the Kaius haunt and the Denver vamps as a whole.

The housing shortage was slowly coming under control. The few haunts still doubling up in temporary homes reached tentative peace agreements with the help of Nichol and Dominic. Though not before several disputes threatened the existence of a few weaker bloodlines.

Orphan vampires continued to outnumber the elders willing or able to take them in, and the housing they were in was becoming unsustainable as the young ones tested boundaries and challenged those in charge.

Andy was taken in only to be returned days later when the elder realized the skittish young vamp had few survival skills.

"Detrimental to existence," the old vampire proclaimed before he drove off.

And then there was the human arm of the conflict. Violence over the political polarization had spilled onto the streets around North America, with opposing sides clashing at rallies and protests while the leadership contenders did little to denounce the aggression. Propaganda on both sides became a constant loop on every news channel, with the truths lying somewhere in the black hole between ratings and reviews.

It was in the midst of the media discussion Audra Put forth the idea of a memorial. A funeral of sorts for those vampires who didn't survive the evacuation.

Nichol's blanket proclamation was stopped short when Audra placed a list of names on the conference room table.

"The humans have had their ceremonies. Let our orphans have theirs."

And there he was a week later, glaring at a tie that was too long in the back and too short in the front while Jonathan chain-smoked in the living room. The freshly pressed suit Bianca sent over was getting wrinkled while he hunched over the ashtray and stared at the floor.

Louis held off on broaching the topic of a memorial

until they were back at the Minks home. His uncertainty over Jonathan's reaction stayed his tongue while the SUV sped down the quiet streets in the predawn hours.

And he would have put the discussion off longer had Minks not stood in front of him in the foyer, arms crossed, while he questioned Louis about why he'd gone silent on the drive.

So he had told him.

Then he watched as Jonathan walked to the coffee table and picked up his pack of cigarettes, lighting one after the other until sunrise came and went before he lay back on the sofa and turned his back.

Yanking the knot apart, he grabbed his phone and went downstairs, leaving his tie dangling around his neck in defeat as he brought his attention to something more important.

"Minks?" he said quietly, crouching at Jonathan's knee.

"Yeah?"

"Are you ready?"

Jonathan looked at the burned-out cigarette between his fingers, crushed it into the ashtray, and pushed himself to his feet. "Nope."

Reaching over to adjust Jonathan's collar, he smoothed down the front of the jacket and took a step back. "We can stay here."

Minks gave him a grim smile and walked around him, grabbing both ends of Louis's tie and making quick work of it from behind. "I'd regret it if I didn't go." He looked over Louis's shoulder. "Better."

They were halfway to the memorial site before Jonathan spoke again.

"A few nights ago, I was thinking about how I would

Katja Desjarlais

give anything to trade places with them."

Louis tensed and instinctively watched Jonathan's hands on the wheel. "Trade?"

Rolling his window down an inch, Minks lit up a cigarette and took a long drag. "My life for theirs if there was some super-being who could make it happen. Nine lives for one wouldn't be a fair trade, but the idea crossed my mind." He exhaled out the window and flicked the ashes. "But what got me—what really fucked with my head—was the more I thought about it, the more I didn't want to do it. Even if it was possible."

Unwilling to interrupt the longest stretch Jonathan had spoken in seven days, he settled back in his seat, one eye on the speedometer.

"Nine for one would be a golden deal," Minks continued, his voice strained as he inhaled deep. "But all I could focus on was what I'd miss out on. What I'd never get to do. Or see. In a century or two, or whenever this shit calms down, I want to go overseas and travel for a few decades. Maybe bike across Europe and Asia. And once I started thinking about that, I started thinking about who'd be doing it with me."

He pushed the spent cigarette butt into the car's ashtray. "I'd always thought I'd convince my brothers to go with me. Maybe even all of us. But the more I thought about a trade, and the more I thought about all the selfish shit I didn't want to let go of, you were kind of in there."

Jonathan's eyes remained locked on the road, his fingers flipping on the turn signal as they slowed and made the right toward the memorial site.

Louis scanned the street for danger and pressed an imaginary brake when they approached the entrance to the parking lot. "Was I driving the motorcycle through

Europe, or were you?"

"Me," Minks replied, pulling into a reserved spot and killing the engine.

Undoing his seat belt, he got out and walked around the SUV, the weight of Jonathan's admission not lost on him as they looked at the crowds pouring into the arena. He reached over and took Jonathan's hand. "I'm game for that."

****

The self-consciousness plaguing Jonathan in the first few minutes of the ceremony was forgotten once Bianca Schumann stood at the podium with Jagger at her side and addressed the solemn assembly seated in the rows upon rows behind him.

His mind drifted in and out of the returning fog as she spoke about the humans who lost their lives during the evacuation. Her voice remained strong while she accepted Jagger's handkerchief and dabbed her eyes.

When she stepped aside to allow Nichol to take over, Louis's fingers tightened around his own.

The tension in the old vampire's muscles was evident through the cut of his expensive suit as he approached the microphone, his hard eyes locked on the wood of the podium. "Vampires do not conduct funeral rites," he began, his voice low.

"Some of us have outlived the cultures our human burial traditions were borne from. Others balk at the reminder immortality is a myth. The very core of vampirism is survival, existence across time. To acknowledge our fallen is to acknowledge our weaknesses and, for some of us, to take ownership of our failures."

He flattened his paper and swallowed. "Tonight, we

break this custom. Two weeks ago, fifty-four vampires lost their lives as they forged toward a safe harbor. And in the wake of these losses sit those of us who survived. I—"

Nichol's jaw flexed, the grinding of his molars audible to the vampires in the front rows while Rhys crossed the stage and joined him. He nodded to Dominic, and the lights dimmed. When music started playing and a familiar face filled the screen behind him, Rhys tilted the mic toward himself.

"Jackson Stojanovski."

Andy was seated with the other orphan vamps to Jonathan's left, his elbows on his knees as he stared at the floor until the photo faded out, replaced by another.

"Gregoire Euripides."

One by one, the photos changed while he read off the names, Mickey taking over when Rhys's voice cracked.

Jonathan braced himself as the number counted down, his throat tightening when Armand's face filled the screen with a picture he was sent months ago from the perimeter patrols.

"Armand Minks."

His oldest brother's smile evaporated as Gino's solidified. A photo taken years back when Gino was dabbling in tie-dyed shirts.

"Gino Minks."

"Nero Minks."

"Theodore Minks."

Mickey's head bowed, and Nichol took over again.

"Xavier Minks."

"Walter Minks."

"Christoph Minks."

Through his daze, Jonathan could make out the sound of people sobbing behind him while the faces of his brothers faded on and off the screen. Each photo was one he kept on his phone where he could bring them up periodically while he wound through mountain roads and ripped across prairie fields.

"Frederick Minks."

"Samuel Minks."

"Minks Silas."

Louis's arm draped over his shoulders while the picture of his sire disappeared with the end of the song. As Audra stepped up to the podium and the lights brightened, he allowed his mind to wander as far from the memorial as it would go.

CHAPTER THIRTY-SEVEN

Louis kept his hand firmly wrapped around Jonathan's as yet another group of people approached them. His attention was torn between monitoring his partner and keeping an eye on Andy, who stood mutely in the corner between Nichol and Simone.

While three of the women took turns hugging Minks, their condolences little more than muffled babbling into Jonathan's suit jacket, his dark eyes caught Louis's.

"Screw this, I'm out," Minks whispered, his voice too low to be heard by the humans swarming around them.

Stepping between Jonathan and the next wave of sympathizers walking their way, he motioned toward the perimeter where the Kaius haunt had taken up position. "Let's start our exit strategy."

Leading Jonathan across the arena floor, Louis attempted to block the constant surge of well-wishers seeking out the last of the Minks haunt, muttering his appreciation for their support and half-heartedly apologizing for needing to leave.

The outpouring of compassion was overwhelming. The majority of people who attended the packed memorial remained in the building to show their gratitude and share condolences with the vampires who had lost hauntmates.

Of them, Jonathan was sought out relentlessly. For the past two hours, Louis kept an eye on him, watching his movements and expressions for signs of anxiousness while Minks graciously shook hundreds of hands and accepted dozens of embraces. At first, he'd answered most of the questions which came his way, but as his responses became shorter and more rote, Louis knew Jonathan was reaching his limit.

"There you are, honey," Bianca greeted them when they made it to their first stop. She reached up to straighten Jonathan's tie and frowned at the mascara stains on his jacket. "Well, I suppose I'll deal with those later. Are you two heading out?"

While Minks was dragged into Bianca and Audra's discussion for a few minutes, Louis joined Mickey and Jagger.

"You guys did well with all this," he said, looking out across the crowded arena.

Mickey ran his hands through his hair and shrugged. "Sure, aside from the fact none of us could actually finish any of the speeches we were supposed to make."

"The women did," Jagg reminded them, his eyes scanning the room. "So the next time they gang up on us for being emotionally stunted, we can bring up the fact we couldn't make it through a memorial without choking in front of thousands of people."

Glancing over at Audra, Mick nodded. "They kicked ass. How is he?"

"Dazed," Louis replied, quiet enough to keep his appraisal from Jonathan's ears. "I'm going to take him home and let him decompress."

As he reached over to take Jonathan's hand, Mickey cut him off. "I want that contract signed and returned,

Forbes. Tonight." When he opened his mouth to make an excuse, Mick's eyes darkened. "That ceremony drove a lot home around here. You're one of us, Louis. Whether you can admit it or not."

Wrapping his fingers around Jonathan's hand, he gave Mickey and Jagger a tight smile and began the arduous process of winding through the crowds to the next outpost where Dominic and Rhys stood.

"Minks," Rhys called out. "Come settle an argument for me."

Jonathan looked at Louis before joining Rhys and Lis. His eyes widened as Lis's cheeks reddened, and Rhys laid out a litany of reasons he and Lis needed to, in Rhys's words, *Christen the arena after the crowds left*. And precisely how they should do it.

With hand gestures.

When Molly snorted and Dominic grinned at her expectantly, Louis leaned against the wall and let Jonathan navigate his own way out of the predicament. If anyone could lift Jonathan's mood temporarily, it was Rhys. And Louis was on board for anything that would ease the weight on Jonathan's mind. Even if it was one of the crassest conversations he'd ever heard.

"We should head out," Minks finally stated, backing away from Lis and Rhys when Lis began rolling her tongue ring between her teeth. "Thank you for everything tonight."

All levity left Rhys's face. "I know we've said it hundreds of times, but anything you need, you know how to reach us. And whenever fucknuts over here gets his shit together and makes good on an offer we've put forth, he'll be able to authorize requests as well without having to go through Nichol."

Dragging Minks away before Dominic got in on the pressure, Louis beelined to where Nichol and Simone stood, guarding the orphan vamps still milling around.

"Louis," Nichol barked as they approached. "Tell that blond kid over there to stay with the group before I castrate him."

Tapping the young vamp on the shoulder when he passed by, he pointed to the others. "Might want to get over there before Nichol Kaius comes for you."

The kid nodded, his eyes wide as he jogged back, taking the long way to avoid Nichol's reach.

"Like a herd of goddamn cats," Nic groused, his lips moving while he counted them up. "Who the fuck decided I should be on babysitting duty here? Because I know it wasn't on any of the schedules and lists I assembled."

Simone leaned in and kissed his shoulder, calming the anger building in Nichol's eyes immediately. "I did. Though I believe it was Audra who suggested it would be good for you to have an organizational focus to center you after the ceremony."

When Nichol looked over the crowd and locked his gaze on Audra, Jonathan shrunk back a step.

"We're taking off," Louis stated. "We just wanted to thank you for putting this together and to let you know you all did a pretty amazing job."

While Simone smiled, Nichol crossed his arms. "We all? You mean the Kaius haunt, right?"

"Who else?" He grinned, lacing his fingers in Jonathan's. "Good luck on the babysitting gig."

The old vampire glanced down at his hand wrapped around Jonathan's. "Minks. Could you give us a minute?"

Jonathan hesitated before moving back. Simone linked her arm in his and walked him to the largest group of orphan vamps hanging out by the exit.

Nichol watched them leave and lowered his voice. "You should have been up there, Forbes."

"Public speaking isn't my thing," he replied, quickly becoming uneasy being in Nichol's sights. "Public anything isn't really my thing."

"It isn't any of ours, either. But it had to be done. Now what's the holdup?"

Knowing he couldn't feign ignorance, he shoved his hands into the pockets of his suit jacket. "I'm still thinking about it," he muttered, focusing his attention on the back wall. "It's a flattering offer and all, I'm just not su—"

"It wasn't made to stroke your ego," Nichol interrupted. "It was made to ensure you had the protection of our name no matter where you go."

Widening his stance, he nodded. "I get it. But I've gone this long without haunt connections. I fly under the radar so—"

"So nothing," Nic spat. "Look around at these vamps I'm watching over right now. Take a good fucking look, and tell me what you think is going to happen to those who can't link up to a haunt? Who have to ride solo?"

Turning to scan the dozens of males chatting quietly amongst themselves, his eyes fell on Jonathan.

"That's right," Nichol hissed, stepping up tight to him. "If it wasn't for you, he'd be with them, sleeping in makeshift dormitories and waiting to see if a vamp past his first century might take him on. Most elders don't want to take in bloodlines that aren't theirs, don't want to become permanently tied to a line that may not be strong enough to fight.

"Because the thing is, Denver isn't the end of the line. At some point, years, or decades from now, vampires will branch out again and reestablish their territories. Where do you think that will leave orphans like you?" Nichol stepped back, his eyes darkening. "Yeah, you, Louis. Right now, you're one of them. How do you intend to keep Minks around and alive when the land wars erupt?"

****

Jonathan tossed his tie over the back of the sofa and collapsed into it, covering his eyes with his hands. "My throat is killing me," he groaned hoarsely as he rifled through his jacket pocket for his lighter and sparked up a cigarette.

Louis sat across from him, toeing off the dress shoes he'd groused about the whole way home. "Maybe cut those out and see how it goes for you."

Arching his head back to exhale toward the ceiling, he shook his head. "Not that kind of soreness. More like that ache you get when you've been wanting to scream and yell for the past five hours, but it wasn't an appropriate time to do it."

Wrestling with his own tie, Louis grunted in agreement. "Do it now. And make it loud enough for both of us."

"Don't have the energy," he replied, turning his attention to his cigarette until it was burned down to the filter. "Louis?"

"Yeah?"

"It was a good ceremony, right? I mean, was it something they would've been okay with, right?" he posited, slipping his phone from his pocket, and scanning through the photos to find the ones Louis must have pilfered for the memorial video.

Louis got to his feet, walked over, and sat beside him. "Yeah, Minks. I think they would've been good with it. Probably a little overwhelmed by the amount of human support, but that's not a bad thing to have right now."

He nodded absently and continued to flip through his old pictures until the pressure in his chest built again. "Isn't there some rule where it gets better now?"

Scoffing, Louis ran his hands through his hair, twisting the ends into bright red spikes. "I think that's the hope but not the reality."

"That really fucking sucks," he muttered, leaning back and closing his eyes. "Because right now, I'm torn between going to bed for the next three months and trashing whatever reminds me of them. Which is everything."

Louis went silent for a minute. "I could try to fix that."

"What, the closet?" he grumbled. "It stills squeaks."

Chuckling humorlessly, Louis leaned back with him. "I'll oil it again tomorrow. No, I could try to fix this. The ache, the misery, the anger."

He sat up to light another cigarette. "How? Stake me? Because that's probably the only option."

"Hypnosis."

Staring at the wisp of smoke rising from the cherry, he allowed the idea to worm into his head. "Would I forget them?"

Louis rested his elbows on his knees. "No. I could try to create a wall in your mind, though. Maybe try to alter the intensity. But I wouldn't touch your memories."

The temptation was high, the concept of existing without the heaviness of his loss bearing down on his every thought and movement holding an appeal that nearly swayed him.

Nearly.

"I can't," he finally said, taking a drag. "Don't….don't take this the wrong way, but I can't do it. It's not that I think you'd fuck around with my head or anything, I just…a break is all I need. I can handle it. I just need a break from feeling this."

They sat in silence. Jonathan burning through two more cigarettes while Louis played with the cuff of his shirt.

"I can give you the break."

Butting out the charred filter, he looked over. "Yeah? How?"

Yanking at a loose thread, Louis snapped it and wound it around his finger. "Same way I do for Mickey."

"Wouldn't that mean a blood exchange?" he asked, getting to his feet and walking into the kitchen. "I appreciate the thought, but those go permanent real fast. And since you don't seem too thrilled with contractual commitment, I'm thinking a blood link would be off the table, too."

Opening the fridge, he pulled out a B-positive and sniffed it, pushing himself to switch away from the topic before he said anything more. "It'll get better on its own. And when it does, we'll plot a ride across Europe."

Louis's footsteps came up behind him, the scent of vamp blood hitting his nose moments later.

"For anyone else, yeah, a blood link would be off the table," Louis said, holding his scored finger in

Jonathan's line of sight. "But this isn't anyone else, Minks. You and me. That's it."

His eyes locked on the bead dripping down to Louis's palm. "It's not your job to take this on."

Louis stepped closer to him. "Yeah, it is. I deal with your shit, you deal with mine. Then we travel through Asia at a safe, responsible speed."

CHAPTER THIRTY-EIGHT

Jonathan's lips parted slightly, and Louis stilled, caught between trepidation and anticipation.

Linking to Minks had crossed his mind dozens of times over the past two weeks. The thought he could ease some of Jonathan's despair became more and more appealing as the nights passed, and Minks only seemed to fall deeper into his own head.

With his flat affect serving as a landing pad for Mickey hundreds of times over the decades, he saw no reason Jonathan couldn't use him in the same way.

But it wasn't solely an altruistic proposition.

Even the spikes of emotion Louis had experienced over his lifespan were mere blips muted by the underlying apathy tempering his reactions and limiting his connections.

Minks ran on a different wavelength.

The guy felt higher highs than Louis did. Experienced greater fear and deeper rage.

And he wanted a piece of it.

Jonathan licked his lips and blinked a few times as he backed up against the fridge door. "What if you want out?"

"I don't."

"But if—"

Louis brought his wrist to one fang and held it there. "I won't. I'm not going anywhere."

Minks slowly lifted his own to his mouth and scored the skin, the scent of his blood filling the air as he held it out to Louis.

Slicing his skin, Louis grasped Jonathan's wrist and brought it to his lips, hesitating until Minks closed his eyes, latched on to his arm, and took the first sip.

The memory of his accidental linking with Molly flashed through his head as his mouth closed on Jonathan's wrist, his attention on monitoring Jonathan's reactions to ensure the young vamp didn't panic the way he had with Molly.

He braced himself for his own disorientation, only to find a subdued warmth flooding through his head when the first drops hit his tongue. As the link formed, Jonathan took a sharp breath, his lips releasing Louis's arm for a moment before he latched back on hungrily.

Louis could feel a gentle probing in his mind, and he stilled, closing his eyes and doing his best to relax enough to allow Jonathan to search out the place Mickey so easily dipped into.

"Woah." Minks exhaled. He swiped his tongue over Louis's healing wrist and held it against his chest as he slouched back against the fridge. "That's the spot, isn't it?"

Resisting the urge to reopen Jonathan's vein, Louis reluctantly lowered his arm and stepped in close enough to rest his forehead against Jonathan's. "Didn't take you long to get in there, did it?" he murmured, sinking into the sensation of the relief flooding through Minks.

"You are really fucking calm." The tension in Jonathan's shoulders and muscles visibly released. "Are you always like this?"

Smiling, he shook his head and linked his fingers

with Jonathan's. "Mickey refers to it as my baseline. You, on the other hand, are all over the map."

He could feel a faint weight as Jonathan settled into his bubble, apparently content to remain in Louis's serenity for a while longer.

"What are you getting off me?" Minks asked, his eyes still closed.

"I'm no empath, so I kind of suck at reading this shit," he replied when Jonathan's forehead dropped to his shoulder. "Anger. Sadness. A lot of bitterness. A little hopeful. Anticipation." Pausing to delve a little further into the emotion running through all the others, he smirked. "I don't even know what that would be called. Charged up, maybe? Whatever it is, I think it's your baseline."

He felt a small rush of amusement drift through the line connecting Jonathan's mind to his. "Minks Sr. always said the same thing," Jonathan mused quietly. "Said I was always raring to go but go where was what worried him."

Louis focused on clinching the line enough to block the incoming emotions while leaving enough open for Minks to continue to relax in his calm.

"Determination," Minks muttered. "I felt that. How weird is that?"

Centering all his thoughts on the noticeable drain of tension in Jonathan's muscles, he attempted to hold on to the contentment.

"That's very cool." Jonathan straightened and leaned back on the fridge, a lazy grin on his face. "Or should I say warm? I could actually feel my mind warming up when you did whatever it was you just did."

As Minks pulled out of his head, Louis gripped his

hand a little tighter, noticing the absence with more intensity than he'd anticipated. "All right," he huffed, stepping back. "To the living room. You look tired."

Jonathan nodded and followed him, veering off to stand at the base of the stairs. "Maybe...up there?"

Joining him, Louis leaned on the repaired banister. "Your call."

Hesitating for a moment, Mink started up the stairs. "I can't hide down here forever. Let's go."

****

Jonathan stood in the hall, looking between the two doors while Louis waited patiently for him to decide whether they would spend the day in his room or the master suite where the haunt leader slept.

"Sofa?" Louis finally asked.

He shook his head. "Just trying to figure out where I fit. I mean, you could have Armand's bed if we go in there, but—" His eyes fell on the door to the master. "It's just kind of hitting me that I'm it now. The Minks haunt is...me."

Louis reached past him, turned the knob slowly, and pushed the door open. "Yes?"

His fingers twitched for a cigarette. The need to focus on something other than this decision grew stronger. "Should I?"

"Yeah," Louis stated, stepping past him. "You should. Come on."

Grateful the choice was made, he entered the room while Louis turned on a lamp and sat on the bed. "I have no problem staying in the hall today if you need space."

Approaching the bed, Jonathan unbuttoned his shirt and shrugged it off. "Could you maybe just, I don't know, lay here? With me?"

Tossing his own shirt onto the floor, Louis kicked off his dress pants and got under the blanket, throwing one arm over his eyes. "Thank fuck. I'm exhausted, and the idea of sitting in the hall for the day wasn't all that appealing." He lifted his elbow while Jonathan hung both of their pants on the back of a chair and placed both shirts on the dresser. "Not that I wouldn't have done it."

He crawled into the bed, and Louis reached over, turning off the light. "Night, Louis."

Louis snatched one of the pillows from his side and tucked it under his head. "Wake me if you need anything, Minks. Got it?"

Nodding, he stared at the ceiling in the red bedroom, the light from the hall illuminating the bright walls and giving everything a faint rose hue.

He was right. Minks Sr. outfitted the master bedroom with crimson walls and a silk ruby comforter spread across scarlet sheets. Heavy garnet curtains lined one wall where a window once was, the cherry-red lamps providing the only light the room would see.

"You know," Louis murmured as he tossed one arm over Jonathan's waist, "trade out the white trim and furniture for black, and this would look pretty damn cool."

Before he could scoff about his sire's reaction to such a move, he stopped and frowned. "I suppose I could, couldn't I?"

"Or leave it." Louis's speech became slurred as he started to fall asleep. "Matches my hair."

He grasped Louis's hand and rolled onto his side, making sure the reassuring arm around him didn't leave while he continued to stare at the little details keeping his eyes from closing.

Nero's art hung on the walls, landscapes done solely in shades of red. The watch collection the hauntmates started for their leader was displayed on the dresser. Each one reflected the personality of the giver.

He knew if he opened the bedside table, he would find a stack of diaries and photo albums, bound in red leather, and ordered by decade. Probably a few of the postcards he himself had sent over the years. Maybe the old wallets Minks Sr. refused to throw out whenever he bought a new one.

Never know when they might have a use.

To his recollection, not a single worn wallet was ever taken out of the pile.

"Louis?"

"Yeah?"

Pulling Louis's arm tighter around him, he forced his eyes to close. "Thanks for not making me do this alone."

"Minks?"

"Yeah?"

Louis pulled him closer, his forehead resting on the back of Jonathan's neck. "It's you and me, okay? We can do it all on our own. Our own haunt."

As Louis stilled, Jonathan settled into the mattress and sought out the warmth in his partner's mind.

****

Louis shoved his buzzing phone between the sofa cushions and grabbed the remote, ignoring Jonathan's pointed look. "I told you when we woke up that tonight is a lounge night and I'm not negotiating that. Movie or series?"

"Series," Minks replied, stretching out on the couch he'd claimed as his own. "I'm guessing that's the Kaius haunt?"

"Do you know any other vamps who would take the time to hook my number up with an auto-dialer?"

Jonathan snorted and lit up a cigarette. "No way."

Tugging his phone free, he answered the call and put the phone on speaker, his eyes narrowing when Rhys's voice carried through the room.

"Thank you for choosing the Kaius help desk. To sign your fucking contract and gain an all-access pass to the Kaius Friends and Foes list, press one. To admit to Jagger you're a window-licking asshole with limited prospects and a penchant for stupid decisions, press two. To hear Mickey play air guitar to hits of the seventies, press three. To listen to Dominic's last sparring match, complete with vocals inspired by Molly's skill with a BB gun, press four. To hear Nichol talk, which no one does, press five. To repeat these options, press six. To connect to the Rhys Kaius personal assistance line, press seven and get your jerk-off hand ready."

Minks choked as he laughed and exhaled at the same time, holding his hand up until he could speak. "Okay. I was wrong."

Louis ended the call and held it out when it buzzed again, swiping the answer button and letting the message play a second time.

Butting out his cigarette, Jonathan ran his hands through his hair and grinned. "What happens if you press seven?"

"Trust me, you aren't old enough for what Rhys would say," he groaned, shoving his phone back under the cushion. "I'll deal with them later."

The night passed in a quiet companionship, the odd muttered comment about the shows the only things spoken.

They needed it. A night without pressure and decisions and weights and questions. One where they could pretend nothing existed outside the walls of the house, where neither of them needed to answer to or for anyone.

Jonathan slipped in and out of the sadness tinging everything in his mind. Louis tracked carefully and timed each swing, switching up their viewing schedule whenever Minks spent too long in his own head.

As they climbed into the bed in the master suite for the second night, Louis turned off the light and rolled onto his side. "What's the plan for tomorrow?"

"Reality?" Minks huffed, feeling around on the mattress until he found Louis's hand.

Louis leaned forward and kissed him softly. "Fine. We'll figure out what that looks like now at sundown."

CHAPTER THIRTY-NINE

Jonathan stepped outside the house for the first time in three nights and paused, turning around to look at Louis. "Uh, what's that?"

Louis sauntered past him, scrolling through his texts and passing the phone over. "Jagger's calling this a compensatory offering for monetary losses."

Reading the message, he looked back at the motorcycle sitting at the curb, two helmets slung over the handlebars. "That's almost the exact same one. How the hell would they know? It's not like you had any idea what you were riding."

Louis shrugged. "Nichol probably had a hand in identifying it from his aerial footage. Which should scare the hell out of you on principle." He ran one hand over the leather seat and patted it. "Are you driving, or am I? Keys are in the mailbox."

Doubling back to check, Jonathan swung them around his finger. "Better question is straight there or long way around?"

Louis slicked his hand through his hair and put his helmet on, frowning as he adjusted the built-in mic. "This is a shit-ton more comfortable than the add-on we had going before. Testing. Testing. *Minks*. I'm testing here."

Adjusting his own, he swung his leg over the seat and bounced on it a few times, admiring the shininess of

the body. "Hear you loud and clear. This is pretty sweet."
As Louis got on, he turned the key in the ignition and
listened to the purr of the engine, waiting until Louis's
hands were on his hips before he toed the kickstand up
and revved it a few times. "I'm officially in love. Remind
me to kiss Jagger and Nichol when I see them."

"Jagg, sure. But if you kiss Nichol, you're on your
own for the fallout. Simone has good aim," Louis called
out, his arms inching tighter around his waist as they hit
the street. "I know you're going to test this thing out, but
I'd appreciate a warning before you do."

Flipping his visor down, Jonathan leaned into his
new bike, the rush of the ride flooding his veins when he
hit the freeway and he kicked it into high gear.
"Goddamn, I didn't realize how much I missed this," he
hollered, grinning when Louis's fingers dug into his hips.
"Faster?"

"I'll give you an hour to do anything you want
before we head to the Kaius haunt," Louis called out.

Creeping the speed up, he smirked. "You're using
this to stall."

"Damn right I am."

Their lounge night had extended into three nights of
escapism, quiet evenings of long conversations, silent
moments, and solemn walks through the large house.
Their discussions alternated between leisurely
arguments about gaming systems and the more intense
debates surrounding the Kaius haunt offer. They talked
plans and travel, obligations, and desires.

And ever present in their more difficult talks was the
fate of the Minks haunt.

Round and round they went, their conversations
becoming circular as Louis waffled over his acceptance

of the Kaius offer and Jonathan wavered on his view of his haunt's future.

Until an unexplored option arrived via Nichol's nightly updates.

"Left or right?" he called into the mic, slowing as they approached the exits.

"Right, then take the second left," Louis instructed, his grip noticeably relaxed since they'd first hit the road.

By the time they closed in on the turnoff to the Kaius haunt, Jonathan had reoriented himself. "Should we make an entrance?" he asked, speeding up and chuckling when Louis's head buried against his back.

"Let's focus on making it upright," his nervous companion muttered, the slight tension rippling through their thin link enough to ease Jonathan's foot off the gas.

Pulling into the large garage, he walked them tight to the black sports car wedged close to the far wall and booted the kickstand down. "Ready?"

"Nope," Louis grumbled as he hung his helmet on the handlebars and spiked his red hair back up. "You sure about this?"

"Are you?"

Louis frowned and stared at the floor. "You know what? Yeah. Let's go."

****

The com room table looked a lot bigger than Louis remembered it with him and Minks sitting on one side while the Kaius males sat on the other, the women standing behind them.

Jonathan's fingers inched across his thigh and wrapped around his hand as Mickey stood up, contract in hand. "Mr. Louis Forbes, sole member of the Forbes bloodline," he opened solemnly. "You are hereby presented with documents amalgamating you with the Kaius bloodline. Once signed and filed, you will be recognized as one of us, a full blood member of the Kaius haunt. Should you agree, you will carry the benefits and the detriments of affiliation with our line. Your wars will be ours, ours yours."

Mickey placed the document down while Nichol slid a pen across the table to him, all eyes watching while he read through the contract he had committed to memory weeks ago.

Jonathan gave his hand a squeeze as Louis turned to the last page and signed the final empty line at the bottom. "Okay. You're stuck with me."

Molly let out a piercing squeal that visibly shot through Nichol, his hazel eyes almost glowing as he barked at Dominic to shut her up. Audra's and Simone's admonishments almost drowned out Jagger's and Mickey's voices while they congratulated him. Rhys stood at the back of the room, observing the mayhem and winking at Jonathan when his eyes widened at the speed in which the formality of the signing dissolved.

By the time Nichol got the room back in order, Minks was sitting back in his chair and enjoying the show. Elbowing him lightly, Louis leaned in. "I can't believe you talked me into aligning with this anarchy."

"It's for the greater good."

They waited until the room went quiet again. Nichol's death glare bore into each hauntmate one at a time until the place became more subdued.

"So, we had a reason for doing this," Louis opened, pushing his chair back a fraction and hunching forward on his knees. "We, Jonathan and I? We've been talking. And we were thinking about the Minks' house and how big it is."

Nichol crossed his arms and sat back. "Yeah, we have room for you two to move in. We can easily repurpose the house for our new residents."

Jonathan looked at him and cleared his throat, his nervousness spiking enough for Louis to feel it without trying. "Well, we had another idea. We thought…maybe…I…we…"

"What Minks is trying to sputter out here is we want to take on some of the orphan vamps," Louis stated. "We have the space, the time, and enough know-how to run a half-decent household. And who better to do this, right?"

The room went silent as the Kaius males sat back in their chairs, stunned.

Louis watched Rhys's brows shoot up, his expression one of total bafflement. Mickey looked equally confused, his head tilted as though the angle would help him process the declaration. Jagger glanced over at Dominic, who nodded his affirmation that yes, Jagg read that correctly.

Only Nichol's face remained unchanged, save for the slight shift in his gaze as the wheels began turning in his head.

Minks nudged him. "Andy?"

"Right," Louis exclaimed. "Andy is nonnegotiable. We want him no matter what. And we figured any others who are the last in their lines. The ones riding solo now."

Folding his hands on the table in a manner Louis hadn't seen before, Nichol leaned forward. "You realize you're asking to take on the responsibility of undisciplined newborns," he clarified. "Regulated feeding schedules, monitored sleep patterns, skill development, defense training, control of impulsivity, implementation of consequences, enforcement of rules—"

"Audra and I could help with some of that," Bianca stated, pulling up chairs for herself and Audra. "We can put together a chore list, maybe even teach the vamps how to clean and do laundry since most came from wealthy haunts with Tenders."

"I could run a special training class three times a week until I'm fully recovered," Simone offered, ignoring the growl rumbling from Nichol. "I'm sure Jagg could walk me through age-appropriate skills."

Molly spun a seat around and bounced excitedly. "Lis and I could help with the shopping until they're all settled. They'll need clothes, maybe some books and stuff to do, phones, laptops—"

"I can order laptops and phones," Nichol barked, earning a glare from Dominic. "Fine. Louis, Minks? You two really think you can do this? Do you understand the responsibility you're walking into?"

Jonathan nodded solemnly while Louis relaxed back in his chair, having gained the approval of the haunt's women and therefore sealing the approval of the others. "We'll always have you guys for backup and babysitters." He grinned, tapping the signed contract. "When can we get this started?"

****

Jonathan stood at the entrance to Nero and Christoph's room, garbage bags in hand, while Louis waited behind him with a stack of empty boxes and a few large plastic bins.

"Are you sure you want to be here for this?" Louis asked. "I can do the bedrooms while you scrub down the basement bolt-hole."

Shaking his head, he stepped into the room and flung the closet door open. "No, I definitely need to be around for this. I'll put the things I want to hold on to in the bins. Anything the incoming guys might want can go in the boxes for them to go through when they settle in, and we'll trash the rest."

One by one, he pulled shirts and pants off their hangers and passed them to Louis to fold, setting one shirt from each brother aside for the keep bin. While Louis dumped the dresser drawers of socks and underwear into the donate bins, he loaded the keepsake bin with items from the bedside tables, adding a few art pieces and photos before putting the lid on.

"All the art stuff can be boxed," he mused, looking over the collection of supplies Louis removed from the desk drawers. "Hopefully, one of the guys will get some use out of it."

Louis whipped a black marker from his pocket and labeled the box, setting it in the hall. "Are we sticking with the bedding, or do you want to redo it? Better make that call now before Bee comes in here and makes it for you."

Examining the nondescript comforters and sheets, he shrugged. "Why don't we keep it and let them decide once they're here? We'll toss it through the wash later."

As they moved to the next bedroom, Louis's nose wrinkled, and he crossed his arms. "Are we supposed to teach them financial responsibility? Should we give them allowances and let them decide on what they want? Or how does this work?"

Tying up the garbage bag and tossing it down the stairs, Jonathan leaned against the doorframe. "Allowances would probably be a good idea until they have some impulse control. Nichol said he'd be putting all the orphan accounts in trust, so they'll have access once they're a little older. I'm more worried about them staying out all night and getting caught out of the house for the day."

Louis opened a box and set it in the middle of the room, going to the desk first. "GPS seems like an invasion of privacy, but we're technically responsible for them. Are we getting them cars? Maybe two to share or something?"

Sitting on Samuel's bed, he began emptying the nightstand. "I never thought about that." He frowned and turned a CD over in his hands. "We have a lot of shit to figure out in the next six nights."

"Stability, accountability, opportunity, guidance, and unconditional acceptance," Louis stated, echoing Audra's advice from the night before. "We'll figure out the details when we have to." His declaration was followed by a worried look. "Do we need to be looking into online education courses? Maybe we should write that down."

As Louis pulled out his phone and added education to their growing list of things they needed to consider, Jonathan emptied the last of Samuel's mementos into the keep bin and moved on to Frederick's

CHAPTER FORTY

Jonathan held back a laugh when Louis adjusted the collar of his shirt for the third time and craned his neck to look up the stairwell of the makeshift vampire orphanage. "You're fine."

"This damn shirt's too tight," Louis grunted, spiking his hair up and checking the stairs again. "You sure we have everything ready? Audra and Bee stocked the fridge, but I didn't count how many of each blood type we have. We could have an issue if too many prefer one over the other."

"Then they'll make do until tomorrow." He smiled, knowing Louis wasn't going to settle any time soon.

The past six nights had gone by in a blink. Dozens of small panics were avoided with the reminder they could deal with whatever arose once the vamps were under their roof. Hundreds of minor decisions were already made, from room assignments to chore lists to schedules and routines. The women of the Kaius haunt took up nightly residences in their home for the past three nights, going over calendars and timings and offering advice on everything from conflict resolution to living room seating.

Of course, the women also brought a multitude of new concerns to Jonathan and Louis.

How would they handle arguments between the hauntmates?

317

Did they believe in physical repercussions as most haunts did or were they open to alternative discipline methods?

Had they decided on a plan should they disagree on discipline? Did they know they needed to present a united front at all times?

Did they have any activities planned to build haunt cohesion?

Would they have an open-door policy in their bedroom?

The last one had caused Louis to scoff loudly before he schooled his expression and replied with a calm, "No way in fucking hell."

With the countdown on, Louis woke several times the day before, nudging Jonathan awake to pose issues they hadn't considered.

What if one wanted to leave?

What if they weren't strict enough, and the vamps went bad?

What if they were too strict, and the vamps went bad?

What if the young vamps didn't like him?

"Maybe we should have had Nichol print out questionnaires for them like we talked about a few nights ago." Louis reached down to grab Jonathan's hand. "Where the hell are they?"

Rhys sauntered around the corner and down the stairs, arms extended. "It's like organizing a group of cats," he announced. "Pack your fucking bag. That was the whole instruction. And here we are, forty-five minutes later and Nichol's about two minutes from eating one of them."

Louis moved toward the stairs. "Damnit, Rhys.

Don't leave Nichol alone with our boys."

"They're fine, *Daddy*," Rhys chuckled, jumping the last four steps. "Seriously, though, they're a little skittish, so keep the nervous pacing to a minimum." He looked over at Jonathan. "Are you sure you don't want us to come back with you for a night or two? Jagg said he'd drive in."

There was a rumbling of footsteps on the second floor, and he shook his head. "We'll be good."

Nichol appeared at the top, his boots thumping as he stormed down the stairs. "Get. Down. Here."

A line of young vamps filtered down the stairs, their eyes on Nichol as they inched past him and stood by the door, small backpacks slung over their shoulders and all wearing identical black shirts and hoodies.

Face to face with the ten newbies, Jonathan swallowed and stepped closer to Louis. "That's a lot of responsibility."

Nichol walked behind the line, tapping each on the head as he named them off, his voice dripping with annoyance. "Ryan, Brandon, Andy, Zachary, Justin, James, Joshua, Jeremy…hot damn, enough with the J names…Aaron, and another J, Jesse." Standing in front of the young vamps, he crossed his arms. "This is the J-King Jonathan Minks and Louis Forbes, your new haunt leaders."

****

Louis waited in the hall while Jonathan checked in with Justin and Zach before closing their door and leaning against the wall, pushing his hands through his hair. "Does this count as surviving day one?"

"I'd say everyone in bed only three hours past sunrise constitutes a successful first day." He walked into their bedroom and held the door until Jonathan followed him. "So?"

Minks pulled his shirt over his head and tossed it toward the hamper, rolling his eyes when it fell a foot short. "So I think we got this," he stated, his eyes darkening when Louis stripped down to his boxers and scooped up the shirt from the floor. "What are the chances any of them are early risers?"

"Doesn't matter if they are," he replied, stalking toward Jonathan. "How far would they get? The sidewalk? Lock the door."

Jonathan backed up, flicked the lock, and popped the button of his jeans. "You're not exhausted?"

"Oh, I'm very fucking exhausted," he murmured, caging Minks against the door with his arms as he nuzzled his shoulder. "I'm also very, very revved." When Jonathan lolled his head back and gave him full access to his throat, he dragged his fangs along the tempting artery. "You sure you're up for this?"

Amid the mayhem of bringing home their new young charges hours earlier, something had shifted in Jonathan. While the heartache remained a constant hum through their link, desire had filtered in.

A hand grazing Louis's ass while he rinsed out ten cups.

A murmured innuendo regarding the isolation of the laundry room.

A heated stare and a tongue running along one fang while Jonathan stood at the back of the living room and watched Louis lay out the basic ground rules to their new brood.

But even with the lust amping up from Jonathan's side, the last thing he wanted to do was push for anything his partner wasn't ready for.

He could wait. For as long as Jonathan needed him to.

Minks reached between them and gripped him through his boxers, sending Louis's eyes rolling back. "Up for it, want it, need it..." Jonathan's fingers tightened around him, and his other hand slid up Louis's chest slowly. "Louis?"

Running his tongue along Jonathan's jaw, he buried his hands in his hair, his hips jerking when Minks began to work him. "Yeah?"

"We, uh, damn," Jonathan grunted when Louis tugged at his hair, kissed him hard, and unzipped his jeans. "Things got busy, and I...ooooookay...was going to say it before but...oh fuck."

The more flustered Minks became, the more turned on Louis became. He slid his hand into Jonathan's boxers and grasped him, pumping him slowly while Minks began panting. "We've had a lot on our plates," he murmured into his ear as Jonathan's lust fed his own, an intoxicating warmth winding through the desire and into his head. "Hold still."

Jonathan froze, tilting his ear to the door.

"Not them." Louis smirked as he focused all his attention on flooding Jonathan's mind with the same warmth Jonathan was filling his own with. "Feel that?"

Minks closed his eyes for a moment. "That...that's intense."

"Yeah, well, you make me intense." He leaned forward to brush his lips over Jonathan's. "Things got busy, and I was going to say it before—" He grinned against Jonathan's lips as he echoed his words." —but I love you, Minks. And I'm not just saying it because I'm really, really horny right now."

Jonathan exhaled. "I was waiting for the right time, but yeah, this works," he murmured, pulling Louis tight to him. "I love you, Forbes. And I'm not just saying it because I'm really, really horny right now."

The urgency Louis felt earlier drained from him as they kissed leisurely, taking their time to enjoy the first calm moments of happiness either of them had experienced in ages.

"So it this the Forbes-Minks haunt or the Minks-Forbes haunt?" Jonathan groaned when Louis ground against him.

"Minks-Forbes," he murmured, rather liking the sound of it. "I fucking love it when you breathe like that."

Minks let out a strangled laugh, his head thumping back against the door as Louis tightened his grip and pumped him faster, almost losing his rhythm when Jonathan mimicked his tempo, his panting becoming more raspy and uneven.

The combination of Jonathan's muscles tensing under his hand, his heavy breathing, and the lust pummeling into Louis's mind was making his own control precarious. When Minks dropped his head to his shoulder and bit down, he lost the battle and erupted, slamming his hand against the door to steady himself as his knees almost gave out from under him from the intensity of his climax.

"Shhhhh." Jonathan laughed gruffly into his skin, holding Louis to him until he regained his senses. "You'll wake one of them upoogodrightthere…"

Using his shoulder and knee to keep Minks in place when his hips bucked against his hand, he doubled his efforts to send him over the edge, his eyes locked on Jonathan's reactions.

The way his Adam's apple moved when he swallowed.

The tautness of the tendons along his neck as he arched his head.

The flexing of his jaw muscles while he gasped for air.

Louis could feel the burst of euphoria in his mind moments before Jonathan came. The sensation radiated through his own body as he fought to center his attention on memorizing the curve of Jonathan's throat and the moan that escaped before Minks clenched his teeth.

When Jonathan's muscles went slack and the glazed look in his eyes faded, Louis grinned. "Right there?"

"Oh yeah." Jonathan sighed. "Right there." He shook his head and tucked his hair behind his ear, his nose wrinkling when he looked at the punctures on Louis's shoulder. "Ah, damn. Sorry."

Running his thumb over the blood on his skin, Louis held it out for Jonathan, a chill running through him when Minks wrapped his lips around it. "You can do that any time you fucking wish," he stated, his lust already building again. "Bed?"

Jonathan nodded and reached over to the dresser to grab his pack of cigarettes. "Give me a minute to have one first."

"Uh, no," he replied, taking the pack and setting it down. "We have young ones around. Smoking is an outside-only activity now." Backing toward the bed, he shrugged. "And since the sun's high in the sky, you're out of luck."

****

Jonathan woke up and carefully eased his arm off Louis's back before he rolled over to check the time.

One hour until sunset.

Turning back, he pressed up tight against his lover's side, the coolness of Louis's skin easing the demanding heat of his erection through the thin fabrics of their boxers.

No naked sleeping until we know if we have any day wanderers, Louis stated hours ago, the desire in his gray eyes unmistakable as he slowly tugged his boxers onto his slim hips.

Stretching his senses, he listened for any sounds of life in the still house before he trailed his fingers along Louis's spine and rocked his hips against his thigh.

"Whatever you think you're doing, do it more," Louis muttered into his pillow, grunting when Jonathan slipped his hand under his boxers to grip his ass.

Smirking, he pushed himself up on one arm and leaned over to kiss his way from Louis's muscled shoulders down to the small of his back, earning another muffled groan as Louis's hips shifted against the mattress.

He could feel his lover's lust ramping up exponentially through their link. It drowned out the calm apathy and ran alongside a stream of contentment.

And he needed this.

Needed to stay grounded.

Needed to remain connected.

Needed to be wanted and desperate to hold on to the highs he felt with his partner.

Easing Louis's boxers off, he tossed them toward the hamper and crawled on top of him, straddling his hips and running his hands across the expanse of his back.

Starting with the base of Louis's neck, he dug his thumbs into the muscle and massaged in slow, steady circles along his spine, shoulders, and biceps while Louis groaned in melted appreciation.

Sitting back on his haunches, he moved his attention to Louis's muscled thighs, his desire ricocheting up when Louis moaned a long, low *fuuuuuuuuuuuck*.

His erection kicked, and he gripped it tight, all hope his quick strokes would satisfy it vanishing when Louis rolled onto his back beneath him and licked his lips, his own length laying long and hard against his stomach.

"So, uh," Louis muttered, his gray eyes locked on Jonathan's hand, "you're gonna need to step-by-step me through this."

Surprised, he released his grip and leaned forward on his elbows, his hair falling forward and veiling them. "Never?"

"Nope."

Taking a sharp breath, he nuzzled Louis's jaw. "We don't need to do anything new for you right now."

"Oh, we definitely need to," Louis growled, reaching down and digging his nails into his ass with one hand while he pleasured himself roughly with the other.

The combination of Louis's lust in his head melding with his own set every nerve on fire, and he ground himself against Louis, one hand slapping at the bedside table. Finding the drawer handle, he yanked it open and felt blindly for the bottle he'd tossed in a few nights prior. His chest heaved with the effort to keep his raging hard-on under control, his fingers fumbling the lid a few times. "You sure?"

Arching up to kiss him roughly, Louis scraped his fangs along his throat. "Yeah, Minks, I'm sure."

With a deep breath, he squeezed a dollop of watermelon-scented lube on his fingers and reached down between them, sinking into a kiss that was all tongue and zero finesse. "We'll go slow," he ground out through gritted teeth, his imagination doing nothing to help his control issue. "And we can stop anytime, okay?"

Stroking himself a few more times to ensure he was nice and slick, he lined himself up and pushed in slowly, tucking his hair behind his ear to watch Louis's reaction. When his lover moaned, his neck arching back and his fangs lengthening, he pushed in further, inch by inch, until he was fully sheathed.

His unneeded breath was ragged, the sensation of being buried deep inside Louis while nails raked down his spine, almost sending him over the edge. Concentrating on not coming, he waited until Louis gripped his ass impatiently before he moved his hips slowly, pumping in and out at a snail's pace while his arms trembled. "You okay?"

"Very fucking okay, Minks," Louis ground out, meeting his thrusts and grunting when he shifted angles a fraction. "God, do I ever want to sink my fangs into you right now."

"Ah, hell yeah," he groaned, his speed increasing as he reached down to grip Louis's erection, its thickness hot and heavy in his hand.

The sharp tips of fangs grazed his jugular, and he shuddered, his toes curling when Louis broke the skin and sunk in deep. He grabbed the headboard for leverage, his other hand stroking Louis's erection at a punishing pace as he pounded into him.

Vaguely aware there was no way the vamps down the hall couldn't hear them banging the headboard clear through the wall, he clenched his teeth in a half-assed attempt to silence himself as he felt Louis's length swell and kick in his hand. His own orgasm barreled through him, and he succumbed to the feeling of fangs embedded inside him while he remained deep inside his lover.

CHAPTER FORTY-ONE

Jonathan stood at the top of the staircase, arms crossed, as he glared at the males jostling for the television remote. "We're walking out that door in ten minutes, whether you're ready or not. Andy, I want that dishwasher emptied before we go."

Andy nodded and jogged off to the kitchen without a word, grabbing the remote out of Jesse's hand and throwing it up the stairs as he passed.

The kid had good aim, even if he still refused to speak more than a dozen words a night.

"Did Ryan get the sidewalk shoveled off?" Louis called from the bathroom before emerging, a look of annoyance on his face as he tried unsuccessfully to spike his hair up. "Josh used up the last of the hair product. Again. Remind me to put in for a triple order when we see Bianca."

With the first chaotic month behind them, Louis and Jonathan were slowly adapting to their new reality.

Slowly and clumsily.

The first week was deceptively calm, the young vamps doing little more than eating, sleeping, and nodding in agreement while the two of them reviewed rules, walked through expectations, and laid out boundaries. All attempts to bond were rebuked, met with sullen expressions, averted gazes, and silence.

The second week was decidedly less peaceful.

James was the first to break the barrier, approaching Jonathan early one evening to ask about the motorcycle parked out front.

"*Yours?*" he'd uttered, standing in the open door, hands shoved deep into his pockets.

Pulling the keys off the hook beside the door and grabbing the helmets off the top shelf of the closet, Jonathan had nodded. "My new toy. Want a ride?"

Jeremy was waiting at the door by the time he and James returned.

The first reach across the aisle opened the gates for the others, giving Brandon and Justin the nerve to ask about the gaming systems Nichol sent over. Their unopened boxes sat in a pile in the corner of the living room and once Ryan heard the opening theme of a boxing game, he'd jumped in, setting off the first noisy evening of the new haunt.

By the end of the second week, fights over shower times and blood types began, the overtly hostile Aaron being the instigator of most of the discord. Verbal sparring was quickly replaced by full-on physical blowouts, the walls and decor of the house taking a beating as Aaron took on any hauntmate who crossed him. Jonathan and Louis had lain awake for hours after every fight, quietly discussing the young vamp with the hair-trigger temper and leery eyes while their whispered conversations were interrupted by their daytime wanderers, Andy and Jeremy.

Although neither male spoke much, they both seemed to settle when Louis and Jonathan joined them in the living room, silently watching television until they drifted off.

Jonathan rapped his knuckles on Josh and Ryan's

door. "That sidewalk better be shoveled," he called out. "We're heading out now."

Ryan flung the door open and ducked under Jonathan's arm, the music from his earbuds loud enough to be heard crystal clear by everyone who remained upstairs. "I need to sit up front to charge my phone."

His announcement brought along a wail of protests from downstairs, with Jesse pouncing on the claim for the front seat of Louis's SUV before the others remembered they were taking two vehicles.

"All south and eastbound are riding with me," Louis hollered as he emerged from their bedroom, shrugging his jacket on and stopping short when Jonathan stepped in front of him and pushed him against the wall. When he leaned in for a kiss, Louis smirked. "We're five minutes behind schedule."

Jonathan dove in any way, rewarded with a talented tongue looping and flicking over his fangs. "We're always behind schedule now. You grabbing Aaron?"

"Yeah," Louis huffed, glancing at the closed bedroom door. "He better be ready." Pounding on it with his fist, he raised his voice. "Hear that, kid? You better be in that SUV in one minute flat or I'm changing the Wi-Fi password."

Despite the cursed grumbling coming from inside the room, Aaron stalked out of his room and down the stairs, his phone tight in his hand.

"Are you dropping him off with Audra?" Jonathan whispered, checking inside the room to ensure Andy's side remained untouched by Aaron's temper.

Louis nodded. "They're meeting up at the library downtown. Mick will be on-site in case he takes off again." With a final attempt to spike his hair, he jogged down the steps. "Save your game, get your shoes on, and let's *go!* Who's with me?"

As the males grumbled their annoyance under their breath and got to their feet, Jonathan headed into the kitchen to check the calendar. "Bianca didn't go through the hassle of color-coordinating your schedules to have you ignore them. Aaron's riding with Louis. Jesse, Jeremy, Andy, and Zach, you four are training with Simone and Jagg, so I'll drop you off on my way to the blood bank. Josh, you're hooking up with Molly and Lis there, so make sure you toss those coolers into the back. Ryan, Brandon, James, and Justin, you're tagging along on Rhys's patrol, so get in with Louis and we'll meet you at the training center afterward."

Louis cringed. "We'll talk about Rhys and what to expect on the way there. Get going, and I'll be right out."

The house emptied, leaving Jonathan and Louis alone.

"Louis?"

"Yeah?"

Hooking his keys on his thumb, he rocked back on his heels and tucked his hair behind his ear, a familiar pressure in his chest building. "Could you maybe go out on the patrol with them? Just, I don't know, keep an eye on things?"

"That's the plan," Louis replied, reaching over to give his hand a squeeze. "Someone's got to keep Rhys in line, right? I'll let Audra know I'll be picking up Aaron after the ground patrol is over."

Nodding, he exhaled loudly. "And you'll be careful, right?"

"Minks?"

"Yeah?"

Louis opened the door and crossed his arms, watching Justin and Ryan beating on each other in front of the open passenger door while Brendan and Josh cheered them on. "I wouldn't leave my enemies to deal with this mayhem alone. I'm sure as hell not leaving you to do it."

****

Louis leaned against the SUV and watched Aaron slink out of the library, his shoulders hunched while he scented the air and scanned the parking lot for danger. "Hey," he called over. "How'd it go?"

"Fine."

It was always fine. Three sessions a week, and it was always fine.

"All right," he said, pushing himself off the car. "You get in. I'm going to touch base with Mikhail before we head back to the patrol headquarters and get the others. Their debriefing should be wrapping up."

He sauntered into the library, brows lifting when he spotted Audra reaching across a table to collect her notepads and pens while Mickey crouched down and blatantly stared at her backside under the guise of lacing his boot.

"Subtle," he muttered too quietly for Audra to hear.

"I'm a fucking ninja." Mickey grinned, pursing his lips at Audra when her head whipped around, and she caught his line of sight. "A bad fucking ninja. Need me to keep an eye on the kid while you two talk?"

Glancing out the window toward the SUV, he nodded. "He's chilled down a bit in the past week, but only when I'm close by."

As Mick walked out the door, Audra came up to him, her analytical cat eyes narrowed. "Mickey intimidates Aaron," she stated.

"So do I," he scoffed. "That's why the house is still in one piece."

"No," she said slowly. "He has a reluctant respect for you. Until he gets his temper, his core, and his bitterness under control, he's using you as his conscience. His regulator." Sliding her notebooks into her purse, she waved at the young vamp who was watching them warily from the front seat of the vehicle. "He never wanted to be a vampire. His sire was much like yours, I believe." With a cheerful smile, she looked up at him. "Good luck this weekend. We hit some nerves tonight."

Mickey patted his shoulder as he walked over to the car. "You can return him, you know. The option's there."

"No fucking way. That kid is mine," he stated, opening the driver-side door. "I'll text you tomorrow and let you know what time the guys will be playing online so you and Simone can link in with them. No gaming until chores are done, so it might be late. Night, Mick."

He eased onto the street, anxious to get back to the patrol headquarters so he could reassure Jonathan the rest of their vamps 'first night on patrol had gone without a hitch and they were safe.

The eleven texts Louis sent throughout the night wouldn't be enough for Minks until the guys were secured at Louis's side and on their way home.

"Forbes?" Aaron hunched over his phone.

"Yeah?"

"Why not?"

Signaling his intentions, he slowed and made his turn. "Why not what?"

Aaron adjusted his position, keeping his face angled

away. "Return me? I was surviving just fine at the holding center. And I'd survive just fine out there."

"You'll survive just fine anywhere," he replied, speeding up. "Like me. But you might as well survive just fine in a nice suburb with guaranteed meals and a state-of-the-art washing machine. Get your foot off the dash."

****

Jonathan scooped up three socks from the living room floor and added them to the shirt and two hoodies he'd collected from the kitchen. "We need to get on them about this," he stated, glancing under the sofa and using his foot to pull another sock out from under it. "We have six hampers for a reason."

"Maybe we can have Bianca come by next week and do another laundry lesson with them," Louis called over from the foyer, where he was organizing shoes and boots. "I think Thursday's a slow night, so we can book her in." Wrinkling his nose as the closet door squeaked closed, he stood. "Though I suspect those boys are more focused on Ms. Schumann than her lessons. Maybe we should book Nichol."

Doing a final walk-through of the living room, he glanced over at his half-empty cigarette pack, snatched it up, and walked over to the closet to tuck it onto the top shelf. "Why not Friday? It's completely empty."

"Rhys and Lis are babysitting Friday." Louis grinned, setting the last pair of boots in a row. "You and I are having another date night. Audra insisted it was a necessity for us to do it frequently because, in her words, *It's beneficial for the children to see that their parents are putting time and effort into maintaining and building a cohesive relationship.*"

Smirking, he followed Louis up the stairs. "Date night? Where are we going this time?"

"The theater downtown has a midnight movie showing, so we can start there, then we can drive around and enjoy the absolute peace and silence until sunrise."

Memories of the first date rose fast and hot in his mind. The sensation of Louis's hand snaking down his boxers to grip him as they rode the bike along a deserted path near the outskirts of the city. The rumble of the motor through him when he slowed to a stop, the threat of crashing becoming imminent the longer the strong hand worked him.

The look in Louis's eyes when he got off the bike and returned the favor with his mouth.

Realizing he'd begun breathing in anticipation of another night off, he refocused on the task at hand.

They hit the hallway and Louis bent down to pick up a pair of boxers outside the bathroom. "Neanderthals, all of them."

Aaron and Andy's door opened a crack, and Andy peered out into the hall.

"Back to bed," Louis stated, holding the boxers up. "Yours?" Andy shook his head, and Louis leaned against the wall. "Everything okay?"

"Just checking," Andy replied quietly. "Night."

They waited until they could hear the mattress creak before going into their own room and shoving the collection of dirty clothes into the hamper.

Jonathan pulled his shirt over his head and stretched. "We should get him into something outside of the house. A class of some kind without the others."

"I was thinking he might be interested in one of those anime groups I saw advertised at the library,"

Louis mused, hesitating at the door. "You okay if I keep this open tonight? James was a little off after working the patrol, and I want to make sure I wake up if he wanders during the day again."

Nodding, he got into bed and tossed his arm over his eyes. "No problem. I'm not waking for anything. I can't believe how tired I always am now."

The mattress bounced as Louis got in, the short-lived blanket battle beginning and ending in his favor. "I wonder if Rhys and Lis would take them out of the house for the night so we can, I don't know, sleep?"

"That would be amazing." He grinned when an arm flopped heavily across his chest. "Don't get too comfortable. Someone's door just opened."

He could feel Louis's nose wrinkle against his shoulder, followed by a triumphant chuffing. "That's Jeremy's gait. Looks like you're on call tonight."

Sliding out from under his arm, Jonathan sat on the edge of the bed for a moment and ran his hands over his face. "I'm up. I'm going." He leaned over and kissed Louis's arm before he pushed himself to his feet. "Forbes?"

"Yeah?"

"I don't regret this. Exhausted as I am, I don't regret this at all."

Louis opened one eye and cracked a smile. "Me either. Especially since I get to stay in bed. Good luck." With exaggerated movements, he rolled over and buried deep into the blanket.

Jonathan stood at the foot of the bed for a moment before heading down the hall. "Jeremy?" he whispered, creeping down the stairs.

"Here," the young vamp hushed from the living

room. "Just can't sleep again."

Sitting on the sofa opposite him, Jonathan passed over the TV remote and lay back. "Mind if I hang with you?"

Jeremy mimicked his position and turned on the television. "You don't have to wait up with me every night. You can head to bed if you need to."

Louis appeared at the top of the stairs, pillows in hand and red hair spiking out in all directions as he joined them in the living room. "And miss out on our routine? Screw that. I'm not going anywhere."

Tossing one pillow at Jeremy, Louis sat on the floor by Jonathan's legs and stretched his arms across them, resting his head on Jonathan's thigh. "See if there's a shark documentary on, Jer. Minks loves those things."

A word about the author...

Katja Desjarlais is a music teacher by day and a paranormal romance writer by moonlight. She is an unapologetic music addict and has an obsession for bad Bach puns despite her irrational aversion to Baroque. Her favorite words include "plethora" and "dapper," and she is physically repulsed by the word "moist." Katja's interest in the paranormal can be traced to her early childhood film choices and to the revolving book collection on her phone.

Desjarlais lives in the Okanagan Valley with her husband, three children, and two black cats. Her ideal summer vacation is traipsing through the United States with her family and attending heavy metal concerts.

katjadesjarlais.wordpress.com

Thank you for purchasing
this publication of The Wild Rose Press, Inc.

For questions or more information
contact us at
info@thewildrosepress.com.

The Wild Rose Press, Inc.
www.thewildrosepress.com

www.ingramcontent.com/pod-product-compliance
Lightning Source LLC
Chambersburg PA
CBHW051134030726
47504CB00004B/869